SWEET PAIN

SWEET PAIN

Richard Posner

M. EVANS AND COMPANY, INC.   NEW YORK

Library of Congress Cataloging-in-Publication Data

Posner, Richard.
  Sweet pain.

  Summary: Unable to get along with her parents,
suffering from a lack of self-worth, and in need of a
happy, secure and loving relationship, Casey is physically
abused by her new boyfriend; and while she longs to break
away she is also irresistibly drawn to him.
  [1. Violence—Fiction. 2. Parent and child—Fiction]
I. Title.
PZ7.P8384Sw 1987   [Fic]   87-8930

ISBN 0-87131-501-7

M. Evans and Company, Inc.
216 East 49 Street
New York, New York 10017

Manufactured in the United States of America

9 8 7 6 5 4 3 2 1

For Jarrod, Mark, and Alayna

Chapter One

CASEY THOUGHT, I'M GOING TO GET VIOLENT, AS SHE LIS-
tened to the noisy truck motor out front. She focused on
it with all of her concentration as she gripped her paperback novel. She felt her body tense in the lounge chair
and her chest tightened with frustration. She *didn't* want
to hear truck engines on this hot August day.

The truck wasn't going away, and Casey began to seethe.
In a couple of minutes she'd go around front and yell,
but she figured she'd give this jerk a little longer to get
lost. Forcing herself to breathe in and out, Casey scrunched
up on the webbed chair and stared between her knees at
the new swimming pool. Sun flared from the water and
blinded her, even through her big round sunglasses. She
shielded her eyes with a cupped hand. The water looked
like a lake in hell, fiery and black.

CRASH! The truck had dropped something right in
front of her house. "Damn!" Casey said, and sat upright.
Her lean sprinter's body pointed like an arrow. She dog-
eared her page and slapped the book down on the plastic
table next to her. With quick grace, she rose from the
chair and stood barefoot on broiling concrete.

A second crash made her yelp in surprise. What was

going on? Casey headed for the fence gate at the side of the house, but she hadn't taken four strides before the gate slammed open.

"Huh?" she said foolishly. A section of stockade fence nosed through the open gate like the prow of a ship. A straining young man carried the fence section. Casey couldn't figure out how he did it by himself.

"Where do you want it?" the kid grunted.

A voice from the other side of the gate said, "All the way in the back." That was Daddy's voice!

"Oh, *right*," Casey remembered. "The *fence*." The fence would close in the whole backyard because of the new pool. Daddy had *said* it was being delivered today. Suddenly, Casey didn't object to the gurgling truck motor. This was interesting.

Casey followed the bobbing fence section as it floated past the swimming pool and up the slope. The kid was on the other side of the section, and Casey could see the claw of a hammer hooked onto the bottom edge. *That's* how he does it! she thought. She used her own arms to mimic the way he'd slipped the hammer under the section and then leaned the entire weight against his shoulder.

"Casey," Mr. Gordon said.

She turned. Daddy stood just inside the fence gate, in his old Army Reserve T-shirt and a pair of jeans. His curly hair looked orange in the brilliant sunlight and his skin looked paler than ever. "Hi, Daddy."

He looked at her with a disapproving expression and gestured with one hand. "Uh, do you think you could put something on while these men are here?"

Casey became aware of her yellow bathing suit with the huge cutouts on both sides. It was also slashed at the thighs, so it showed a *lot* of her. She felt suddenly embarrassed. "Daddy, don't be *old*."

"Casey!"

She made a silent raspberry with her lips. With an exaggerated flounce, she went to the picnic table, reached beneath the umbrella, and snatched up a lacy white beach jacket. She turned to watch the kid throw down the fence section as she knotted the jacket's cord around her waist. The thin material made her feel the dampness that coated her skin.

"Happy?" she asked.

"Yes."

She shook her head. "It's not like I'm going to give the guy hot flashes. I mean, this body does not drive men into ecstasy."

"Could you watch your mouth?"

She dropped into the lounge chair. "Here at the convent, we just read and do silent prayer."

Casey picked up the paperback, but she peered over the top of it to watch the kid come back down the slope. She *knew* this boy. From where? He was tall and strong-looking, with light, flowing hair. She couldn't place him but she liked looking at him. He moved like a prizefighter, balanced on the balls of his feet. She could see muscles moving under his white T-shirt. They weren't the muscles that come from pumping iron; he was ropy and tight, with a narrow waist and a firm rear end.

She giggled to herself. God, if Daddy knew what she was thinking, he'd lock her up. But she liked the foamy tingles that rolled down her back. She imagined holding this boy very tightly and kissing him hard on the mouth.

Don't fall for anybody now, jerk, she warned herself.

She couldn't handle that, for sure. Not another louse like Mark Simon who'd make her cry until her throat got raw. For Casey Gordon, love meant pain; she'd learned *that*. She always found the wrong guy, and he always did a number on her. She'd done Mark's homework, typed his term paper, lent him money, bought him a gold ID bracelet, and given him every drop of love inside her. And in return he hadn't bought her even a gumball ring—and he'd cheated on her, canceled dates, and left her sobbing in her room on Prom night.

Creep, she thought, as she relived the nightmare. It made her feel ice-cold inside, even as her skin cooked. She let the paperback rest on her lap; her damp hands were doing a number on the book. It was Faye Pollack's book, and Faye had told her not even to bend the cover back.

The foxy guy returned with another fence section. This time he stayed on her side when he lugged the fence up the slope, and she could watch the way he bulged out at his shoulders and across his back. His T-shirt rode up and she saw a tanned slash of skin and the waistband of his undies. She snickered.

The screen door opened and Mom looked out. She wore an aqua beach jacket over her bathing suit and she looked pretty good, though she was getting a little chunky around the middle. But her tallness covered it. Mom wore her elegant-looking eyeglasses and her hair was done up, and she looked really rich and brilliant. She wasn't that brilliant, and not that rich either, not since Dad's heart attack. But Mom was committed and strong, so very strong.

"Hey, you got a beer?"

"What...?"

He stood over her, and his head eclipsed the sun. Casey couldn't see his features, just a black oval, and of course his long, powerful body stretching from the sky to the patio. He smelled sweaty.

"A beer." His voice sounded amused. "I could use a cold one."

"Oh," she said. "I'll ask my—"

"Hello, there," Casey's mom said.

Casey gasped. She'd forgotten that her mom had come outside. Of *course* Mom had come outside; that's what had started Casey on her reverie.

The boy looked over at Mrs. Gordon and, for some reason, Casey felt a chill pass through her, like a sense of danger.

"Hi," he said. "I wondered if you had a beer."

"Yes, of course," Mrs. Gordon said. "I'll bring it out to you." She turned to go back into the house. "Oh," she added, "if you get too hot doing that, feel free to jump into the pool."

"Thanks," he said.

The screen door slammed. Wow, Casey thought, Mom is being nice to the proles. Well, Mom was really psyched up about the new swimming pool. Dad had bought more land in the back, and when the pool was being dug, the neighbors had kept coming over and watching with green-eyed envy. This got Casey's mom turned on. Any evidence that the Gordons were getting richer made Mom go singing through the day, and even made her lovey-dovey with Dad.

Casey made a visor of her hand and smiled up at the boy. "I love how you carry those fence sections."

"Yeah?"

"Do I know you from somewhere? I think I recognize you."

"Maybe it was the night we made love in the laundro-mat," he said.

"Huh?"

He laughed, and it was that nasty little laugh that clicked in her memory. "Oh, God, you're Paul VanHorn."

"No," he said. "It's: Oh, Paul VanHorn, you're God."

She felt a little disappointed. "Very funny, hyuk hyuk hyuk. Did they ever let you graduate?"

"Yeah. I had to go to Logan's office the Monday after graduation and get the diploma. They pulled down the shades."

"I'll bet." Her eyeballs were throbbing from the sun. "Do you think you could move over a few feet so I don't go blind looking at you?"

He shifted. Still uncomfortable, she stood up. Dizziness rushed over her; she'd moved too suddenly, and it was too hot. His hand slipped under her wrist and locked on, preventing her from falling. She swayed a little and felt her tuna fish sandwich come spinning into her throat. She sucked a deep breath and told herself not to puke.

"You okay?" he asked.

She nodded. The backyard spun slowly, like a merry-go-round. "Thanks," she said. "I was sitting too long."

He looked up and down her body. "You don't seem too long to *me*."

She tilted her head and made a sardonic face. "Are you really as much of an asshole as they said?"

She expected him to go "Hee-haw" or something, but to her surprise, he looked hurt. "That was a crappy thing to say."

She flushed. "I'm sorry. I guess it's just your reputation."

"No problem."

Her eyes picked out tiny black capillaries of soil that sweat had etched into his neck. His eyes gleamed an intense blue, maybe more intense because she saw them through sunglasses. His face was sculpted, very strong and bold. His mouth looked sensuous. She wished he didn't make her squirmy inside.

It was weird meeting Paul VanHorn like this. She hadn't known him when he was at Westfield High School, but everyone knew *about* him. He was supposed to come from a screwed-up family, and the story said he was a super-bright guy who hardly did any work. He'd flunked out of half his classes, the ones he didn't drop. She knew he hadn't been allowed to attend graduation ceremonies because he'd shredded and spray-painted his official senior T-shirt and worn it wrapped around his naked torso during an assembly. He'd worn bikini underpants to the senior banquet and slam-danced with his friends. Lots of stuff like that. But people also said he was angry and sensitive and mixed up. He'd gone through a few girlfriends, most of them from other schools, and nobody knew *anything* about *that*.

"Are you going to college?" Casey asked.

"No."

"Just delivering fence sections?"

"I'm making money. That's what counts."

"I guess so."

Simultaneously, two other guys brought back another fence section and Casey's mom came outside with a tall bottle of Miller. Nobody in Casey's family drank beer, but Mom always kept a case in the garage for workmen. Mom assumed all manual laborers drank beer.

"Here," Mrs. Gordon said.

"Thanks." He accepted the bottle and tilted back his head, and his Adam's apple bobbed up and down as he guzzled. Rivulets of beer ran down his chin and seeped under his T-shirt. Casey remembered now that Paul's hair had been shorter in school; in fact, he'd flaunted a Mohawk for a while, and an earring. She looked, and saw the grayish spot in his earlobe.

She watched the other workmen as they dropped the fence section. One guy was young and huge, with a white belly that protruded from an open plaid shirt. The other man was about sixty, leathered by sun and wind. As they trudged back down the slope, Paul called out, "Hey! You dropped it!"

The older man looked at Paul with disgust. The fat kid chuckled. Casey's mom, said, "Anything else I can get you?"

"No, thanks, ma'am," Paul said, with a snide little smile. Casey wanted to slap his face.

"Tell the other men the same offer goes for them," Mrs. Gordon said.

"I surely will, ma'am."

Mrs. Gordon turned to her daughter. "Casey, when you get a chance, I'd like you to run to King Kullen for me. I need a few things for supper."

"Do I have to?"

"No," Mom said coldly. "You sit here. I'll do it."

"I get the message," Casey said.

"You have a real attitude problem," Mrs. Gordon said. "Work on it." She walked away and slammed the screen door. Casey sighed. Paul said, "Get hassled a lot?"

"All the time. She's so into her business that she never gets organized. She forgets half of what she wants to buy and I wind up running around for her."

"Yeah, you look busy."

"Who asked you?" She went to the picnic table and poured cold lemonade from a red plastic pitcher into a yellow plastic cup. She drank it in three gulps.

"Want some beer?"

She looked at him. "No."

"Sure you do. Bet you want to take off all your clothes and jump in the pool with me."

"What a jerk," she said. She laughed despite herself. "All I want to do is sit in that chair for one afternoon and let my brain rot. I've been working eight hours a day at Waldbaum's. I've been up at the track getting in shape. I've been memorizing college catalogues. I've had a lousy summer—again."

He drank another mouthful of beer. "You're on a treadmill."

"So?"

"Want to be?"

"Don't analyze me, okay? My track coach analyzes me all the time. 'How do you feel about it?' That's his favorite line. Like he cares."

"Whoa. You're pissed off."

She looked at him. "Yeah, a little. Everyone pushes me. My times are never fast enough, my grades are never high enough. I have to get minimum 95 in everything. Getting an 85 is like failing. I get punished for it. Man, I'm not that good. If I don't make Yale, my dad's going to throw a second coronary. They've already made it perfectly clear that his first one came from overworking himself so he could afford college for me. That's a nice thing to live with."

She couldn't believe she was saying this to him. She stalked over to the table and refilled the cup. He watched her with hooded eyes. The older man and the fat kid came back with another fence section. "Hey!" the old man yelled. "You want to move it, Paul?"

"On my way." He set the bottle on the picnic table. "Hate to leave you like this."

"Go ahead. You're not getting paid to hear about my problems."

"But you're interesting," he said. He smiled a very sweet smile and jogged out through the gate.

Casey let out a long breath. Whoa, she thought. She took her cup of lemonade and ambled to the pool, crossing a patch of hard dirt. Dad had started to build decking around the pool, but he hadn't gotten this far. Casey looked down into the water. It lay calm and shiny, like blue Lucite, and she could see the pattern of the liner all the way to the bottom, which was sprinkled with ochre dirt. The concrete around the diving board was almost dry, but some damp gray spots remained. Casey remembered when the backyard had ended here. She'd liked the depth and sadness of the woods, the way the trees seemed to curve toward the house like a sheltering dome. She'd liked the way the afternoon sun had slivered through the trees, making dappled shadows. Now the sun just sat there, sizzling. But at night she could see lots more stars.

Paul came back with another section. She could almost feel the pain in his joints and muscles. Casey liked the way the fence sections formed a path of yellow rectangles down the slope. Daddy had already set fence posts into the dirt, and they stood like the rough bars of an animal cage. There were a few scrubby trees left on the property, but no grass. They could now see the house on the next street, and Casey hated that. All this destruction so her little princess sister could have her own pool to play in.

Paul suddenly stood at the shallow end of the pool, his chest heaving. Casey said, "Take it easy."

"Why?"

"Okay, *don't* take it easy. Kill yourself."

"Whatever you say."

She made an exasperated sound. "Idiot."

So abruptly that it made her lose her breath, Paul's body arched over the pool steps and he dove into the shallow end. He broke the water with a slap. Somehow it scared Casey to watch him swim. Had he worn a bathing suit, it would have been okay, but he wore his filthy clothes and it was as if he polluted the pool. He swam two or three laps, with powerful strokes. Casey worried about Mom or Dad coming back and giving her hell for allowing this. She wished he'd get out.

Finally, he stopped swimming and grabbed the ladder. He tossed his head to make his soaked hair fall back. He grinned up at her. "Beautiful."

"I think you should get out."

"Mommy going to yell?"

"Come on."

"She said I could use the pool."

"Not in your clothes."

"Oh, yeah." He pushed off from the side, and unsnapped his jeans.

"*Damn* it!"

Laughing, he crossed his arms and worked off his wet T-shirt. He made a ball of it and tossed it onto the ground alongside the pool. He swam a few more laps, but now the sun rippled over his back. Casey trembled.

Finally, he hauled himself out and stood at the side of the pool, streaming water. His flat stomach went in and out like a bellows, and his chest gleamed. He smiled boyishly. "Nice pool."

"Thanks."

He put his hands on his hips. "You have a towel, or do you just want to watch me drip?"

"Huh? Oh, sure." She hurried back to the patio, dropped off her lemonade cup, and grabbed a striped towel from a beach chair. Paul now smelled of chlorine and sun. He daubed himself with the towel and then scrubbed his hair, which hung like shaggy fur.

"Thanks," he said, and handed back the towel.

His eyes roamed over her, making her feel self-conscious. She was glad now that she wore the beach top. But her long, well-muscled legs were his to see, for whatever they were worth to him. And her mediocre face and a nice spray of chest freckles.

"Want to go out sometime?" he asked.

She gaped at him. "Where?"

"Saudi Arabia."

She laughed. "Sorry. You caught me by surprise."

"Have you recovered?"

She tried not to get webbed in his eyes, but it didn't work. She felt her throat tighten and her stomach grab. "Yeah, sure. Give me a call."

"I will." He smiled again and walked away, with a confident, sexy walk. Casey held the towel in both of her hands, the warm dampness pulsing against her palms. She wondered why she was so afraid of him and why she had agreed to date him. And she'd agreed the first time she'd looked up at him. He knew it, too.

You really do like the pain, don't you? She rolled her eyes upward, as the next fence section was carried through the gate.

Chapter Two

FAYE POLLACK SQUINTED UP AT CASEY AND SAID, "PAUL VanHorn? You're going out with Paul *VanHorn?*"

Heather Newcombe said, "You're nuts," as she did a pirouette in the sand. Lillian Purcell sat on the crumpled blanket with one leg stretched out and an expression of martyred pain on her face.

"Well, I haven't gone out with him yet," Casey said.

"I heard he killed a girl once," Lillian said.

"Oh, for God's sake." Casey shook her head and looked out at the gray ocean as it heaved and rolled. Millions of sparkles bounced off the water, and a seething mist filtered pale light through the air.

"I heard that, too," Heather said, a little breathlessly. She kicked off into a few jetés and then raised her arms and went *en pointe,* as much as she could on the beach.

"It should make for an interesting date," Casey said dryly. She liked how the sea wind blew back her hair.

"Where's he taking you?" Faye asked.

"He's not taking me anywhere," Casey said. "He asked me if I'd go out with him and I said he could call me."

"And he hasn't called you?"

"No."

"Aha," Faye said. She lay back against a blow-up pillow, her permed hair cushioning her head. Her long, bony form looked undernourished in a violet bathing suit with a flounce at the chest. Faye never got suntanned, no matter how much she stayed outside.

"Why are we here?" Casey asked suddenly.

"Jeez," Faye said, "we're getting deep."

Casey laughed. "No, I mean why are we on the beach? It's disgusting out."

"I don't know," Faye said. "We talked about where to go and we came to the beach."

Lillian whimpered in pain and bent over to rub her leg. Her mass of chestnut hair blew wildly in the damp wind. She wore a white bathing suit which showed off her revoltingly terrific bosom to good advantage. How was it, Casey wondered, that a virginal little creep like Lillian was so well endowed?

"Does it hurt bad?" Casey asked. She figured *one* of them would have to ask, or Lillian would keep whimpering.

"Yeah," Lillian said tightly.

"What did the therapist say?"

"He laughed." Lillian stretched as far as she could, trying to touch her toe. "He's a maniac. He can't wait to strap me into that machine. Torture is his specialty."

"Is it getting any better?" Casey asked.

Lillian shrugged. "It still hurts."

Faye said, "You should see another doctor."

Lillian made a face. "The next nearest sports medicine center is in Nassau County. Since my mom uses my car, I can't depend on getting there."

Heather did toe touches now, and Casey marveled at how smoothly she doubled over. Casey secretly thought that Heather had thick legs for a dancer, but she was really serious about it and had performed in recitals. "*I'm* going to need therapy soon," Heather said between bends. "The pain is getting bad."

"You work at it too hard," Faye said. She had taken a

shiny apple from the Styrofoam cooler and she bit into it with a sharp crack.

"I know," Heather said morosely. She straightened up and shook back her white-blonde hair. Her big turquoise eyes blurred with tears. Heather almost always had tears in her eyes.

Faye asked, "Heard from Jon lately?"

Jon was Heather's eternal love of the moment. He was a six-foot Viking type who was taking Air Force training out West. "Yes," Heather said. "I got a beautiful long letter from him two days ago. He is so sad, Faye. He really needs me. He's like a little lost boy."

"Aren't they all?" Faye said caustically.

Heather spun away, her lower lip jutting. Casey gave Faye a recriminating look. Around them, the beach was nearly deserted. Some decent-looking boys were playing catch with a Nerf football at the water's edge. They had terrific builds, but they seemed too dumb to bother with. A couple of family groups had braved the grim weather. About thirty yards down the beach, a fat woman watched two toddlers as they kept falling into the foam.

But otherwise, it looked like The Day After. Casey *knew* it was dead because she didn't hear the usual cacophony of boxes blasting eighteen different kinds of music. Their own box sat mutely next to the cooler. They'd played snippets of two tapes, gotten bored with each one, tried the radio, and then shut the thing off. It was that kind of day.

"Let's get out of here," Casey said. "We're all going to get arthritis."

"I've already *got* arthritis," Heather said tragically.

"I'm ready to go," Lillian said. "I want to get some clothes on and get warm."

"What's doing for tonight?" Faye asked. She dropped her apple core into the sand and dug a hole for it with her fingers.

"I have choir practice," Lillian said.

Faye said, "*I'm* free. For about the next twelve months."

Casey smiled. "We could go to the movies."

"We've seen everything," Faye said. "Unless you want to go all the way to Commack. I think they've got a couple of new ones."

"Nah," Casey said. She dropped onto one knee and massaged her thigh, which had begun to cramp.

Heather hugged herself tightly. "I think I've got a ballet class tonight. I'm not sure. It was supposed to be Thursday night but my teacher canceled."

"So it's you and me, Casey," Faye said.

"I guess so."

"Unless Paul VanHorn calls you."

"Will you lay off?"

"Will you go if he calls?" Heather asked.

"Oh, *man!*" Casey stood erect. "What is the big deal? I'm old enough to date."

"Not old enough to die," Heather said.

This made even Lillian laugh. Faye chuckled her private chuckle, which never quite became a sound. Casey put her hands behind her neck and lifted her sticky hair. "Who told you he killed a girl?"

"Oh, it's just a story that went around," Faye said. "Remember a few years ago when they found that girl's body under a pile of leaves? And that sick kid was leading tours up there before the cops found out?"

Casey thought for a minute. The waves broke with a rush and hiss. "Wasn't that out West or something?"

"I think so," Faye said.

"So?"

"Well, everyone really got into that, how creepy it was and what would *we* do."

"I remember," Lillian said. "My teacher did a lesson on it."

Heather said, "We had to write a story on it. I wrote one about a girl who was preserved in ice. She had long blonde hair flowing behind her back, and she was in ice

21

because her lover couldn't bear to see her get sick. She had this cancer that was going to rot her skin—"

"Thank you, Heather," Faye said. "We get the idea."

Casey grinned. "So that's when the story went around?"

"Yeah," Faye said. "Somebody knew one of Paul's girlfriends and heard that the girl's family moved away because of what Paul had done to her. Pretty soon, people were saying that Paul had strangled the girl and buried her body by the motocross pits at Exit 52."

"That's where the movies are now," Heather said.

Faye searched the cooler for something else to eat. "Right. So of course the body is buried under the parking lot where nobody will ever find it."

Lillian said, "Didn't Paul used to ride motorbikes?"

Faye came up with a Chips Ahoy cookie. "Uh-huh." She bit into the cookie. "That's how he knew about the place, see?"

A huge roller boomed against the jetty and the spray showered them. Already tense from the conversation, they all yelped, which made them giggle nervously. Faye said, "Yuk!" and scrambled to her feet like a heron. Part of the blanket lay sodden. A lacy necklace of broken shells and strewn seaweed marked the new border between mud and sand.

"Well, we either go home or move back," Casey said.

"Home," Lillian said firmly.

They packed up. Lillian asked Faye to help her up and she stood grimacing for a minute, then nodded bravely and limped in tentative circles. This let her get away with not folding the blanket or gathering up the junk. The girls gave Lillian dirty looks but nobody told her off.

Heather walked on ahead, lost in thought, as they trudged back to the parking lot. Lillian limped behind. Casey said to Faye, "She had that knee surgery eight months ago. Doesn't it ever get better?"

"Not if it's more fun this way."

"Why don't we just let her limp along by herself?"

"You want to?"

Casey sighed. "How do you get to control things like Lillian does?"

"With a big vulnerability act," Faye said. "And you believe in yourself."

Casey threw her arm around Faye's jutting shoulder and felt the gritty rub of Faye's bathing suit against hers as they slogged through the sand. "How do you get to do that?"

"Stay dumb so you don't see the truth?"

Casey laughed. Her calves hurt from pushing against the sand. Her old cartilage injury flared. If this was a damp autumn, she'd suffer in the meets.

They let go of each other to make better progress. "Casey?"

"Yeah?"

"Be careful, okay?"

"With what?"

"With Paul VanHorn."

"Faye—"

"No crap. I'm going to be lonely with all three of you guys wrapped up in your obsessions."

"I'm not obsessed, Faye."

"But you *get* obsessed. I've gone through it with you."

Casey laughed off the jibes. "If Paul VanHorn calls, I *may* go out with him, just to see what he's like. But I *can't* get involved. I've got too much to do. I want to get into college and *out* of Westfield High School. I want to move far away and get plastic surgery and start again."

Faye looked at her. "Casey, I worry about you. I don't think even you know what goes on in your brain."

"Yeah, I do," Casey said softly. "That's the trouble."

Lillian groaned and Casey and Faye turned toward her. With a mutual sigh, they trekked back through the sand to help their friend.

* * *

As it turned out, Faye had to drive into Brooklyn with her mother, because her aunt had been rushed to the hospital with chest pains. So Casey wound up on the family-room sofa, curled in the lotus position, watching TV. She'd popped the tape of *Death of a Salesman* into the VCR and sat in the dark, her eyes shining. She held the remote control in her hand, and wore a hooded sweat shirt and a pair of shorts.

She could hear Mom and Dad in the brightly lit kitchen; they were talking finances at the table. Between Dad's real-estate deals and Mom's flea market sales, they spent a lot of time with the calculator and all the papers spread out. Casey knew if she went into the kitchen to stare into the fridge, she'd get dirty looks.

On the screen, Dustin Hoffman was doing that incredible scene with his boss, and Casey got goose bumps all over again. Most of Casey's friends would think she was nuts for watching *Death of a Salesman* for fun. It was schoolwork. But Casey liked it. She liked *Macbeth,* too, but she didn't talk about it because you were supposed to hate Shakespeare.

Through the family-room window, she could see the pool illuminated against the blackness. In the playroom, which used to be Grandpa's room, JoAnne was playing. When Grandpa died, nobody had asked Casey what should be done with the room. It just became JoAnne's playroom, filled with the toys everybody bought her. This was in addition to JoAnne's *bedroom,* which was Doll City. Well, JoAnne was the Miracle Baby, the baby Mom and Dad weren't supposed to have.

Casey bit her lip. She didn't care. It was easier to hate everybody. It didn't do much good to talk.

Daddy suddenly walked in. He glanced at the screen. "I can't believe you're actually watching a decent program."

"It's good," she said, sniffling.

"Yes, I know it's good. But look what it does to you. Your mother is the same way. She watches old Bette Davis movies with a box of tissues at her side."

Casey smiled, as the wetness touched the corner of her mouth. "'What's Hecuba to him or he to Hecuba that he should weep for her?'"

"Oh, right—*Julius Caesar.*"

"*Hamlet.*"

"I don't think so, Casey. I think it's *Julius Caesar.*"

She resisted the urge to fight. "Whatever you say."

He sat, unexpectedly, in one of the big stuffed chairs. Casey wasn't sure how to react. She didn't want to watch the play with him. She didn't want his comments on it, or his attempts to show off his learning.

"So what's up?" she asked.

He shrugged. He still wore his business shirt, but he'd taken off his tie and opened his collar. Dad was in good enough condition, though he had love handles. He went to the health club twice a week. Still, he looked pale and tired. His hair clung damply to his forehead.

"You want to watch this?" she asked.

"No. I just wanted to chat. I don't get to see you much."

"No problem."

"I don't like that tone of voice."

She turned the remote control over and over in her hands. Her chest tightened. "I'm sorry. I'm in a bad mood."

"Well, I can understand. You're under a lot of pressure. You've been working hard this summer, and we're proud of you."

He didn't *sound* proud. He sounded like he was going to pick a bone with her. Dad never sat down to talk to her unless he was going to lecture. And he always lectured after Mom had bullied him into it. Most of the time, he acted frightened of her and kept to himself. She wished she could love him, but he'd hidden behind Mom all these years and she really didn't know him very well. "Thanks," she said.

He smiled. "I love the way you do that."

"Do what?"

"Curl up on the couch. If I tried it, I'd be in traction."
She smiled. "Oh. It's no big deal."

"Not for *you*. Did you do any running today?"

At once, the pressure was there, as if a valve had been turned. "No."

"What *did* you do?"

"Went to the beach." She stared at the screen, which showed a commercial. "I know how much I need to run before the season starts. I'll be in shape."

"I'm sure you will," he said. "And believe me, if the team doesn't win, it won't take anything away from how good you are. But I worry that the whole senior letdown thing will make you cut back, and that would be a terrible waste."

"I don't have a senior letdown thing," she said. "I'm taking BC Physics, Honors English, Concert Choir, AP Calculus, College Sociology, College Journalism..." She ticked off the subjects on her fingertips. "And Mr. Young doesn't let any girl on the team hold back. I'm going to be ass-deep in work."

"Watch your mouth, Casey."

She blew a breath upward, making the airstream lift her hair. "Sorry."

On the TV screen, Willy Loman and his sons were all talking at once, none of them listening. Mr. Gordon looked defeated. "Your sarcasm is ticking me off, Casey."

"Well, I don't know what you want. If I'm not studying or running or working, you get so nervous. You think you have to stay on top of me every minute."

"Well, you've shown us that it's necessary. You've always been bright, but we've always had to prod you."

"I know."

"Well, doesn't it bother you at all? Listen, I *know* how much you can want to let go. I let go myself a couple of years back and we almost lost this house. But I got it back. I beat the odds on my heart. And your mom beat the odds with JoAnne. Everything we have is ours because we kept fighting."

"Well, I'm not a fighter."

"Are you *proud* of that?" He leaned toward her. "Do you think it's okay that someone with your talent keeps falling off the wagon so easily? Look at that semester you were absent twenty times. They told us you had a phobia about school. Can you imagine what that did to us?"

"Give me a break," Casey said, flopping back against the couch. "If you don't like my attitude, why don't you just punish me some more? That's your response to everything else."

"That's a lousy answer," he said. "We punish you when you deserve punishment, and that's not the issue here. We prod you because we want you to be excellent, and we have a right to want that. You have too much going for you to give up on yourself. Taking all the right subjects isn't enough. You're nearly eighteen. It's about time you supplied the spark. We appreciate your achievements, but we're tired of leading you by the hand."

His words fell like punches, finding her soft, unprotected parts. It hurt more because she knew he was just Mom's emissary and maybe he didn't even believe what he said. "Okay, okay," she said. "Don't worry, I'm not going to fall off the wagon."

Mr. Gordon nodded. "That's good to hear."

Mom's voice came inquiringly from the kitchen. "Is everything all right in there? Should I call the police?"

Daddy smiled tightly. "No problem," he called back. "Just a little father-daughter combat."

"Understood," Mom said.

Mr. Gordon pressed his palms against the chair's arms and stood up. "Friends?"

Casey picked up the remote control again. "Sure."

"I know this hurts you," he said awkwardly. "It hurts me, too. But I know what you'll be facing."

"Okay."

The phone rang shrilly, making her jump. Since the phone sat on the table next to the couch, she pounced on it. "Hello?"

"Glub glub."

"Who is this?"

"The Creature from the Black Lagoon. Do you get off on kissing a guy with fish lips?"

Her heart thudded and she felt cold even in the sweat shirt. Daddy was looking strangely at her. "Who is it?" he asked.

Casey waved a hand at him. "Talk straight, Paul."

"Okay. I want to take you to a movie tomorrow night."

The room seemed to lean forward and listen. Why was this such a big decision? "Uh...yeah, I guess so. Sure."

"Great. I'll be there at seven."

The phone clicked. Daddy was staring hard now. "Casey?"

She clutched the phone receiver, light-headed. She wished she'd said no. But she couldn't wait to see him. Faye appeared in her mind, and Casey banished her. It was just a date, not a big deal.

Chapter Three

OWEN YOUNG KEPT HIS EYE ON CASEY AS SHE SPRINTED around the far side of the track. He appreciated her hungry strides and fierce concentration. She wasn't breaking any records this afternoon, but she was fighting.

"Go!" he yelled to her. "Come on! Dig!" He didn't think she heard him. By now she'd be wrapped in a cocoon of rushing wind, her head pounding and her heart a drumbeat. Owen knew the sensations. His own muscular legs tingled now with sympathetic pain. He wore a tank top and gym shorts and his tanned skin seemed to glow in the afternoon light.

He smiled ruefully. He knew the girls sometimes sneaked looks at him, and called him a fox. A balding fox, he thought, as he pushed back his thinning hair. They loved to make jokes about his sunburned forehead, and they went into mock mourning when he wore his glasses in English class. He didn't wear the specs for practice, though. There was a limit to how much he'd surrender to the ravages of time.

"Aces!" he said, as Casey slowed to a jog. The other girls whooped and clapped encouragingly. Casey managed a weak smile as she shook out her arms and sucked in air.

Owen walked over to her and slipped a strong arm around her trembling shoulders. "Nice," he said.

"Too slow."

"It's heavy out today."

"No excuses."

"Come on," he said. "When do I make excuses? I'm brutal."

She smiled, and her slender body yielded to his squeeze. "My time was way off."

"*Off,*" he corrected. "Not *way* off. You went off balance in the downside turn. Try using your arms more."

She nodded. He let her go and watched her walk in tight little circles. "Cramped?"

"A little."

"Work it out. I think we're going to break."

He went to a bantam-sized girl with cropped hair who waited with a clipboard. "How'd she do, Amy?"

The girl looked at the clipboard. She'd just penciled in Casey's time on a chart. "Fourteen-three."

Owen felt a small vacuum of disappointment. "Two seconds off."

Amy gave him a sympathetic look. Owen walked away and gathered his thoughts. Sometimes he couldn't take their beautiful, caring eyes. It hurt to love the kids as much as he did, and to get as involved as he got. It tore him apart to go to each graduation, to hug them in their flowing black gowns and feel their wet faces against his neck. It was bad enough when the courts took your own kid away from you. To lose a hundred more every June was rough.

But he knew he wasn't going to change. I'm just a cockeyed masochist, he thought wryly. He'd keep coaching these intense girls, and he'd keep teaching English. He'd keep entering marathons he could never win. What made it worse was that he *liked* doing it.

He dismissed his reflections and went back to the long wooden bench where the girls had gathered. Some of them sat with knees apart and heads lowered. One girl idly flipped a towel. Casey Gordon put one sneakered foot on the edge of the bench and massaged her cramped thigh. Other girls sprawled on the yellow grass.

Owen gestured for Amy to give him the clipboard. He let his eyes touch each of the girls. "Okay," he smiled. "You ran your butts off. Unfortunately, you stank."

They gave mock cheers. Owen smiled again. "Actually, you didn't look bad at all. You're rusty from a summer of stuffing yourselves with ice cream and lying on the beach getting suntan oil *r-u-b-b-e-d* into your shoulders." He contorted his face into a travesty of rapture. The girls laughed. "We lucked out in one way. The first meet on"—he checked another sheet—"September eighteenth is against Greenfields and they finished last. Not that we underestimate any rival, but it gives us a shot at a win." More laughter. "*Un*fortunately, on November fourteenth, we have to face Northville for the first time and we have *got* to be ready. If we lose to them once, we won't meet them again."

He let that sink in, and watched Casey. Each year there was one student, maybe two, who became special. He thought that, this year, it might be this hard-driving, complex girl. She wrote surprisingly good poetry; her eleventh-grade English teacher had shown Owen some of her verse. Most poetry by high-school girls was greeting-card jingle, but Casey went for the heart.

Now Casey was going to be in Owen's Honors English class *and* on the track team. He wanted to help her develop her writing. He wanted to find out what animated her. He laughed to himself. What he wanted was to be her friend, until she graduated. The only problem was, Casey kept it all inside, tightly locked with a heavy chain. The way she ran, falling and bleeding, reminded Owen of himself years ago. But he'd run for the joy of it. Casey seemed to be running *from* something. And when she got hurt, she seemed pleased, as if she'd deserved it.

"Now," he said to the girls, "we've got a couple of weeks before Greenfields, but one of those is the first week of school and that's hectic for you *and* me." He glanced at the molten sky. "It also looks like there's going to be a record heat wave. But we still have to practice. Every day. No excuses. If you have sweat glands, prepare to use them now."

The groans rose in a tragic chorus.

Casey said, "You think *you've* got problems. *I've* got him for English."

Owen grinned. "True. Physical training and intellectual training, back to back."

"That's exciting," she said.

"Okay, ladies," Owen said. "Go home." He jerked his thumb upward and they slowly scattered. Owen watched as Casey retied her sneaker laces. She scooped up her gym bag and Owen said, "Casey?"

She stopped, and looked at him. "Yeah?"

"What does Casey stand for? I haven't gotten my official class rosters yet."

She smiled. "Katherine Claire."

"Impressive name."

She averted her eyes. "Yeah, well unfortunately, I didn't turn out as impressive as the name."

"Hey, what's with the sad song?"

"Sorry."

Owen felt a surge in his heart. "Don't keep apologizing. Casey's not worse than Katherine, just different."

She looked at him without emotion, her eyes shielded. "That's for sure."

He'd lost her. "Okay. I was just curious. I'll call you Casey."

"Whatever."

"Take care. Rest the leg."

"Right. 'Bye."

Like a deer released from a trap, she turned and sprinted down the slope. Owen cursed himself for being a clod. Wearily, he gathered his own equipment and stood for a moment, sweating. The deserted track mocked him as cruel ghosts ran its perimeter.

He forced himself to brighten. There'd be time to get through to Casey Gordon. He shouldered his bag and trekked toward the school building.

Casey spent half the afternoon trying to figure out what to wear for her date. She lifted dresses and skirts from her closet, stared at them, and hung them up again. She opened and shut bureau drawers, which wasn't easy because some of them were overstuffed. The white sunlight pressed against the windows, but air conditioning kept the room cool. Finally, after a lot of cursing and ten minutes of sprawling on her bed feeling sorry for herself, Casey chose a pink gingham dress that looked summery and feminine.

She took a long, steamy shower and used baby oil soap. She scrubbed her hair, which was ratty from practice, and combed creme rinse through the tangles. Her stomach fluttered as she wriggled a shift over her underwear. She didn't want to eat supper in her dress.

With wet hair slapping her neck, she racketed downstairs. Daddy was out back grilling hamburgers. She went outside and got smacked by the heat. "Whoa," she said. "It's *bad* today."

The barbecue smoke stung her nostrils, and she stood behind her father, watching him squirt ketchup onto the burgers. "Hi, baby," he said.

"Hi, Pops." She stood on tiptoe and kissed his stubbled cheek. "Patio Burgers, huh?"

"Yup." Patio Burgers were his specialty; they always elicited jokes about throwing meat on the patio. "I think Mom wants you to set the table."

"Do I have to? I was hoping to just eat and get ready."

"For what?"

"Date tonight."

"Oh." He always looked mortally hurt when she had a date. He bent over the acrid smoke and his eyes watered. Casey turned at the sound of splashing and saw JoAnne in the pool. At eight, Casey's sister was a spindly monkey, with muscular legs from her gymnastics class. She bounced up and down in the shallow end of the pool, her little head bobbing amid an archipelago of inner tubes and rafts.

"Casey?" Dad said. "The table?"

"Yeah, yeah." She looked bleakly at the picnic table, which was shaded by a big fringed umbrella. Mentally, she made a list: paper plates, plastic utensils, paper cups, napkins, mustard, salt, pepper, salad—oh, damn, that would get her hands smelly from oil and vinegar.

The muffled ring of the doorbell roused her from her misery. She tried to peer through the back door. "Who the heck is *that*?"

"Who?" Dad asked.

"Don't you hear the bell?"

"No."

She laughed. "I'll see who it is."

"Don't forget the table."

"*Yes!* All *right!* Don't get apoplexy." She shook her head and went into the house. Her bare feet felt slippery on the foyer tiles. The front door was closed because of the air conditioning, and Casey could just make out a humanoid shadow through the white curtains.

"Who is it?" she called.

"Rapist."

"*What?*"

"Open up."

Baffled, she said, *"Glenn?"* thinking of a friend who sometimes had a strange sense of humor.

"Thanks," the voice said.

She realized her goof, with a rush of embarrassment.

"Oh, no! Paul!" She opened the door. Paul grinned at her from behind dark sunglasses. He wore a white sports jacket over a pastel-blue T-shirt, and white slacks and shoes. He looked absolutely gorgeous and he was attracting attention from other kids in the street.

"What are you doing here?" she demanded. "You're supposed to pick me up at seven."

"No watch," he said, holding up a bare wrist.

"I haven't eaten yet."

"Me either."

Her heart did a Thumper imitation. "Listen, I'm not even dressed—"

"You mean that's a skin condition?"

"Will you *stop*?" She sucked in a breath, trying to slap her fluttering mind into submission. "I guess you could eat with us; Daddy can make more hamburgers."

He smiled more suavely. "I don't want to eat hamburgers with Daddy. I'll take you out."

"Oh." She tried to assimilate this change in plans. "Well, I have to ask. Could you stay here?"

"I guess."

She smiled, delighted to see him and madly excited. She sprinted through the house and out the back door, letting the screen door slam. Mr. Gordon looked sharply at her.

"Listen," she said, "my date is here early."

"Huh?"

"The guy who's taking me out."

"Who's taking you out?"

"*Daddy*." She tautened her lips, to stop herself from chattering. "There's a guy taking me out tonight. I told you, remember?"

Mr. Gordon had closed the grill cover, and he held the redwood handle with one hand. "Yes, I remember."

"So he's here now instead of at seven, and he wants to take me out to supper."

"I'm making supper."

"I know," she said. "But he wants to take me out. Do you mind if I don't eat with you guys?"

Daddy put on his hurt-angry expression. "Well, yes, I mind. We don't give up the family dinner on a whim."

Frustration bubbled in her throat. "It's not a whim, Daddy. The guy is standing out front waiting for me."

"So let him wait. Or tell him to come back."

"I'll ask Mom," she said tightly.

"No, you won't. After dinner, you may go on your date. If this fellow doesn't think you're worth waiting for, he isn't worth going out with."

"That isn't fair!"

"Neither are you." He turned back to the grill.

"I can't believe this. I can't believe I have to tell—"

The back gate opened. The sudden scrape and squeak made both father and daughter look. To Casey's horror, Paul sauntered into the backyard. He seemed to glow in the sinking sunlight.

"Hi," he said. "I'm Paul VanHorn."

"Yes?" Mr. Gordon said.

"I'm taking Casey out tonight, and we have reservations at Clams Unlimited." Paul leaned on the serving cart next to the grill. JoAnne had stopped splashing in the pool and stood straight and silent, looking with delicious terror at the interloper.

"What?" Mr. Gordon said.

Paul scratched the tip of his nose. "The thing is, sir, that a scout from Yale will be there. He was out at the track today watching the team. Now these scouts aren't allowed to talk to the girls, but if he happens to be in the same restaurant..."

Mr. Gordon looked at Casey. "Is he serious?"

Casey couldn't speak.

"She didn't want to tell you," Paul said.

Mr. Gordon said, "Are you nuts, or what?"

Casey could only shake her head. Mom came out of the

house, carrying the napkin holder. "Oh, hello, Paul," she said cheerfully.

Mr. Gordon stared at his wife. "You know him?"

"Of course I know him," Mrs. Gordon said, as she adjusted the angle of the umbrella. "He delivered the fence."

Mr. Gordon looked back at Paul, and recognition brightened his face. "I didn't recognize you."

"It's the sunglasses," Paul said.

Mrs. Gordon said, "Are you here for Casey?"

"Yes, ma'am," Paul said. "We're just having a hard time getting her out."

"Excuse me?"

Casey shook her head *No!*, and Mr. Gordon said, "I told her she had to have dinner with us."

Mom nodded. "Well, Casey, he's right. You can't spring things on us like this."

"It's my fault," Paul said. "I came early."

"Oh." Mrs. Gordon sized up the situation. Casey made hard fists out of her hands. "Well, Ron, that seems like an extenuating circumstance."

"But I'm cooking the hamburgers."

"I can reheat what we don't finish. I think we can show Casey some leeway."

Daddy's eartips reddened. Casey knew she was playing Mom against Dad, but she didn't care. Daddy said, "Fine. If that's what you want to teach her." Viciously, he flipped the burgers. One dropped between the grates of the grill and he snapped an obscenity. Paul beckoned Casey to go with him. Casey said, "I have to get dressed."

Paul made weird faces and rolled his eyes toward Casey's father. Casey giggled. Mom said, "Paul, why don't you wait out front. She'll be along."

Paul shrugged, and ambled back through the gate. Mom looked reprovingly at Casey and said, "Try to make your arrangements more conscientiously next time."

"I will," Casey said. "Thanks! See you guys tomorrow."

Daddy was grabbing at the protruding edge of the fallen Patio Burger and hissing curses, so Casey didn't wait for a reply. She heard Mom yell, "JoAnne, come out of the pool, please. Dry up and change for supper."

JoAnne whined *"N-o-o-o-o!"* as Casey let the screen door slam behind her.

As she leaned back against the red vinyl seat of Paul's 1980 Oldsmobile Cutlass, Casey laughed. "You're out of your mind."

"I know," he said. He drove casually, a hand palming the top of the red steering wheel. The radio blasted rock music, and the engine roared. They raced past scrub trees toward a pink and violet sky.

"You're lucky my dad didn't call the cops," Casey said. "What kind of story was that? A *scout*?"

"I was trying to get you out."

"First of all, Yale wouldn't send a track scout to Westfield High School. And why wouldn't a scout be allowed to talk to me?"

"I don't know," he said. "I made it up."

"You almost got me grounded forever. Thank God my mom came out."

"Good old Mom."

She turned sideways to study him. He'd shaven quickly, because there were a couple of tiny scabs on his cheek and neck. His sandy hair whipped in the warm wind. He sort of grimaced as he drove, and his fingernails tapped a rhythm on the roof. The jacket fit him loosely; it was a cheap knockoff of the Italian original. She'd seen it in Caldor's.

"Where are we going?" she asked.

"Clams Unlimited."

"Really?" Oh God, Casey, you sound like a junior-high jerk. "That's kind of expensive."

"You're worth it."

She felt her neck get warm. Her dress was scoop-necked and it shaped her nicely. She felt girlish and sexy at the same time. She'd fluffed her hair with the blow dryer and put on light blush and liner and a touch of lip gloss, just enough to make her mouth look moist. She wanted to look good for him.

"I don't want you to feel obligated," she said. "You only asked me to the movies."

"I got off work early," he explained. "There wasn't anything to do at my house, so I figured I'd see if you were ready."

She impulsively touched his arm. "I'm a little worried," she said.

"Why?"

"They say some pretty terrible things about you. Nice girls aren't supposed to date you."

He laughed. "Yeah, I know. I didn't fit in with all the cheerleaders and preppies. I wasn't even smelly enough to be a dirtbag."

His anger was almost palpable. He'd opened a secret trapdoor and she'd gotten a glimpse of demons chained in a cellar. But he'd shut the door again, and now he hummed along with the music. Casey felt scared, but somehow close to him. Maybe it was a stupid fantasy, but she thought that she could become very important to Paul. She was getting the hot flushes and the scoops in her stomach that meant she was falling.

He broke her reverie by spinning the steering wheel sharply to the right. Casey caught her breath as the car swerved, slowed, and jounced over the gravelly shoulder of the highway. She felt weird stopping on a major road. Other cars whipped past, rocking the Olds. She could hear twilight wind, and she could see the western sky aflame with dusty scarlet.

"What's wrong?" she asked.

He hitched himself sideways and looked at her. "I'm nervous," he said.

"About what?"

"About the good-night kiss. You know: Am I *getting* a kiss? Am I *not* getting a kiss? It bums me out."

She laughed, more startled than amused. "What?"

"So I wondered, could I get a good-night kiss now? Then I can enjoy the evening."

She wondered if he could hear the drumming of her heart, because it sure deafened *her*. What did she do now? Boy, oh boy. Lonely road, night falling, Paul VanHorn the girl killer. Would he bury her under the road divider? Daddy would be *furious*.

That made her laugh out loud. Paul scrunched up his face in a little-boy expression. "Did I make a funny?"

"No," she said. "I just don't—I don't know, Paul."

He smiled reassuringly. She *hoped* it was reassuringly. "I'll make it easy. No hands."

She thought she would stop breathing. He put his hands behind his back. The car's motor kept running, *chug chug chug*. Clouds raced like sculls across the lavender river of sky, and the horizon turned blood red. *Whoosh* went another car past them. Casey could see headlights stabbing the blue dusk.

Her mouth was dry. Her hands rested stiffly in her lap, and boy, were they damp. She could feel her deodorant melting under her arms. Paul leaned toward her and she stiffened and pulled her head back. His lips brushed hers. She sat utterly still and her pulse kicked her throat. He pressed his mouth to hers very softly. His lips felt cool and dry.

She shut her eyes. His hair smelled of hot afternoon sun. She sensed moisture on his forehead. She returned the pressure of the kiss, but kept her mouth firmly shut. Her heartbeat roared in her ears. This was ridiculous. She had *kissed* before. She had *more* than kissed. What was the problem?

Then his mouth was gone. Her eyes flickered open. He sat in a casual, nonthreatening way, one arm over the wheel. She let out a long, rattling breath.

He sat quietly for a long, long time. She died inside, not knowing what to say. She didn't think she could say anything, anyway; the roof of her mouth was sucking up her tongue. Darkness seemed to close over the car like a black hood over a birdcage. Say something, she begged. Please.

His fingers reached out and brushed aside a strand of her hair. "Wow," he whispered. "You are a sex machine."

She gaped for a full five seconds before her laughter came rushing. He turned to face forward and gunned the engine. This is going to be some relationship, Casey thought.

Chapter Four

THIS SUMMER, GLENN LINDSTROM'S MOM WAS DONATING HER house for the semi-official Back to School party. For the first time ever, Casey was torn about going. She'd always loved this gathering of friends, except last year when she was going out with Mark Simon and she'd spent the whole night crying while Faye handed her tissues.

But now there was Paul. Casey didn't want to spend a Friday night without him. She agonized over it for days after Glenn called her. She thought of calling Glenn back and saying she couldn't make it this year. But then she imagined how great the party would be, so she thought of telling Paul she was busy Friday night. Would he mind? Sometimes he got awfully moody. If he broke up with her because of it...

Finally, Casey decided to bring Paul to the party. Why not? she thought defiantly. So he *wasn't* one of the gang. It was getting boring anyway, with the same kids every year. Paul was off-the-wall and fun; he'd stir it up a little. And anyway, what about two years ago when Heather had brought that Italian exchange student she was in love with? And Lillian had brought that deaf girl three years ago when she was into teaching the deaf. So guests *were* allowed.

Casey called Glenn on the portable phone and stood by the picnic table in her backyard, watching Dad and two neighbors hammer up fence sections. "Glenn, is it okay if I bring a friend?"

"Sure," Glenn said. "Who is it?"

She took a deep breath. "Paul VanHorn."

The hammering echoed back and forth across the yard. JoAnne and two of her friends ran screeching around the far end of the pool.

"Glenn?" she said. "Are you there?"

"Yeah," he said. "I guess you can bring Paul. Is he going to do anything weird like throw people in the pool?"

"No," she said. "He's a nice guy."

"If you say so."

"Hey, Glenn, if it's a hassle, forget it."

"It's not a hassle," he said. "He's just not everybody's favorite guest. But if you're vouching for him, it's no problem."

Boy. He wasn't just dripping sarcasm, he was spouting it. And he was making Paul *her* responsibility, which was pressure she didn't need. But it was suddenly important for Casey to show off her boyfriend, to prove how great he was. "Don't worry," she told Glenn. "He'll behave."

They hung up, and Casey pushed down the phone's antenna with her palm. She chewed on the inside of her mouth. She should have told Glenn to go suck ice. Well, she'd made her decision, and Casey stuck to decisions the way captains went down with their ships.

Casey and Paul arrived at Glenn's house at sunset. It had been a hot, clear day, and now the sky seemed to fall in gently pleated drapes of gray and pink. Rooftops were sharply silhouetted against the dusk. The air smelled of cut grass. Glenn's mom answered the door and Casey smiled warmly at the thickset, ginger-haired woman in her usual housedress and slippers. "Hi," Casey said. "This is Paul VanHorn."

"Hi, Paul," Mrs. Lindstrom said. "Everyone's in the back."

Casey and Paul went in. To Casey, the scrubbed little house was a familiar friend. She had spent a lot of growing-up time here. She'd been here as a gangly kid in elementary school, lying on her stomach with Glenn in the family room and working on projects. She'd watched the big color TV, from "Sesame Street" right through MTV. Mrs. L. had always produced bowls of heavenly hash and plates of Oreo cookies. More recently, she had sat at the kitchen table listening to Casey cry, or complain, or ask questions. Casey's heart sang with good feelings when she came here.

And suddenly she felt as if she had violated the house by bringing Paul into it. Paul had never been a kid here. But it's too late to cop out, thought Casey: As good old Macbeth said, "I am in blood stepped in so far..."

"If you get bored later," Mrs. L. said, "we're going to get a little Trivial Pursuit tournament going."

"Super," Casey said. She asked Paul, "Do you play Trivial Pursuit?"

"Sure."

"*Great.*" Casey grabbed Paul's arm with both of her hands and leaned against him. He wore a Hawaiian flowered shirt, white ducks, and sandals. She'd put on a clingy lemon sundress that showed off her tan and sporty plastic earrings that jiggled when she moved.

She led Paul out through the sliding door in the family room and into the backyard. Faye sat in a lounge chair, eating taco chips from a bowl. Lillian was in the pool, showing how she did laps in therapy. Heather wasn't around, but a few of the other kids were. Glenn wore a Great Adventure T-shirt and shorts and fiddled with the speakers he'd set up on two folding chairs. Pop-rock thumped into the backyard.

Casey said, "This is Paul, everyone. Paul, that's Faye Pollack, and Glenn Lindstrom, and Lillian Purcell is in the pool, and that's Tracy Blayne, and Jenn Coleman, and Charlie Drucker..."

She pointed at each kid, and each said "Hi," or gave a little wave. Casey perspired. What a case of nerves, and everything was going fine. She scanned the rectangular picnic table, which had been draped with a plastic cloth and was laden with goodies. "Let's munch out," she said to Paul.

Glenn sidled by and said, "Don't fill up too much. We have the pizzas later."

"Oh, right," Casey said. To Paul, she added, "That's a tradition of the Back to School party."

Paul smiled.

Glenn said, "You look good, Case."

"Thanks. You look good, too." She filled her eyes with Glenn, and an eddy of love warmed her. God, they must have been eight or nine when they first met. He'd been this marshmallow of a kid with white hair and no neck. He was hyperactive and always ran around singing commercials. Poor Mrs. L. had gone through it with him. But he'd outgrown it, and the fat, too. Now he stood six feet tall, with ashy hair and an open, sweet face. He had a great body from lifting weights and playing on the football team, and he *still* sang commercials.

Glenn looked at Paul and said, "We've got all kinds of chips and some cheese and punch and soda. Tell me if you don't see something."

"Miller," Paul said.

Casey squeezed Paul's arm. Glenn said, "No beer."

"How about drugs?"

"Funny," Glenn said. He looked with reproach at Casey

and moved away. Casey worked a knot of anger from her throat.

"Come on, Paul," she said. "Don't do this."

"Do what?"

"Act crazy."

She felt his arm tense up. "Who are they, the Fortune 500?"

Casey pursed her lips and slipped her hands from his arm. "Okay. I don't want to get into a stupid argument."

"Is this a test?" he asked.

"No. It's just tough for me. I wish you'd understand that. I'm being pulled in different directions."

"Not by me."

She nodded. "Yeah. By you."

He moved past her and cut a hunk of Jarlsberg cheese. She looked up at him as he nibbled. He looked big and powerful. The sky darkened to a rich blue. She could see the first stars burning whitely. Amber lights came on in the backyard, and the pool was illuminated from underwater. Behind the steady thump of the music, Casey heard crickets rasping. A dog barked relentlessly down the block.

"How am I pulling you?" he asked.

"Isn't it obvious?"

"No."

She looked up at him. "I like you," she said. "A lot."

He stuffed the rest of the cheese into his mouth and gazed at her in a troubling way. "So I've got to be a good boy with your friends."

"That's a lousy way to put it."

"But true?"

She sighed angrily. "Yes. Okay. I want to be your girlfriend and I want to keep my other friends. Am I being selfish? Are you going to make it a choice, Paul? That would be a pretty rotten thing to do."

He nodded. "Yeah, it would be."

"Huh?"

He grinned. "I love to watch you squirm."

She felt relief, but he wasn't kidding around, not completely. She'd felt something snakelike about the way he'd turned the screws on her mind. "So what are you saying?" she asked.

He began to move his hips suggestively. "Let's dance. It's a party, right?"

She shook her head, laughing, but felt jammed up inside. She reached out and touched his fingers and let the music move her body. The other kids clapped and cheered and Casey flushed. But a few of the others began to dance, too, and she felt less on display. Paul was a smooth, confident dancer, and he kept his eyes locked with hers all the time. She returned his gaze with full power, sending him urgent messages: I think I could love you, Paul. Please don't hurt me. She tried to read *his* messages, but she knew that her own hopes and desires would fill in the words. She thrust her arms in the air and pumped her hips and moved her feet. It felt good to dance on the cool stone patio, with the stars coming out.

The dancing and talking went on for a while, and then the music stopped. Everyone looked toward the speakers, where Glenn stood shyly. "Okay, pizza time," he said. There were cheers and groans. "Listen," he went on, "it's gonna take about an hour to get it, so we better start ordering."

"Who's going for it?"

"Steve and Jerry, who else?"

That brought huge groans. Casey touched her fingers to her face and laughed along. For a moment, she forget that Paul stood next to her. Glenn yelled, "Come *on*, guys, let's do it. Faye's going to take down the orders—how many slices, what kind of junk you want on it—and then we can figure how many pies and what you owe."

His voice was drowned by other chatter, but somehow everyone got the idea that Faye was sitting at the picnic table with a pad and pencil. Bodies crowded around her. Faye scribbled down the orders and said, over and over, "One at a time...was that two cheese?...who said that?..."

Casey moved toward the crowd, grabbing Paul's hand. "What do you want, Paul? Cheese? Mushroom?"

Paul looked annoyed, "What is this, you order pizza and then wait for it?"

"Yeah," she said. "We do it this way every year. Once we tried to take the orders over the phone, you know, calling everyone who was coming to the party, but it got fouled up and some people didn't come and we were stuck paying for them."

"This is crap," Paul said.

"Oh, come on. I know it's high-school stuff, but don't be upset about it."

"I'm not upset."

"Good. What should we order?"

His eyes were distant. "What do you want?"

"I'm boring. I just like cheese."

"Get cheese."

She squeezed his hand, which stayed limp in hers. "Are you sure? You can get anything—anchovies, sausage, peppers. Go wild."

"Get cheese."

Once more, her chest constricted. "Okay, if that's what you want. How many slices?"

"Whatever you want."

She blew out a breath. "Why are you doing this, Paul? I thought we'd settled everything."

"Yeah, we did. I'll be back."

He twisted his hand free of hers and disappeared into the house. Casey stared after him, terrified.

Glenn was at her back. "Case, did you and Paul order yet? We're about ready."

"Cheese," she said numbly. "Uh...four slices, I guess."

Glenn leaned across the table and told Faye what to write down. Faye began to total the orders. Glenn returned to Casey. "Where'd he go?"

"Bathroom, I guess."

"Bladder problem?"

"Get a life," she snapped, and walked away. She stood by the stockade fence and wrapped her hands around two of the points. She heard Paul's Oldsmobile roar, and a minute later, his headlights rippled along the fence. Her throat tightened, and her eyes filled. What was wrong with him? She couldn't figure his mind.

And she couldn't figure *her* mind, either. She knew she was hooked on him. He could be so tender, so funny, and then he pulled idiot stunts. Maybe that's how he killed his girlfriends. He drove them nuts.

"Hi," Faye said.

"Go away."

Faye patted her shoulder. "I know you really mean that, but I'll stick around anyway. I haven't talked to you tonight."

"I know."

"I hate it when my friends fall in love. You all get crazy and nobody can talk to you."

The night air felt chilly and suddenly damp on Casey's skin. She smelled rain on the wind and when she looked up, she didn't see the stars anymore. "Oh, God. It's going to rain on our pizza."

Faye laughed. "That's deep."

Casey gripped the fence more tightly, until her palms hurt. "What's with him?"

"You tell me."

Casey shrugged. "Maybe he's just shy. I don't think he really feels comfortable. And he has this reputation and Glenn was giving him a hard time before."

"So *we* drove him away, huh?"

"Come on," Casey said. "Don't start on me."

"Well, someone has to start on you," Faye said sharply.

"I mean, what did you expect? You knew he was off the wall. He probably freaked out watching all of us act like jerks with the pizza. He *had* to notice that you were part of us and he wasn't."

Faye's words were soothing, like Ben-Gay rubbed into her legs after a meet. "I hope you're right."

"Well, see if he comes back. I mean, if he leaves you here forever, that's got to be the end of it."

Casey looked harshly at Faye. "Don't sound so hopeful."

Faye's eyes got steely. "Don't jump all over me. I'm sorry I can't be more gung-ho about him. If he's so adult, he should be able to take our antics, you know? We're not retarded here."

Faye punched the fence and stormed away. Casey spun back and pressed her body against the peeling wood. She heard Lillian climb out of the pool, to sardonic applause. Then someone yelled, "She's fainting! I need help!"

Yay, Lillian, Casey thought.

The rains came a few minutes after Steve and Jerry got back. Everyone screamed, "Hurry!" as the hot boxes were handed over the gate and set up on the picnic table. Mrs. L. brought out paper plates and napkins and a plastic bucket full of ice. Eager hands slid dripping triangles of pizza from the boxes. Eyes looked anxiously heavenward as the food was ransacked. A panicky voice asked, "Where's the other sausage pizza? Didn't you order it?" Through all of this, Casey sat on a beach chair at the far end of the patio. It had been an hour now. She began to believe that Paul wasn't coming back and that she'd have to make a big decision about ever seeing him again. What made her feel really lousy was that she knew she *would* see him again.

Faye brought Casey two slices of cheese pizza. She sat down with Casey, and Casey managed to eat the stuff, though she choked on it. It started to drizzle. Everyone groaned and ate faster. The drizzle intensified and lightning zapped the western sky. When thunder split the night, everyone went into a Keystone Kops routine to get pizza, tableware, and bodies into the house. Casey busied herself helping.

A bunch of kids went home, since the small house was now crowded and stuffy. Rain lashed the backyard, blowing the tablecloth and scattering pizza boxes across the patio. Glenn brought out the Trivial Pursuit game and the rest of the kids huddled around on the family-room carpet. Someone put an Eddie Murphy movie on the VCR, and a few kids watched that. Since there were about twenty kids around the game board, they chose teams of five, which made the game a marathon. By the time five teammates finished arguing, nobody remembered the question or where anyone's game piece was supposed to be. It didn't matter much, because they were laughing too hard and making too many dirty jokes to care about accuracy.

It was the kind of moment that Casey had always cherished, but tonight every laugh felt like a dentist's drill. She sat with her legs folded and her hair damp. Faye knelt behind her. The family room was muggy and smelled of rain and pizza. Glenn sat opposite Casey, legs sprawled. He was trying to read a question. "Okay...this is a green question..."

"What's green?" Jerry asked.

"SN," Glenn said.

"Snot?"

"Right. It's a snot question. It's about mucous."

"Gross out."

"What is it really?"

Casey said, "Science and Nature, you idiots."

Glenn deadpanned, "Science-and-nature-you-idiots. Weird."

They giggled like morons—all except Lillian, who was

in the kitchen with her leg up on a chair. Two girls sat with her and kept asking her if she could breathe.

"Come on," Glenn said. "Let me read the stupid question."

"A question can't be stupid," Faye said. "Only people."

"Come *on!*"

From where she sat, Casey saw Paul walk in. Her chest drew tight, like a belt on its last notch. Paul looked okay. He wasn't bloody or anything, and he wore the same clothes. His eyes found Casey's, but they said nothing.

Through continuing laughter and commentary, Glenn read the question: "What's the most popular form of suicide among American males?"

Silence crashed down. They could all hear the steady patter of rain and the distant rumble of thunder. "Great question," somebody said.

"Why don't we take a poll?" someone suggested. That made them laugh again.

"Well, come on," Faye said. "It's our question, team. What do you think?"

Jenn Coleman said, "Slitting your wrists, I guess."

"I don't know," Tracy Blayne said. "I think *girls* slit their wrists."

"Guys do, too."

"Yeah, but not *mostly.*"

"Pills," someone said.

"No, guys don't take pills."

Faye said, "I don't know. What *is* the most popular form of suicide among American males?"

Paul had stopped at the archway leading into the family room. "Guns," he said.

He got a good reaction. Some of the kids sitting in front of him craned their necks to see who it was. Faye looked at him and said, "You sure?"

"Yeah," Paul said.

Faye said, "Okay, guys, Paul's on our team. The answer is guns, right, Glenn?"

Glenn flipped the card over. His face turned red. "Firearms."

"All *right*."

There were protests. "He can't be on your team. He wasn't even here."

"He was on the bench," Faye said.

Casey whispered, "Cut it out."

"Just trying to help."

"Don't." Casey got up and smoothed out her wrinkled dress. "'Scuse me," she mumbled as she clumsily stepped over and around people to make her way out of the family room. The others let her pass, and nobody looked at her.

She finally stood in front of Paul. She smelled liquor on him. Not a lot, but enough. "Where'd you go?"

"I rode around," he said. "Stopped for a drink."

"Why?"

"Couldn't stand the kiddie party."

"You could have said something."

"Why should I?"

"Because I was *with* you. I would have taken a walk with you, or a drive."

"Would you have left?"

She looked fiercely at him. "Yes. I would have. What's your problem, Paul?"

He stared frozenly at her. "I'm going home. If you want to go, I'll take you. Otherwise, get a ride."

She sighed. "I'll go now. I'm not having much fun, anyway."

The truth of that hit her like a water-filled balloon. For the past hour, without Paul, she'd been with her friends just like it had always been, and yet she'd been blue. How did a guy do that to you, anyway?

With embarrassment, she went into the kitchen and said good night to Mrs. L. She also said good night to Lillian, who had her head back with an icebag on it. Then Casey went to Glenn and said, "Glenn, I'm going."

He looked up at her. The dice were in his hands.

"Okay. Nice to meet you, Paul."

"Likewise," Paul said.

Casey wanted to slap Glenn's face, and she wanted to hug him and tell him how much she loved him. But she didn't do either. She just said, "G'night, everybody," and waved.

The others waved back and said good night. Casey locked eyes with Faye for an instant. Faye's look held sympathy and concern, but it also said good-bye.

Casey let Paul escort her to the door and outside. The rain had stopped, but the air was drenched. Cars swished through the shining street. The air stank of rain. Casey shivered in her light dress, even though it was warm.

She slid into the car and buckled up, and he slid in next to her and started the engine. The drive home was slow and tense. When they were a few blocks from her house, she said, "How much did you drink?"

"Three Scotches."

"Where?"

"Bar on Portion Road."

"I see."

He gave a small laugh. Beads of sweat glistened on his temples. Casey leaned back and nursed a fearsome headache. Her sinuses felt clogged.

He pulled up on her driveway, dousing the headlights. He kept the windows closed and they fogged up. Casey sat rigidly and unbuckled her seatbelt. "Well," she said, " 'Bye."

He half turned. "Don't be a jerk."

"*Me?* You've got the wrong one, buddy."

"Hey!"

She stared ahead, focusing on little pinball drops of rain rolling down the windshield.

"I said, 'Hey'!"

She turned to him. He looked seedy and attractive, like

Bogart in the old movies. A passing car threw sudden cold light on his face.

"I'm sorry," he said. "Some things aren't easy, you know?"

She nodded, feeling tears wanting to come. "I know."

"You still want to go out with me?"

She could only nod.

"Come here."

With her throat shut down and her temples pounding, she shifted in the seat. Her arms went hungrily around his neck and she pressed herself tightly against him. She opened her mouth and kissed him with all of the feeling that had been building inside her. He pulled her closer and he tasted of whisky.

She felt tears sliding from under her closed lids. She let the kisses go on and on, never wanting them to end. She touched her fingertips to his cheekbones and ran them down the side of his neck. Finally, the waves of emotion began to subside and she rested her wet cheek against his chest. One shirt button poked the corner of her mouth. She could hear his heart beating. "Paul...," she murmured.

"Sit up."

His voice was so icy that it didn't make sense for a second. She slowly sat up, staring at him. "What's wrong?"

He pointed at her, and his voice sounded thinner. "Don't ever take me to that kind of crap party again."

"Paul, I didn't mean anything—"

His fingers struck like a snake's fangs, and her cheek vibrated with the slap. "Don't answer back," he said. "Just listen. Don't put me with your crap friends."

"Okay, I won't—"

The second slap came harder and faster. It made her yelp in surprise, and her jaw throbbed. Her hand went to her face. "What the hell are you doing?"

He stared coldly at her, like she'd turned into slime. "Just listen, okay?"

She was shivering. "Paul—"

"Shut up!" He hit her again, this time across the back of her head. The sound was a hollow pop. He was breathing rapidly.

"Oh, God," she whispered. She wondered why she wasn't more frightened, but all she could do was try to think of what to say to make him stop.

He turned around in the seat so that he faced the windshield. He gripped the steering wheel tightly and he bowed his head so that his forehead touched the rim. More cars passed, and illuminated him for brief seconds. The rain started up again, splatting against the windows.

Casey couldn't take her eyes from him. There was blood in her mouth. Her head throbbed. She kept her hands in her lap and twined her fingers. She still tasted his kiss. She didn't want to leave the car. She didn't know *what* she wanted to do.

"Go into the house," he said.

"Paul, I don't understand this."

"Forget it."

"I can't forget that you hit me. I want to talk about it."

"Later."

"How could you hit me? What's going on?"

"Damn it!" He pounded both fists on the steering wheel, once. He leaned back, against the headrest, so that his chin jutted toward the roof. He shut his eyes. "Are you stupid, or what? Go to bed. Get your teddy bear. You want me to say I'm sorry? I'm sorry. Now get out."

She was shaking. "Yeah," she whispered. "All right, Paul." She fumbled for the door handle. "Don't call me again, okay?"

"Whatever you say."

"I mean it."

He exhaled wearily. "Get out."

She ducked out of the car and shut the door viciously. She stood in misty rain, looking at him through the windshield. The car's engine roared, and the headlights flared on, making bright wet circles on the garage door. He backed up, and his tailpipe scraped the road. He drove down the street, disappearing around the corner.

Casey kept staring at the empty street. At the curb, dented garbage pails gleamed. The white streetlights looked frosty. Maple trees ruffled in the wind. Casey hugged herself and sobbed wrenchingly until she thought she would pass out. Then she stumbled to the shrub bed in front of the living-room window and threw up.

Chapter Five

FOR A LONG TIME, CASEY'S ALARM BUZZED, AND SHE DIDN'T
know what it was. In a horrible nightmare, she was at
Great Adventure, in a flume that suddenly was a rope
bridge over a chasm thousands of feet deep. She got
dizzy, and she had to walk the bridge, but it swayed. She'd
never been so scared.

Then she woke up, enough to slap the top of the
clock-radio and silence the alarm. She felt her heart
pounding, so hard it hurt. She kept her eyes shut and
told herself it was only a dream.

But as her sleep faded, she remembered the real nightmare. She looked at the glowing red numbers on the
clock. Six o'clock. Time for her morning run.

All right, she thought. Today we start from scratch.
We're gonna really get in shape.

Her determination made her feel euphoric for a few
seconds. But when she got to the bathroom and looked
into the mirror, Casey lost it. Her whole face was puffed
out, and her left cheek was gross. A purple and yellow
bruise sat right under her eye. She touched her finger to
it and hissed. It was tender, and felt squishy.

What was she going to tell Mom and Dad? Couldn't he have hit her in the stomach or something? The creep.

She bent her head and sluiced cold tap water on her face. Then she stepped out of the long, peach-colored T-shirt she'd slept in and stood under the shower. She scrubbed her hair and lathered every inch of herself, including the bottoms of her feet. She wanted to wash him away. The only bad thing about the shower was that it hurt to let the spray hit her face.

Back in her room, Casey put on a tank top and shorts, then sat on the edge of her bed to lace up her running shoes. Hazy gold light sliced the raspberry carpet. Outside, cars rolled past. She loved this time of day.

She poured a glass of orange juice. Luckily, Mom and Dad were used to her morning runs, and they didn't bug her. She drank the juice by the stainless steel sink, in the middle of the big kitchen with its bay window, feeling miserable and alone.

Why didn't I smack him back? she asked herself angrily. When she remembered just sitting there and letting him hit her, she felt her stomach heave. What a jerk.

She rinsed out the glass and went outside. The air was damp and mist hung against the cornflower-blue sky. The trees that lined the street looked top-heavy with dark green leaves. A cool breeze shivered through her wet hair.

She stretched out and then began to jog her usual route, up Roberta Street and around the big, long curve past the satellite dish in Longman's side yard. She could hear the soft thump of her sneakers against asphalt. Her thighs ached right away, especially where she'd pulled a muscle a couple of weeks ago. Perspiration broke out on her face and back.

No way am I going to quit, she thought grimly. She wished she could keep running until she was out of the development and on the expressway, and then in some other state, on a strange highway, running past farms, grazing cows, and barns with silos. She dreaded coming back home. All those questions:

"What *happened* to you?"

"Oh my God, Casey, did he *hit* you?"

"I want the truth."

"Do I have to call the police?"

Thinking about it made her run harder. She began to pant, and her lungs burned. Then she remembered that she'd upchucked in the bushes. She wondered if that stuff stayed overnight, and if Daddy would see it and ask her what it was.

She blinked away sweat, and the salt touched her tongue. Okay. She'd cover the bruise with makeup. She'd stay out of sight today, and by tonight it would probably be better. Except she'd get the third degree about what had happened after she and Paul left the party.

Well, she had to take some lumps. So they'd get on her case about what a creep Paul was. At least she hadn't gotten in too deep. In a way, she was lucky.

She broke stride and yelped as pain shot through her leg. "Damn damn damn," she said, as she limped along with her hand against the back of her thigh. She was right on Greenwood Road, with a million cars whooshing by, and probably every jerk behind the wheel was staring at her.

She managed to work out most of the cramp, but she was shot. She limped all the way back up Carla Street, and had to walk way out in the road three times to avoid the arcs of lawn sprinklers. Once she got spattered anyway. Behind her, a big green garbage truck squealed and the garbagemen clanged cans. Terrific. The garbage truck always woke up Mom. She'd probably be in the kitchen with her cup of coffee and her *New York Times*, just waiting.

Casey bit her lower lip and vowed to get away with it. No questions. She couldn't take it. As she renewed her determination, her head filled up with Paul, the way he looked while he was dancing on Glenn's patio. Her skin remembered how he felt and her mouth tingled with his kiss. She missed him, because it was over and she wasn't seeing him again.

Idiot, she thought. Stop it. Stop it. Stop it.

Suddenly, Casey laughed. The way she was limping, she probably looked like Lillian. But Casey was so stupid, she pulled this kind of stunt with nobody around.

The mall was a zoo; it was the weekend before school opened, so all the mothers were dragging their little darlings around to get them new jeans and sneakers. "I hate when they bring their kids," Casey told Faye.

"Me, too." Faye's cheeks caved in as she sucked the last of a Coke through a straw. They sat on a gray metal bench in front of the health spa so they could watch the hunks go in and out.

"I mean," Casey continued, "they know the kids' sizes, right? Why do they have to put them through torture?"

"Yeah," Faye said. She jammed the straw up and down in the crushed ice at the bottom of the cup, then shook the cup and sucked again to get the dregs of the soda.

Just then, a little blonde boy screamed and waddled ahead of his mother, who shrieked at him. Casey shuddered at the awful sounds. "Why'd she bother having him?"

"It was fun at the time," Faye said.

"Yeah, sure. Oh, Jeez, look at that!"

Casey nudged Faye. A huge guy had come up to the desk at the entrance to the spa. Faye made a face. "That's grotesque."

He wore a yellow tank top and his deeply tanned skin was stretched over enormous muscles. His biceps were the size of bowling balls. "How can he move?" Casey whispered.

"He rolls."

Casey lifted her legs up onto the bench and hugged her knees. "Can you imagine him on *top* of you?"

"Give it up."

Casey giggled. The hunk went into the spa. "Where would you hug him?" she wondered. "My arms would just make it around his *leg*."

"Sounds like something you'd do. Then he could drag you around."

"Thanks a lot."

"Don't get paranoid. Anybody ask you about your injury?"

Casey stiffened. "What injury?"

"The one to your brain," Faye said acidly. She pointed with the wet straw. "That one on your face that you tried to hide. I mean, if you're going to put on enough makeup for a prostitute, it's kind of a tip-off."

Casey gazed gloomily ahead, her chin resting on her knees. The racket of the hammering gave her a headache. They were still working on stores in the new wing of the mall. "I banged my face against the car window."

"How?"

Casey glared at Faye. "What do you mean, 'how'? Like this, dummy." She lunged forward and said, "BANG!"

"You had Mr. Epstein last year, right? You're picking up his sick humor."

"Well, what did you want me to say?"

"I meant, was it an accident or something?"

Casey faced front again. Two workmen passed by, in T-shirts and baggy pants. The smell of chocolate brownies came overwhelmingly from Mrs. Fields. "No. We were making out and I was shifting position."

Faye just looked at Casey for a moment, with cool eyes. "What kind of position were you in?"

"Get out of here, will you?"

Faye made a sour face and got up to toss out her Coke cup and straw. She came back and stood over Casey, one bony hip jutting out. Faye looked like a scarecrow in shorts and a summer blouse. "So how was it?"

"Huh?"

"Making out with Paul? Inquiring teenagers want to know."

"You're disgusting." Casey let her legs drop and flung an arm across the back of the bench.

"You were the talk of the party."

"I'll bet."

"Everyone figured he was going to dump your body on Blue Point Road."

Casey rolled her eyes heavenward and clicked her tongue. "I'm sure they're really disappointed."

Faye chewed the inside of her mouth, seeming to consider what to say. She looked around with extreme ennui. "I have to start shopping someday soon."

"Here?" Casey asked. "It's ridiculous. How about if we hit the flea markets."

"Sounds good. I need belts and shoes."

"I need pants. But I hate what they're wearing."

"You mean like those?" Faye jutted her chin and Casey looked at a pair of chunky girls in tight-fitting pedal pushers. One pair was white with big yellow flowers and one was a patchwork of Day-glo green, blue, and pink.

"That's gorgeous," Casey said. "They walk like they've got constipation."

Faye gave one of her eerie silent laughs. "You really should have taken Creative Writing."

"Oh, yeah. More pressure. I've got to do two research papers this year, and all my college essays, and track, and take the AP exams. I really wanted to do more writing."

"Oh, it's cake for you," Faye said. "Anyway, Mr. Anderson has had about twenty novels published."

"I know. He never lets anyone forget it. But nobody ever heard of any of them."

Faye smiled. "He's also a dirty old man."

Casey pursed her lips. "Sure. That's why you want to set me up with him."

The noise had become a roar, like ocean waves in Casey's head. Her cheek throbbed like mad. The afternoon and evening stretched before her like years of a prison sentence.

Faye was watching the workmen, over Casey's head. Casey realized that Faye hadn't said anything for a long time. "Did we die?" she asked.

"No. I was just watching your boyfriend. He's pretty sexy."

Casey thought that if she ever found herself in a thunderstorm and a million volts of lightning zapped her, it would feel like she felt now. She sat up very straight and hoped to God that Faye was kidding, or wrong. "What are you talking about?"

"I'm talking about the mating habits of the newt."

"Faye!"

"All *right*. Didn't you know he was working in the mall?"

"No."

"Oh, sorry. I guess you were too busy banging your face against the windshield to ask about his employment."

"Shut up, Faye."

"Yeah, right. See you later."

"No! Don't go."

Faye squinted at her in exasperation. "What's the matter with you? Did you have a fight with him or something?"

"Yes."

"You want to sneak away?"

"No."

Faye made a tight-lipped smile. "*Ho*-kay. Casey's got it bad, and she's going to act like a major fruitcake. Just feed me instructions slowly. Talk me through this."

Casey clenched her fists and let waves of conflicting emotion rock her. "I don't know what I want to do."

"Why not just go away? You can always call him tomorrow."

Casey wished she had the guts to turn around and look at him. But she didn't trust herself. She could feel her insides turning to soap suds. Hatred, like a drumbeat, crashed against her ribs. But more than anything she was scared out of her wits. Her skin crawled at his nearness.

She said, finally. "Let's go to A&S."

"A&S it is."

Casey took a deep, rattling breath and stood up. "Come on," she said urgently.

"Too late, he saw you."

"Oh, crap."

Faye stared hard at her friend. "Casey, is something wrong?"

Casey shook her head.

"What's going on, Casey? I'm scared. Do you need the police?"

Casey tried to keep her eyes steady as she looked at Faye. She could feel herself filling up. "Don't be a jerk."

She felt him come up to her. She could feel his breath on the back of her neck. "Hi, Case."

Oh, man. Everything was pumping and floating and jerking around inside. Her mouth had dried up. Her palms were damp. Faye's eyes held bewilderment.

"Can I talk to you?" Paul asked.

His voice felt like hard fingers pressing into her shoulders. Casey cursed herself for not getting out of there faster.

"Just for a minute," he said. "I have to get back to work, anyway."

Well, all right. He was here. It was probably best to finish it formally. If there were no loose ends, she'd sleep better. But she swore she'd scream her head off if he so much as touched her. "Okay," she croaked. "Just for a minute."

Faye smiled weakly. "Well, I'm off to A&S. In fact, I think I'll hit the *shoe department.*"

She stressed the last two words. Casey nodded tightly. "Okay, I'll meet you there in two minutes."

"'Bye." Faye waggled her fingers and then turned and strolled away. Soon she was swallowed by throngs of shoppers. Casey looked longingly into the alien mob, feeling stranded.

Paul said, "How about a slice of pizza or something?"

"I'm not hungry. I just had lunch."

"Do you mind if I get something?"

"Why should I mind?"

"Come on."

She made her mouth a pencil-thin line and turned around. She felt her body swell and contract, like an accordion, as she looked at him. He wore a Van Halen concert T-shirt and a pair of faded Wranglers, with ugly work shoes. His wrist veins had popped from hammering, and grimy perspiration covered him. His eyes seemed dark and hooded and a lick of damp hair had pasted itself to his forehead.

"I meant what I said. Only two minutes."

"I know."

They started to walk, through sun that filtered down through the skylight. Casey kept her mouth shut tight, refusing to make small talk. They emerged in the Food Court. Thousands of people sat at little square tables. Casey's nose filled with the smells of pizza and chow mein. Paul found a table and stood as Casey sat down. "Sure you don't want anything?"

"Nothing."

She wanted some pizza more than anything, but she'd die before she let him buy it for her. She watched him thread his way to Sbarro's. Casey brushed crumbs from the table. In the center of the white Formica lay an amorphous sticky stain, probably from soda. Casey touched a surreptitious finger to her cheek and blinked at the stinging pain. What a mess. Boy, in the movies they slapped each other in the face all the time and nothing happened.

Paul came back with two slices of sausage pizza on a paper plate and a big cup of Coke. He sat down and began to eat the first slice. He lunged a little to catch the cheese and sauce, but some strings of cheese stuck to his lip and stretched back to the plate. The smell of the pizza made Casey's stomach lurch with hunger.

Paul jerked his chin at the plate. "Hf fthr sls," he mumbled.

Casey caught herself laughing, and forced her jaw shut. She looped her handbag over the back of her chair and leaned back in what she hoped was a blasé pose.

Paul swallowed and washed it down with Coke. Casey could remember last night in the car, but it didn't seem to have anything to do with this boy.

He heaved a sigh. "Look," he said, in a fumbling voice. "I have a temper. I always did."

"You have a sickness," she said with a surge of fury.

He stopped, and seemed to square himself to take her abuse. "Okay. I usually keep a lid on it. I...don't know why I did that last night. I feel like hell."

"You ought to feel like hell. You're a creep." She didn't believe she was saying this to him.

"I left the party because I was scared," he said. He let the pizza sit on the plate now, and Casey had to restrain herself from grabbing it.

"Scared of what?"

"Of not fitting in. I knew you had these bonds with them, and it got me pissed off."

"Okay. So?"

He shrugged and drank some more Coke. "I don't know. I kept hoping I'd run into you so I could tell you I was sorry."

"Sure."

He really looked sad. "Yeah, okay. I can dig why you won't give me a break."

"Oh, come on," she said, leaning toward him. "Do you *think* I should give you a break?"

"I don't know. I'm mixed up about it. I'm crazy about you, Casey. I know that sounds like a jerkoff thing to say after I...did that stuff. I didn't get any damn sleep last night. I put my hand on the phone about fifty times to call you. I wanted to tell you I was working here, to come down and talk. I didn't believe it when I saw you."

Casey had taken Paul's straw wrapper, and was busily working on tearing it up the middle and twisting the ends. She was on a cliff now, and when she fell over the edge she'd tell him it was all right, that they could start over. But she clung onto that cliff with white knuckles. Not this time. Not again.

"Well, you saw me," she said. She sighed and looked around, afraid to meet his eyes. "How do you get all these jobs?"

"This was through my uncle," Paul said. "He's a foreman for another outfit. The fence company wasn't giving me enough work."

"Work for what? Are you going to college?"

He shook his head. "Nah."

"Why not? Why are you going to waste your brain?"

He smiled. "Are you worried?"

She crushed the straw cover in her closed hand. "Don't be a jackass."

"I can't go to college," he said. "My father's on welfare. My mother works three jobs. We never had any money, anyway. We lived in a tent in Eisenhower Park for a year."

Casey looked at him. "Is this for real?"

"Yeah, it's for real. You can check it out. My father worked for this construction company up in Massachusetts. We lived in this neat house in the country. Really pretty. But he got greedy and took us all to New York and he tried to start his own company. He went broke pretty fast. Then he became a drunk."

"Oh, man," she said in a soft voice. "I can't imagine living like that."

"So anyway, I have to bring in a salary."

He continued to eat the now-cold slice of pizza. Casey's brain raced. "You know, Paul, you could register at Suffolk Community—"

"Oh, sure. Thirteenth grade."

"No, come on. You could take one course at a time, and still work, and meanwhile you'd be piling up credits. Then you can transfer to any college whenever you want to. I mean, it's not terrific, but at least you're getting somewhere."

She could see his eyes considering. She was reaching him. "I could go down there and ask about it."

"You really should," she said.

He crunched the pizza crust. "Thanks," he said. "You got me thinking."

"Well, let's not get hysterical," she said, but her heart was bounding.

He put his hands palms-down on the table. "I mean it," he said. "I'm glad you don't hate my guts totally."

"Of course I don't hate you totally," she said, as she stepped off the cliff. "I just hate what you did."

"Well, so do I."

The people in the mall seemed to stop eating and walking, and for an instant she felt she was in a tableau of wax figures. She looked at the pink and yellow neon signs and at Paul, who looked so tired and so young. He was a little boy, a smart, mixed-up, angry little boy.

"Oh, Paul," she said sadly. "Why did you have to be an asshole?"

"I don't know," he said.

"Didn't you feel how much I cared about you? Why'd you screw it up?"

"Casey, would you give me another shot? One date. If I can keep from crapping out, we can think about the next one. I don't want to give you up."

Her cheek burned. The back of her head still hurt. "I don't know what to say, Paul. You could be doing a job on me. This whole soap opera about your family, and now suddenly you're inspired to go to college. It sounds great, but everyone always said you were a con man."

He stood up with an abrupt, violent motion. "I gotta go."

"Hey, don't get ticked off at *me*."

He subsided. "I'm not. I don't blame you. I loused up."

She stood up, too. "Paul, you don't have to louse up anymore. You can change."

"If you say so."

"Oh, damn it, what do you want from me? Am I supposed to fall into your arms because you've got problems?"

"No."

She breathed in and out, four or five times, as a vise squeezed her chest. "All right. One date. I want to go where there's a crowd. And I'll meet you there."

He smiled his devilish little smile, the one she'd seen the first time she'd met him. "Boy, you drive a hard bargain."

"You bet your ass."

"Well, I'll see my ass and raise you an elbow."

Her laughter popped out; she couldn't stop it. He touched her shoulder, very briefly, with two fingers. She almost didn't know it had happened.

"I have to get back," he said.

"Okay."

"I'll call you up."

"Okay."

There was a pause. "I'm going to go to Suffolk and register. I mean it."

"Okay."

"Jesus, say something else."

"I don't know what else to say."

He smiled. "Take care, Casey. See you soon."

"Sure."

He seemed to want more, but he held back. He wrested himself away and strode headlong through the crowds. Casey stood like an idiot by the table. On an overwhelming impulse, she grabbed the untouched second slice of pizza. It was stone-cold, the pointed end curled up, the sausage circles hard. She bit into it and chewed ecstatically. She gobbled down the whole thing, including the burnt crust. Then she picked up his Coke and finished that.

She suddenly, absurdly, felt good that she could go to the A&S shoe department and tell Faye that she and Paul had patched up their fight. She didn't have to explain to Mom and Dad why she wasn't going to date Paul anymore. These things lifted a load from her heart. She was filled with a sense of future. She wanted to turn him around. Love could do that.

Casey grabbed her handbag and walked away from the table, smiling. If only her face didn't hurt so much, she could pretend nothing bad had happened at all.

Chapter Six

OWEN YOUNG LOOKED OUT OVER ROWS OF EMPTY DESKS still warm from young bodies. He heard shrill voices in the hallway and the sandpaper shuffle of kids rushing toward the exit.

He closed his grade book with a sigh and reached for the lid of his attaché case. Casey Gordon appeared at the doorway. Owen's heart jumped; Casey had sat very quietly in class today, writing something in her notebook. She hadn't come up to his desk afterward.

"Hi," Owen said. "What's up?"

She hugged her books to her chest and tilted her head a little. She looked shy and appealing. "I forgot to ask you before..."

"Yes?"

She slid her lower lip under her upper lip and looked upward, gathering courage. Then she said, "Could I have a recommendation letter for college?"

He was a little disappointed. He hated writing those things, and about forty kids would wind up asking before December. "Sure. But write me a note to remind me. Otherwise I'll forget."

"Okay. I don't need it right now, anyway. My guidance counselor said I should get it."

"It's a good idea. Any particular school, or just general?"

She shrugged. "General, I guess."

He knew he was trying to prolong the conversation, hoping she would stay and maybe open up. "Any ideas about where you want to go?"

"Well, Mom wants me to try for Yale and Stanford and Dad wants me to go to Northwestern, for journalism."

"Pretty impressive."

She smiled. "That's the idea." She seemed content today. She'd even run smoothly this morning, without knocking herself out.

"Where do *you* want to go?" he asked. The wind picked up and cooled the perspiration on his back. He could smell rain in the air. Casey glanced toward the windows and her eyes dreamed. "I'm thinking about Wesleyan; they have a good poetry program."

"Good choice. If you need any help with your application essays, just ask."

"Sure. Thanks."

"Well, now I've made you miss your bus." He felt like a rat.

"No, I'm getting a ride home."

"Don't keep a ride waiting." She smiled politely, and shifted her books. She moved to go, and Owen said, "Casey?"

"Yeah?"

"If that was a poem you were writing today in class, I'd love to read it."

Her cheeks reddened and she dropped her eyes. "I'm sorry."

"Don't be ridiculous. Writing poetry in English class isn't a crime. I like your stuff. I think you could be published."

She made a self-deprecating face. "I doubt it."

"Come on. You know you're good. Show me anything you write; I'll play editor."

She straightened up and gave him a warm smile. "Okay, maybe I will. I've got a trunkful, though. You'll be sorry."

"No, I won't."

"Okay, Mr. Young. I gotta go."

"Sure. See you in the morning."

"Don't remind me." She freed one hand to do a gag-me gesture. Then she was gone, and there was only empty hallway.

Owen blew out a breath and shut his attaché case. He felt locked out by Casey Gordon. She was a terrific wall-builder. And he was angry because the great Owen Young, Master Communicator, couldn't scale the wall.

He smiled at his honesty and lifted the briefcase. He'd drown his sorrows at Burger King. Tomorrow was another day.

Paul called Casey that night and said, "I registered for two courses today at Suffolk. English and Bookkeeping."

"Paul, that's terrific!"

"We're celebrating tomorrow. I'll pick you up at school."

"No—"

"Be there."

That was enough to give Casey a night of thrashing around. She agonized over whether to ride with him until her clock showed 3:20 A.M., and then she fell asleep for an hour and got up at 4:30 to get ready to jog.

By 2:00 P.M., Casey was running on fumes. She'd actually fallen asleep for a moment in Calculus, but she'd remembered the trick of holding a pencil upright so it would drop when she nodded off. She got her second wind in Concert Choir, since she had to stand and sing. She went outside at the end of eighth period and stood amid throngs of kids who scattered to the yellow buses lined up at the curb.

This is ridiculous, she thought. She looked around, too

distracted to answer Gina and Laurie when they called hello or to notice when Eddie shouted something obscene from his bus window. Then she saw Paul's Oldsmobile idling by the teachers' cars.

Casey squeezed between two buses, wrinkling her nose at the fumes, and hurried across the parking lot. Paul wore dark sunglasses and smiled beautifully at her. As the buses groaned and lurched forward, Casey slid into the seat next to Paul and shut the door. She noticed a towel covering something in the backseat.

"Hi," she said to Paul's profile. "Congratulations."

"Thanks." He glanced out the window and gunned the motor. She sat back against the seat and fluffed out her hair with her fingers. White sunlight etched the dirt spots on the windshield. Paul worked his way out of the crowded parking lot, ahead of the buses, and soon they were heading north.

"Where are we going to celebrate?" she asked.

"The pond."

"What pond?"

"My pond."

"What?"

"You'll love it."

She skittered with nervousness. "What's in the backseat?"

"Picnic."

"It's the middle of the afternoon."

"Good observation."

He sounded so chipper. Casey spent the ride straining her neck to watch traffic. She tightened at every red light, waiting for him to touch her, but he didn't. She was a total wreck by the time he stopped on a winding side road across from a picturesque old mill with a water wheel.

"Where the heck are we?" she asked.

"Pond."

He got out and slammed the door hard, then raced around and opened her door. She stood by the car as he reached into the back and took out a real honest-to-God picnic basket. "You're crazy," she said.

"Always was. Come on."

He pranced coltishly ahead of her, down a pathway that led between gently sloping meadows of pale grass. Casey followed. She felt girlish in her matching top and shorts. He wore a beautiful rugby shirt and dark jeans.

The sudden quacking of ducks made Casey look toward the pond. It was the deepest cobalt blue she'd ever seen, and it mirrored trees and sky so the water looked a million miles deep. A magnificent willow tree overspread the bank, dropping fringed fans of green. She could smell rich, warm earth, and summer grass, and a fishy rottenness from the pond itself.

"This is so beautiful," she said softly.

"Like it?" Paul asked. He stood proudly by the pond's bank, holding the basket. He grinned like a kid.

"I love it. When did you find this?"

"School trip."

"Be serious."

"Cross my heart." He dropped the basket. Immediately, two inquisitive brown ducks waddled up on the bank, their belly feathers dark with water. They quacked comically and poked their dripping beaks at the basket. Casey giggled.

Paul said, "Get outta here!" and made shooing motions. The ducks clamored furiously and scattered, then slowly waddled back again. Paul said to Casey, "It was sixth grade. We went to see the grist mill." He pointed up the hill. "I got bored with the lecture, so I came down here. The cops came to look for me."

She shook her head and blew a stray hair from her eyes. "You were always a problem."

"Come on. Let's picnic."

Exhilarated, and uncertain, Casey made her way down to the bank of the pond. She looked at Paul as he sprawled in the grass. He gazed at the pond, his eyes hidden behind his shades. He reminded her of a magazine ad for men's cologne.

She sat down to watch the ducks, a couple of feet away from Paul, and wrapped her arms tightly around her knees. The brown ones floated near the bank, sometimes plunging their heads into the water. A little farther out were sleek ducks with feathers of iridescent blue and green. She became aware of lacy insects that hovered just above the pond's surface.

"This is outrageous," she murmured.

"I like it," he said. "No radios. No cars. You know, nobody listens anymore."

She looked at him. "That's pretty deep."

"Yeah?"

She turned back to the pond. "You're right. We carry our little Walkmans everywhere."

"There's no *environment*," Paul said. "Most kids just hear the top forty, every minute of their lives. At the beach, in the car, doesn't matter. What's that do to your brain?"

"We never see anything, either," she said.

"Right."

"Like those ducks. Look how the sun makes them sparkle. I love colors. Even at a concert, you know? Everyone watches the lights and the explosions, but nobody *appreciates* it. I love it when there's a red light on the singer, and it's so deep and rich. And when there's yellow smoke and lights whipping around.... Everyone thinks I'm weird."

Suddenly, she saw a huge white swan. She nearly cried at how gorgeous the swan looked, against blue water and blue sky.

"This is so great, Paul," she said. "I can't believe I'm sitting here."

"Let's eat," he said.

She shifted as he pulled the towel from the basket. He

reached in and held up a package of Hostess cupcakes. "Caviar?" he said.

She laughed, with her fingers against her lips. "Terrific."

He tossed her a package and she caught it and unwrapped the plastic. Suddenly ravenous, she bit deeply into a cupcake, and brushed crumbs from her mouth. He held a cupcake in one hand and rummaged in the basket with the other.

"Some vino?" he said, and held aloft a bottle of California Cooler.

"No, thanks."

He tugged his sunglasses down so they sat on his nose, granny-style. "Are you serious?"

"Yes."

"You don't do wine coolers?"

"Come on, Paul."

He spread his arms in a comforting gesture, still holding the cupcake and the bottle. "I assumed you'd had the experience."

"It isn't that. I'd just rather not."

He smiled at her discomfort. She suddenly felt idiotic. What was she worried about, Mom smelling it on her breath? Here she was with ducks and swans and Paul and cupcakes and wine. It was so romantic and only Paul understood that she needed this.

"Okay," she said.

"*Yeah*," he said, in mock lustfulness. "The woman becomes a harlot."

She grabbed the bottle from him and twisted open the cap. "Where'd you get such a big vocabulary?"

"Big vocabulary book," he said. He opened his bottle and took a long drink. Bad move. It reminded her of the Scotch on his breath that other night.

"No, really. I thought you flunked everything."

She nervously took a sip of the cooler, which was ice-cold. It tickled her nose and her throat, and tasted strange against the chocolaty sweetness of the cupcake.

"Yeah, I flunked a lot of crap. What's that got to do with education?"

"Are you going to dump on the system?"

"Why? Are you *for* the system?"

She thought about it, even though she didn't want to think about anything with the sun sweeping in bright sails across the trees. "I don't know. I like school."

"Always got straight A's?"

She gave a closed little laugh. "I never had much choice."

"Oh, right. Mom and Dad expect 95's."

"They sure do." She drank a little more freely and felt herself getting a small rush. She was stupid to do this when breakfast had been her most recent meal.

"Why?"

She stared at him. "Why?"

"I asked you first."

"I don't know. They set standards for me. I remember even as a little kid, they always got me educational toys. I wanted a My Little Pony Dream Castle one year for my birthday—"

"When *is* your birthday?" he asked. He chugged the rest of his cooler and delicately put down the bottle, holding it by its neck.

She lowered her eyes shyly, feeling a surge of excitement. "October tenth."

"What do you want?"

"What I want isn't expensive."

"How about if I blow up the school? POW. No more crap."

"Don't be stupid, Paul."

"Want it both ways, huh?" He laughed. "You get pissed if I rank on school, but you're pissed at your parents for making you go."

"I never said that."

"You deny it?"

"Yeah, I deny it." A shroud of shadow rolled over the

scene. "I like school okay. I just get sore at my mom and dad for a lot of things. Like that My Little Pony Dream Castle. They got me this learning gym instead. I cried. I really cried."

He sat up and took out another cooler. "Poor kid."

She felt so good talking about this. She complained to Faye, of course, but it wasn't the same. It was almost as if Paul could *do* something about it, kill her parents and make it look like an accident. Oh, Lord, she was getting wasted. On a stupid wine cooler.

"Every year Mom would go to school to try to choose my teacher," Casey said. "I was always so embarrassed because the teachers would point me out. And Mom always examined my homework, every night, and if she didn't like the assignments I was getting, bam, she'd be on the phone. Every teacher I ever had hated my guts."

She felt her throat burn. Paul leaned on an elbow and looked at her. "Even now?"

"Well, it wasn't so bad once I got to junior high. Mom couldn't keep up with all those teachers. But baby, if I get less than 95, I get grounded for two weeks."

"Ever happen?"

"Oh, yeah." She tilted back her head and finished the last of the cooler. Her head buzzed. She let herself fall backward and felt the grass blades tickle her neck. She gazed giddily up at the sky, watching cloud ghosts as they haunted the soft blueness. "I get sick before a test. I puke the night before and I get massive headaches. And I've got to bring every test home, and if I fail, Mom makes me answer every question or look it up."

"Why do you put up with it?"

"What am I supposed to do? They've got the power."

"Bull. What can they do to you?"

She plucked a grass blade and ran it across the ball of her finger to make it tickle. "It's not so bad. They're pretty decent most of the time."

"Yeah, two beautiful people."

"No, really. They never hassled me about dating. I have this friend Gina, she's eighteen and her parents won't let her go out. They're from Italy, really stone age. My mom is just—well, she's got this thing about superior genes. Her side of the family are all professors and musicians and she thinks I ought to have the same genes. I know she sounds loony when I say that, but she's not."

"What about your father? He have anything to say?"

She touched the grass blade to her chin, then her upper lip, slowly and sensuously. The smell of clover touched her nostrils. "Daddy never shows any emotion, except when he gets upset. He's got a hot temper." She giggled. "He's funny when he gets into a snit. He once threw a whole orange across the garage. It squashed into the car window."

"Another nutjob."

"No," she said, feeling guilty. "He's okay, too. He feels inferior to Mom, I think. She's way smarter than he is. He tries to come on smart, but he always gets things wrong and he never admits it. He doesn't like me much." She became sad. "I think he wanted a boy or something. He always called me Flamingo when I was a kid, because I was gawky. Now he's scared of me. Like when I got breasts, he wouldn't look at me."

"Stupid man."

She heard him move to where she lay. She smiled and ran the grass blade over the bridge of her nose. "He lectures me a lot. He thinks I waste my potential. So does Mom. And my teachers. I guess I'm overloaded with potential. Do you think I've got potential, Paul?"

"Yeah," he said.

She raised her head and looked at him. He was right next to her. She could see the pores on his nose. He'd taken off his sunglasses. "You never did tell me how you got educated."

"I read a lot," he said. "When I was a kid, I bought a million comic books. I took books out of the library and read them all night, until my father started tearing them up."

"So why'd you flunk out, you jerk?"

He tenderly took the blade of grass from her fingers and laid it aside. With his own fingertips, he pushed back her hair and traced her eyebrows. Casey shut her eyes and listened to her heart do a timpani solo. "Because I was tired of assholes. All the kids were assholes. The teachers were assholes, too. So I busted their chops. I had a good time doing it."

"You were obnoxious."

"They were obnoxious to me."

"That's no excuse."

"I don't need an excuse. You think you have to be a good little girl, even when you're being crapped on."

"No, I don't."

"Come on, Casey. You're afraid of somebody not loving you, so you do all these tricks like a little dog, and people kick you in the butt anyway."

The ugly truth of his words hit her like punches. She *did* feel that way, and he knew it. He knew the inside of her heart.

"Don't talk like that," she said. "It gets me depressed. I don't want to be depressed anymore."

"Don't run away, Casey."

"I won't. But I just don't want to talk about sad things."

He smiled down at her. She smelled his skin and hair, and saw tiny pearls of perspiration on his lip. The skin of his face was drawn tight and was a little bit freckled. She locked her hands together around his neck. She pulled him down and kissed him passionately. She wouldn't let him stop. He moved his hands over her face and then down her sides. She felt his fingers on the exposed skin of her stomach.

"No . . ." she said, in a travesty of her voice.

He broke her grip. She opened her eyes wide. His face was flushed.

"Please, Paul."

He playfully slapped her behind. She gasped. He laughed and sat up. "Did you think I was going to rape you?"

Relief mixed with confusion in her shaking body. She sat up, too, and brushed back her mussed hair with her hand. "I didn't know *what* was going to happen for a minute."

"I love you, Casey."

He didn't move when he said it. He just said it, sitting up straight and still.

"I love you, Paul," she said, and her throat felt like it would explode.

He gazed at her, and he suddenly looked like a lost puppy. She laughed and grasped his face in her hands and smiled idiotically at him. "Be good to me, Paul," she said. "Please."

"Don't worry," he said huskily. He rubbed the back of her right hand as she touched his face. "With you on my side, I'll make it."

"I'll be there," she said ecstatically. "I'll be right behind you, Paul, every step of the way. I promise."

"Then I'm all set." He leaned toward her and she let him kiss her, over and over and over. She tasted the cupcake and wine in his mouth. He was hers. And she already knew the worst about him, right at the start, so there'd be no bad surprises.

No other guy had given her a picnic by the duck pond. No other guy had made her feel like this. He saw right into her soul, and he quieted the storms there. He understood about her parents, and he loved her for what she was. And she would help him to become what he wanted to be. Oh, man, they'd be so great together.

She bent forward and touched foreheads with him. She looked deep into his eyes and smiled. "I love you so much."

"You're my lady, Case."

"Yes, I am."

He kissed her again, and then stood up, turning away quickly and looking toward the pond. Casey giggled because she knew why he'd turned away. She hugged herself and shivered and looked at the wildly rippling trees and the pond. The wind had picked up and the little brown ducks looked as if they were being blown around on the water. She began to get a headache from the wine.

"More cupcakes?" he asked, finally turning back.

She shook her head. "I can't. I have to get home, Paul. My mom will have the cops out."

"Good," he said. "Let her sweat."

Fear touched her ribs. "Come on, Paul. Please. Just take me home."

He popped a mildly exasperated breath. "Man, you really think I'm a psycho."

"Well, I'm a little nervous, you know?"

"I can see that." He picked up the empty bottles and dumped them back in the basket. "Come on, princess. Back to Mom."

"Don't do that."

"Hey, if I can't tease, I can't love."

She scrambled to her feet, brushing off bits of grass and soil. "Okay. But don't overdo it."

He smiled and she watched him exultantly as he finished packing the basket. She let her eyes linger over him as she thought about how this outlaw belonged to her.

A loud honking made her look at the pond where the swan was announcing her departure. The wind ruffled her feathertips as she drifted around a bend. The brown ducks quacked their snide comments and headed for shelter. A sudden golden light brightened the scene, throwing individual leaves into bold relief. The sky turned rich turquoise and cherry pink. The wind freshened. A flock of black birds exploded from the trees and formed a rippling banner in the sky.

Casey loved the unbearable beauty of it, and at the

same time, she hated the underlying weight in her heart. Defiant, she spun and looked at Paul as he gestured for her to return to the car.

"Come on, baby-girl," he said with a grin. "Are you with me?"

"Forever," she said. She ran to him and he threw an arm around her shoulder. She hugged his waist and walked clumsily up the hill with him, toward sunset.

Chapter Seven

DADDY JUST COULDN'T BRING HIMSELF TO CLOSE UP THE new pool, even though it was already past Labor Day. The fence was up, and the backyard looked like a big yellow sandbox. Mom and Dad gave a barbecue, and the whole gang was there: the Lippmans next door, the Dolces two doors down, and the Gennaros down the block. Casey usually got bored out of her skull at these parties, but she helped out with this one because she was so happy about Paul that she didn't mind playing the good daughter.

She had stayed up the night before with Mom and Anita Dolce and scooped out hundreds of cantaloupe and watermelon balls. Now she was watching the little kids in the pool. It was a total mess. Dad had put a plastic pan of water by the steps so everybody could rinse off their feet, but the little brats didn't bother. They ran through the dirt and jumped like lemmings into the water.

At least Lisa McGuire was around. Lisa was nearly Casey's age. She went to B.O.C.E.S. for Beauty Culture, and she was having hassles with her mom. They walked around to the front of Casey's house and stood in hot, clear sunlight. Lisa smoked a cigarette, and her luxurious black hair glistened. "Is Billy coming over?" Casey asked.

"I don't know."

"Is it serious?"

Lisa made a face. "Yeah. Right."

"How's your mom like him?"

"She don't talk about him. You know her. If it's not Joey, forget it."

"You still like Joey?"

Lisa leaned against one of the white columns in front of the house. There used to be three of them, but after Hurricane Gloria in 1985 there were two. Dad had never replaced the third one. "Who knows?"

Casey got a charge out of Lisa. She got a charge out of pretty much everything these days. She was bursting to talk about Paul, but she was keeping the lid on. Her birthday was soon and she knew Paul was going to get her a chain. Then everybody would know.

"Man, I'm bored," Casey said. She walked a few paces down the driveway and did stretches. The sky was terrifically blue today, with little puffy clouds. The weather had finally cleared up. Even school was bearable, now that she wasn't sweating through her clothes.

"Wanna take a ride somewhere?" Lisa asked.

"Can't. I said I'd stick around. Some of the guys are coming over later."

"Who?"

Casey worked on a knot in her thigh. The meet with Greenfields was this Wednesday and Casey was psyched for it. She'd been running smoothly, inching her times up. Mr. Young said she was in her groove. Yeah. She was.

"Let's see," she said. "Maybe Faye but I don't know, and Charlie, and Glenn, and Stace, I think. So maybe later we can cruise somewhere."

"I feel like getting totally wasted," Lisa said. She dropped the cigarette and toed it out. She wore a pink sweat outfit that made her look cute and girlish.

"Maybe my dad will give you a piña colada."

"Yeah, that sounds good."

Casey giggled. "Fat chance."

JoAnne came charging around the house, soaking wet in her little flowered bathing suit. *"C-A-S-E-Y-Y-Y!"* she cried, in a voice like a fire siren.

"Oh, great," Casey said. She pretended not to hear.

JoAnne went right up to Casey and whined, "Mommy wants you in the back right now to help bring out the ziti."

"Tell her I'll be there in a minute."

"Now," JoAnne persisted. "Right *now.*"

Casey brought her arm up in a threatening motion. "Get out of my face, you jerk."

"You're a jerk."

"Brat."

"Stupidhead."

"Get *away!*"

JoAnne put her hands on her hips and did grinds with a nasty grin. Then she giggled and ran to the backyard. Casey felt her blood pressure rising. "Little turd."

Lisa said, "You want Glory?"

Glory was Lisa's ten-year-old sister. "Any day. Straight trade."

Lisa looked at her wristwatch. "I'm gonna call up Maryanne. Maybe she's around."

"Want to come back with me and serve the ziti?"

"Nah." Lisa's eyes looked at the middle distance. "I'll be back."

"Take care." Casey envied Lisa for just taking off. Since her dad had divorced her mom, Lisa and her sister had the run of the house. Casey sometimes wished that her mom and dad would get divorced. They fought enough. Mean, quiet fights, with a lot of muttering under their breath. But they never talked about splitting up.

Casey swore that she wouldn't be that way. If she stayed with Paul, everything would be straight from the heart. No games. Just like at the duck pond. She figured Faye would be her maid of honor, if Faye was still around.

In the backyard, Daddy was at the bridge table that had been set up with all the liquor. He was mixing up another blender full of piña coladas, but he was swaying a little. He was singing in a weird voice and spilling things all over the plastic cloth. Casey laughed to herself. She thought Daddy was hysterical when he got drunk. It was the only time he really had fun.

Dave Gennaro was sunning himself on a lounge chair by the pool. He was a pretty foxy guy; Casey had sometimes had fantasies about him. His wife was a cute dizzy blonde.

Casey went inside. The kitchen was a total disaster area, with Tupperware bowls all over the place and shreds of lettuce and other gunk on the floor. All the women were in here, talking at the same time. Susie Gennaro smoked a cigarette, one of about five million she smoked during the day. She leaned against a counter, with one arm across her chest.

"Glad you could make it," Mom said to Casey.

"I was just up front."

"Well, I didn't know that, did I?"

"Okay, okay, don't have a hairy. What do you want me to do?"

Mom wore a red bathing suit under a beige beach jacket, and she wore her gradient sunglasses. "I want you to change your attitude."

Casey's face burned with embarrassment. This was nothing new. Mom would start up with her anywhere. Susie Gennaro smiled brightly and said, "How's the running going?"

"Okay," Casey said.

Anita Dolce ignored the clash between Casey and her mother and continued taking big trays covered with aluminum foil out of the refrigerator. She was a tall woman with frizzy hair. Casey wished she would say something now.

Susie Gennaro said, "How many miles do you run every day?"

"Usually I do about two," she said.

"That's all?"

"I'm not on Cross Country," she explained. "I do sprints and hurdles." She really didn't feel like talking about it.

"Well," Susie said, "I wish I had your legs. They're gorgeous."

She exhaled smoke, which hung in rings in the air. Casey blushed, and felt stupid. Mom had allowed the conversation but now she said, "Okay, let's get this stuff out. Casey, I'll come to the door and hand you trays, and you put them on the food table."

"Okay."

She opened the screen door and slid the metal ring so the door stayed open. Grace Lippman, who'd been in the dining room looking for plastic placemats, said, "Are we feeding the kids first?"

"Oh, God, yes," Mom said. "Let's get them done and then sit quietly and enjoy our dinner."

"Amen," Anita Dolce said.

Casey seethed. That meant she'd have to eat with all the little brats. Man, if she'd wanted to be a camp counselor, she could have gotten paid for it.

Brilliant sunlight made blinding slivers on the pool. The kids turned the slivers into froth as they lined up by the diving board and jumped in. They did it over and over again, jumping in, climbing out, running around to the diving board, and jumping in again. They never got tired of it. And the whole time they screamed.

Casey began to think of having kids with Paul. But not like this. Maybe they'd live out West. Or in Hawaii, in a house overlooking the ocean. And every night they'd stand on their deck and watch Diamond Head in the sunset. She'd always dreamed of doing that. With a white flower in her hair—Paul would think she looked pretty that way.

"*Casey!* Heads up!"

She snapped out of the daydream. Mom stood there, holding a tray of ziti with two pot holders. "Sorry," Casey said. She gingerly slipped her hands under the pot holders and took the tray. The ziti was dried out, and the layer of mozzarella cheese on top was burned at the edges. Nothing new.

"Can you make an effort to move it?" Mom said.

Casey cursed under her breath.

"What was that?" Mom asked.

"Nothing."

"That's what I thought."

Casey turned away sharply and brought the tray to the long table they'd borrowed from Dave Gennaro. As she set down the tray, she saw Glenn walk into the backyard.

"Hi!" she said. She held both pot holders in one hand.

"What's doin'?"

"Zero. Where's everybody?"

He shrugged. "They'll be around. I got finished early so I drove over."

He worked at the local Channel store. He looked really tough in a cutoff sweat shirt and shorts. He'd been working out with the football team and he was pumped up.

"Have some burnt ziti," said Casey.

"I just had lunch."

"Please, come on. I have to eat with the little kids."

"Forget it."

"Thanks a lot."

Mom leaned out and called, "*Casey!* Oh, hello, Glenn."

Casey squirmed with fury at the way Mom totally changed her tone of voice. Glenn waved. "Hey, Ms. Gordon."

"Want some supper?" Mom asked. "There's plenty."

"I don't think so. I'm just hangin' out."

"Okay. Casey, want to bring out the rest of the stuff?"

She said it so sweetly. "Sure," Casey said. "I live to serve you."

"Be nice," Glenn said.

"*You* try."

She crossed the patio and Dad saw her. "Hey, Casey. How's my little girl?" He began to sing, at the top of his voice: "My little girl, as sweet as a rose is *S-H-E-E-E* ..."

"Chill out, Dad," she said, a little embarrassed.

He made a pathetic face. "I don't understand. My singing should make you breathe faster, tingle with fulfillment, *swoon* with joy. Are you swooning?"

She laughed. He looked so silly in his Bermuda T-shirt and blue shorts, with his skinny legs and chunky middle. He held a plastic cup with about his ninth piña colada, and he had this goofy grin. She stuck one hand on her hip and tilted her head as she looked at him. "No, Dad. I'm not swooning. Sorry."

"Well, *I* like it. Having fun, kid?"

"Oh, yeah."

"How come you're not stroking away in the pool?"

She wore a tank top and shorts, and her damp hair was combed back and held by a headband. "It got disgusting with all the kids in it."

"Aw, so tell 'em to get out for a while. It's for you, too."

"It's okay, I'd rather hang out with my friends."

"Well, I want you to enjoy that pool. It isn't just for JoAnne."

Casey bit back a tart answer, because Daddy was really being sincere. "How come *you're* not in the pool?"

"No time. Have to mix the drinkees." He waved the cup back and forth as if leading a band. "Mix, mix, mix. It's tough, but someone's got to do it."

She shook her head and laughed. "You're pretty polluted, Dad."

"Yes, I guess so." He shielded his eyes and looked at the pool. "It's a flotilla in there! Rafts to the left of me! Rafts to the right of me! I think I see George Raft!"

"Right, Dad. Slow down."

He looked at her like a sad beagle. "Do you know who George Raft was?"

"Uh uh."

"Boy, I feel old sometimes."

"Who was he?"

"Doesn't matter." He slurped at his drink, smacking his lips.

Mom stood in the doorway, looking disgusted. "Ron, Casey was helping me. Could you talk to her later?"

"Whoops," Dad said. "In trouble again. Go help your mother."

Casey put her hand on his neck, feeling his perspired warmth, and she stood on tiptoe to kiss his cheek. "Try to stay on your feet, okay?" She felt real love for him just for this moment. He was so helpless and stupid right now, and so nice.

The afternoon was turning cooler—it was almost cold—when Casey got to take a walk out front with Glenn. She hugged herself against the fresh wind that tossed the treetops. Clouds slashed the sky. If she looked up in a certain way, she could imagine that all the houses were falling away.

"Thanks for sticking around," she said.

"Nothing else to do."

They trudged up Roberta Street, in the opposite direction from her jogging route. They passed Lisa McGuire's house and the woods behind it. Old tires and other junk littered the sandy hill that led to the woods. Somewhere back there a dirt bike buzzed like a hornet. Casey listened to the crunch of their sneakers on the road.

"I never see you in school," she said.

"We don't have any free periods together."

"I don't have any free periods period!" She shivered, and he hesitantly put a big arm around her shoulders. She gratefully leaned against him, liking the feel of his side rubbing against hers.

"How's it going with Paul VanHorn?"

She wished he hadn't asked. "That why you came around?"

"A little."

"I really hate you as a big brother."

"Well, I hate you as a jerk."

"Har har."

"So how's it going?"

"It's going good."

"Still seeing him?"

She reached across her body and held onto his hand. "Yeah, I'm still seeing him."

"Seriously?"

"I hate this."

"Sorry."

They walked silently for a while. They were in a different development, an older one. They passed two wrecked cars and a gang of dirtbags who hovered around the rusted heaps. In the middle of the road, a fat kid and a dark-skinned kid played with a frisbee. Thousands of crows started racketing at once, calling back and forth in the trees. She could hear Glenn's breath going in and out.

"How far are we walking?" she asked.

"I figured we'd go to the 7-Eleven, for a soda."

She stopped, which forced him to stop. "You have to be joking."

He made an open-handed shrug. "I'm thirsty."

"I don't want to go all the way there. I'll never make it back."

"Want to take a ride later?"

"Where?"

"If the other guys show up, we can go to the movies, or whatever."

"If my mom lets me."

They turned and walked back. She linked arms with him. "Can you believe it's our senior year?" she asked.

"Yeah. I'm up to my ass in college applications."

"You? I figured they'd be driving you around in limos."

He grunted, embarrassed at the compliment. "I've had a couple of feelers."

"You'd better be a star. We're all waiting to say we know you."

"Yeah. Big thrill."

She jabbed him with her elbow. "Come on. You're terrific. We're all psyched like crazy about coming to the games."

He managed a smile. "Hey, how about *your* season? You've got a good shot at some personal records."

"I'm going all out," she said. "I'm pumped."

"Don't kill yourself."

"Not me."

He chewed on his lip as they walked. She stopped again, just at the curve that led back to her block. "What now?" he asked.

"Anything wrong?"

He looked away from her. "Nope."

"Bull. What's the matter?"

"Forget it."

"Don't play games with me, Glenn. We've been friends forever."

He turned back so abruptly that it startled her. His face looked disoriented. "Yeah, well that's the damn problem, so leave it alone."

"What?"

"Nothing. Come on."

"No way. What did you mean that's the problem?"

He looked toward the houses, biting his lip like crazy. He slapped his side uneasily with one hand. "It's no use getting into it."

"What do you want me to do, beg you? I care about you, Glenn. If you want to talk about what's bothering you, I want to help."

He hung his head. Then he looked at her. "You can't figure it out?"

She pretty much *had* figured it out, but she didn't want it to be true. It scared her and hurt her. "Why don't you tell me?"

A Chevy pickup came down the road and made a tight, squealing turn. It kicked up pebbles. Shreds of old, yellow newspaper danced in the air. Glenn said, "I like you."

"I know *that*."

"I wanted to go out with you. Since last year, I guess. But you were all screwed up with that other guy."

She exhaled. The wind went through her. She crossed her arms over her chest and trembled, wishing she'd thrown on her hooded sweat shirt. "How come you never asked me?"

"We were friends for so long, I wasn't sure how to do it."

"Come on. How'd you ask Jennifer DeFeo to go out with you? I mean, she was the queen of the cheerleaders and you were a junior."

He grinned at the memory. "She was pretty easy."

"I'll bet. But you couldn't ask me. What was it, my blinding beauty?"

"I hate when you put yourself down."

"Sorry. I love my beady eyes and freckles and straight brown hair. It's so subtle."

"You're an asshole, Casey."

"Flattery will get you nowhere."

The dirt bike came out of the woods. The kid on it looked about nine years old. The bike bounced and churned up a dust cloud and then whined down the road. Glenn looked openly at Casey.

"I was afraid of you," he said hoarsely. "You write poetry, and you've got such a deep mind."

"Oh, yeah. The Grand Canyon."

"See? You're always saying witty things."

"I am *not*. Will you get away?"

"It doesn't matter, anyway," he said. "I didn't ask you. I

was going to do it at the Back to School party. But you brought Paul."

"Oh, no. Why didn't you say something when I called you?"

"Why?"

"Because I wouldn't have rubbed it in your face."

"I was just being masochistic."

"You sure were."

They let silence come between them. The air darkened. Houses looked like dark blocks against the deep, glowing sky. "So anyway," he said, "that's why I asked you about Paul now. After the party, I thought maybe you'd broken up with him."

She sighed and looked down at the cracked sidewalk. Then she grabbed him and held him with every ounce of her strength. He put his arms around her with great tenderness, and they rocked back and forth. She felt her eyes fill up, and she heard his raggedy breath.

"I love you so much, Glenn," she said into his neck. "I didn't want this to happen."

"Me either," he said. "It's not your fault."

She held on to him, and looked up into his face. "You deserve a lot better than me."

"Cut the crap."

"I mean it. It's just because we were so close as kids, but it's hard to be that way when you're different sexes and you're grown up."

"It still hurts."

She tightened her lips and touched her fingertips to his face. "I'm so sorry."

"I know." He gently pried her loose and kept her at arm's distance. "Don't sweat it. You've still got me on your side."

"I'd break your arm if you weren't. I need you. I'll always need you."

"Any time Paul gets out of line—even an inch—come running. I'll break his ass."

She smiled. "Paul's a cool guy. Maybe you'll even like him someday."

"Don't push it."

She realized that she'd been stupid to say that. "I won't. But don't ever leave me alone, Glenn. I couldn't take it."

"I want you to be happy, Casey. You've never been happy."

She hugged him again. "I'll be happy. I promise."

More cars came around the curve, with their headlights on. She took his hand and squeezed it tightly, and they started to walk back to her house. He'd really chewed her up inside. For a moment, Paul leered over her, a cold, vicious bad guy who held her prisoner while Glenn rode away, and it was Glenn she wanted. But that was idiotic. She thought of the duck pond and of how much she needed Paul.

So why didn't it feel good? Why did needing Paul sit like that whole tray of ziti on her chest? She didn't understand any of it, except that even when she found something that mattered, she made it hurt.

Chapter Eight

CASEY STOOD UP AND PULLED OFF HER DARK BLUE TEAM jacket. She dropped it on the wooden bench and walked over to Mr. Young. His eyes were hidden by sunglasses but his mouth was tight with concern.

"How's the knee?"

She nodded. "Great."

"Sure it is." He knelt in front of her, tucking his clipboard under his arm, and with two fingers touched the bruised welt on the inside of her knee. She hissed, but stood up straight.

He unbent. "I can run Angie."

"No!" She faced him with dark determination. "Don't scratch me, Mr. Young."

He sighed. Hot wind blew his sparse hair and puffed the nylon sleeves of his jacket. "Don't cripple yourself out there, Casey. We're ahead."

"I'm going to run to win."

"I want you to. But I want you to finish in one piece."

The official called over to ask Mr. Young if his entrant was ready. He kept looking at Casey and gestured at the official with a raised hand. Casey listened to the irregular pounding of her heart as she prepared. "I'll be okay," she promised.

Mr. Young hugged her shoulder and pinched the nape of her neck. "Go for it."

Buoyed, she continued over to the official, who wore a short-sleeved shirt and billowing slacks. The weather had changed wildly today. Until a half hour ago it had been chilly, with high blue skies and bright sunshine. But suddenly the wind had shifted, and she could feel the growing heat and dampness.

Casey wore Westfield's blue and white track uniform of tank top and shorts. She was a few feet now from her Greenfields opponent, in light green and dark green. The girl was a redhead, her hair cropped close. She looked like she was all sinew and wire.

The official held out two Popsicle sticks to Casey, concealing their lengths in his hand. She took a breath and yanked one out. Short stick. Inside lane. She heard the Greenfields girl make a disappointed sound.

The girls on the bench clapped and hooted through cupped hands. There were scattered kids and parents in the green bleachers. Far across the grass playing field, some boys hit baseballs. The American flag behind the bleachers whipped and flapped in the wind.

She stretched out by the starting blocks and lifted her head. She saw the first hurdle, a white bracket over the black cinder track. She looked down and felt blood hot inside her head. Her knee throbbed. She'd bashed it in practice two days ago.

"On your marks."

The voice of the official startled her. She glanced to her right and saw Greenfields, arrowed for her start. Her long, pale legs were clear of bruises. Casey looked away. She savored the anger churning in her chest. It helped to get mad.

"Get set."

Casey hunched forward and flexed her knees. She

made a false start lunge, then held herself back. She focused on the track, away from the pain.

"Go!"

Overanxious, she surged forward and lost her balance. Grimly, she righted herself and pushed into a hard sprint. She saw Greenfields' back, shimmering as the wind caught her uniform. First hurdles just ahead.

Greenfields scissored through the air, cleared hers, and ran on. Casey threw back her head, grunting for breath. She flung her body up and cleared the hurdle.

"Atta girl!" Mr. Young screamed, very far away.

Gotta catch her . . . , Casey's brain gasped. Can't screw it up. . . .

She wished Paul were in the bleachers, watching her and yelling for her. Glenn would have been here, if she'd gone out with Glenn. What a stupid comparison. Paul wasn't into team sports. Not a guy who'd gotten kicked out of graduation. And she wondered how he felt about that—if he'd stood behind the chain link fence that day and if his eyes had wavered as he watched the kids in their caps and gowns. Did he feel low? Did he kick himself? What made him care?

Thinking about Paul made her forget how badly she hurt. She leaned into the curve, running through a slice of clear sunlight that poured sudden heat onto her back. Her ribs ached, and cramps stitched her sides. Her ears filled with the rhythmic thud of her sneakers, and she smelled her own sweat.

Second hurdle. She was a few feet behind. Her legs felt like rubber. She leaped on sheer memory. She was over. They were down the straightaway. She could reach out and grab for Greenfields' waistband. For a moment, her pain was outside of her body, like a vial of brown poisons, drained for just this race. She imagined the poisons being injected back into her blood after she'd won. But not now.

She was abreast of Greenfields, and Casey could hear

the soft whimpers of the other girl. Their ripsaw breath rasped on the wind. Raindrops pelted Casey's face. She smelled sweet, warm earth. She ran past Greenfields and approached the hurdle on the turn. She flung herself up, reached for her toe with an outstretched hand, hit cinder, and kept running.

No way..., her brain told her. Don't have anything inside...

It didn't matter. Her brain wasn't in control anymore. She ran the way an exhausted deer would flee a charging lioness. You ran or you went down.

She saw her hurdle. She couldn't see Greenfields, but she heard her. Thump, thump, thump.

She heaved her body upward and knew at once she didn't have enough explosive force. Her right leg bashed the wood as she went over, and by instinct she lifted her leg to avoid tangling her foot in the falling hurdle. She wondered why she felt no pain.

She yelled out, to nobody. She couldn't see. The track rippled in front of her. Why couldn't she see the next hurdle?

"Sprint!" her teammates screamed.

Teammates. That meant there were no more hurdles, only the last taunting stretch of track. The other girls were screaming and clapping. They were on their feet, in front of the bench. Mr. Young was windmilling his arm.

Casey whined through gritted teeth and pumped each arm like a piston. Wind roared in her ears. And then it was over. Suddenly, there was no more track and she was staggering on the other side of the finish line. Her lungs were bags of flame. She put her hands over her face.

Mr. Young yee-hawed and grabbed her. The girls were all over her. She uncovered her face and twisted her head. Greenfields was bent over, hands on her thighs, head down.

Casey laughed, and pushed wet clumps of hair from her forehead. Her shoulders tingled with warmth. She had to take a lap and cool down.

Then she stepped down on her right leg and it was like a white shark had bitten it clean through. She screamed and felt herself fall.

Mr. Young held her up. "Take it easy. Get to the bench."

She let herself be turned and guided. She still felt as if she were running. The bleachers and the playing field spun around her. She swallowed the urge to puke.

Mr. Young was at her outstretched leg. Casey glanced down and saw a mass of hamburger just under her knee. Below the pulsing gash, road maps of blood crisscrossed her shin. She turned away, biting hard on her lip.

Janine, a teammate, sat by her side and held her hand. "You were outrageous, Casey."

"Blew her away, huh?"

"You put this one on ice."

Casey could hear the Westfield kids screaming and clapping. "I can't believe that last hurdle. I needed one inch."

"You'll be okay."

"Sure, I'll—OW!"

Mr. Young was cleaning off the blood and he'd sponged the wound itself. She saw black suns and brilliant purple planets. She fell rapidly, down a long tunnel. A million years later, she saw the overcast sky again. Her head was resting on a crumpled team jacket on the bench.

Mr. Young stood over her. "We've called home. Your mom is coming for you."

"Oh, damn," she said. Her heartbeat had come down to normal, but her arms and sides still felt leaden. "She'll take me to the hospital."

"She'd better," Mr. Young said. "You'll need stitches on this one."

She turned her head aside. "No. I have to meet some-one tonight."

"You might have to cancel it."

"No," she said, more sharply. "I'll be okay. I was just dumb."

Janine said, "*Dumb?* Come on, Casey, you were going flat out. You gave everything."

"You gave too much, at the wrong time," Mr. Young said sternly. "You keep punishing your body that way and you'll need more than stitches."

"It's only a cut," Casey said.

"You know what I'm talking about," he told her. "We'd won the meet. And even if we were losing, you don't drive yourself that way."

Casey listened to her leg pound. Her stomach clutched with fear at the pain to come in the hospital. "You were pretty happy at the outcome."

"It was still not bright. And if you pull that kind of showboating again, I'll scratch you."

She recoiled at his angry words. "I'm sorry," she said. "I just wanted to win."

"I know," he agreed. "But the pride isn't worth the pain."

She smiled up at him. "It's sweet pain," she said.

"No, that's not sweet pain. Sweet pain is when you work through your endurance limit to make it grow. It's not masochism."

"It's not so bad," she said in a weak voice. The hurt was dizzying her, and she felt filthy and damp. But she knew she'd make it to Little Tony's Pizza Restaurant tonight to meet Paul, to celebrate the victory. She'd even said no to the girls on the team, who were going out to Chi Chi's. It had been hard to give up a team celebration. But Paul had insisted on taking her out, and Paul was her guy.

Casey shut her eyes and felt the wind scour her face.

She wished, suddenly, that she were in her bed, with her Pound Puppy. She wanted it so badly it surprised her.

The clock on the wall of Little Tony's buzzed constantly. Casey had never noticed it, because she'd always come here with a bunch of friends. She'd never just sat in one of the booths and waited.

Casey looked at the clock again, for the hundredth time. It was 9:25. Five more minutes and Paul would be an hour late. She yanked her gaze from the clock and looked down into her half-filled paper cup of Coke. Brown droplets clung to the end of the straw and she watched how they glistened in the dim light.

The counter was across from the booths and people waited there for their orders. Casey had watched them come in and go out for the whole hour. Tony pounded and twirled pizza dough by the window. The backwards neon sign sizzled. A skinny kid in a stained apron checked the big black pizza ovens, sliding pies out to see them and sliding them back. A mousy woman got her pie now and carried it out, nudging the door open with her shoulder.

Casey pressed her lips together and swallowed around the lump in her throat. The first fifteen minutes, she'd been scared but excited. She'd actually pulled off the scam she'd worked out with Janine. It wasn't even that tough. At the Emergency Room, waiting for Dr. Cohen to come, she'd calmly told Mom that Janine would drive her to the team party at Chi Chi's. She promised that she'd sit still and wouldn't drink liquor.

Mom had said okay. Mom had really looked scared when she'd picked up Casey. Mr. Young had carried Casey to the car and slid her into the backseat—kind of like sliding one of the pizzas into the oven, she thought with a smile—and Mom had driven without a word. Sure. Mom felt guilty about not coming to the meet.

So with Casey lying in a cubicle in the Emergency Room, her leg wrapped up in bloodstained bandages, it was a pretty good time to ask about the team party. Mom just sat there, stiff and tight-lipped reading a paperback novel. It was tough for Mom to hold Casey's hand, or stroke her hair, or hug her. Mom didn't like touching.

Casey drew in a breath as the door opened. The breath escaped again, as a brawny man came in and went to the counter. Casey looked away, not knowing *where* to look. She'd memorized the 3-D plastic plaque for Riunite on the wall, and the painting of a gondola. She'd studied the phony wood grain of the plastic paneling. She'd looked through the door at headlights. Each time she prayed, Let it be Paul. Please let it be Paul.

After half an hour had passed, her excitement had died. Only idiotic hope remained. She was hungry, and so tired she couldn't sit up straight. The novocaine had worn off long ago, and so had the two Vicodins the doctor had given her. The pain had built up in her leg, and now it throbbed with a cold fury. She kept the leg stretched out under the table, but it felt stiff.

She'd managed to shower, wrapping an Ace bandage around the hospital dressing. It felt so good, washing off the sweat. She'd dressed in a cashmere sweater and a short pleated skirt. She'd fluffed up her hair and she felt pretty.

She sniffed and blinked very hard. No way was she going to sit here in Little Tony's and cry. She looked at the buzzing clock. It was 9:32. She'd have to call Janine to come get her. But she didn't want to leave, just in case. God, how could she be so weak? But she'd sit here forever, until the place closed. She knew she would.

Just then, Paul walked in. She knew it was him even before the door opened. In an instant, her anger lifted and her heartbeat quickened. Okay. He'd gotten delayed. Now they could have supper and make up for lost time.

He saw her and slid into the seat opposite her. She tried to hang on to her renewed euphoria, but she sensed that it was all wrong. He wore a faded concert T-shirt and jeans and unlaced hitops. Dark stubble shadowed his cheeks. His eyes looked red.

"I didn't think you'd still be here," he said.

"I was waiting for you."

"Yeah, I see that."

She kept her fingers lightly on the cup. "What happened?"

He leaned to the side and dug in his pocket. He came out with a crushed pack of cigarettes, and matches. He lit a cigarette while she waited. Reflectively, he let smoke drift from his mouth. "I was working at the mall," he said. "We're doing some overtime, to get this department store opened. Can't beat the money."

Her anger and disappointment crushed her. "Couldn't you have called?"

He gave her a look. "I figured you'd go home."

"So why'd you come?"

He smiled. "I also figured you'd be dumb enough to wait around."

"Thanks."

He sighed, annoyed. He let the cigarette sit in an ashtray. "Look, I'm tired, babe. Don't hassle me."

"I'm not hassling you," she whispered fiercely. "I'm a little pissed off. I had five stitches in my leg today, Paul, and I lied to my parents to come here."

He looked oddly at her. "Five stitches from what?"

She looked down. "I cut myself open on the last hurdle at the meet."

He snickered. "Why you do that jock stuff..."

"I like running."

"Rah rah. Westfield sucks."

"Okay. Forget it."

"And why'd you lie?"

"I told you."

"You mean Mommy and Daddy wouldn't let you see me."

"Or any guy," she said with emphasis.

He took a long drag of the cigarette. "You know, I feel

like a real jerk, being out with a jockette who can't go out with boys. When do you get some space?"

"I don't know," she said woodenly. "If you're so embarrassed, then let's break up now."

"Oh, *man*." He sat back and flung his arm over the back of the booth. They were silent for a long time. Casey couldn't think of anything to say. She was numb with betrayal and with physical pain.

"You eat yet?" he asked, finally.

She shook her head.

"You want to eat?"

She shrugged.

"Aw, Jesus, Casey, say yes or no."

Her throat closed completely, and her shoulders trembled. She barely whispered, "No."

He leaned forward. "Huh?"

"No."

"You don't want anything?"

She shook her head again.

He leaned back with a thud. "Great. So what do you want to do?"

She took two deep breaths. "I want to go home. My leg hurts."

"You want to go home. And then what do I do? Play in the street?"

She managed to look at him. "I'm sorry, Paul. I really looked forward to this. I waited for you. But I'm tired, and I hurt, and you're in a lousy mood."

He gave her a sarcastic smile. "Yeah, well, those are the breaks. I've been busting my hump, Casey. Trying to make some bucks. I mean, I haven't been jumping over hurdles in the Olympics."

"Please take me home."

He looked around. The place had emptied out. Tony was giving them dirty looks. At last Paul stubbed out his cigarette. "Let's go."

He got up and stood by the door. She put her tongue

between her teeth and sighed as she looked toward the ceiling. She tried not to think about the girls at Chi Chi's. She'd have to make up more lies to tell them, about how she'd had this great Italian dinner with Paul, and how he'd carried her to the car because of her leg. She was getting to be dynamite at telling lies.

She slid painfully to the edge of the booth, rested, then gripped the table and hoisted herself up. She could barely put pressure on her foot; searing pains shot up through her leg. She got dizzy and held on to the table for a moment longer.

Tony looked worried. "You okay?"

She flushed with embarrassment. "Yeah."

Tony glanced with disgust at Paul, who stood impatiently with the door half open. Casey worked her pocketbook strap over her shoulder and limped to the door. She sidled past Paul and stood awkwardly on the sidewalk outside. The smells of tomato sauce and baking dough were replaced with smells of fragrant trees and warm night air. Cars whooshed by on Route 25. The tall lights of the shopping center cast harsh white pools on the asphalt.

Paul walked past her and out into the lot where his car was waiting. "Let's go."

She bit the inside of her lip and limped after him. She leaned against his car.

"Could you spare me the acting job?" he said.

She turned her head to look at him. The night breeze raised goose bumps on her skin. "You don't have to work at being a slime," she said. "You do it naturally."

"Oh, now we're going to dump, right?"

"Did you forget it was supposed to be a celebration?"

His keys were in his hand. He slammed the car's hood, making a startling bang. "Yeah, I forgot. Sue me."

"And why were you working, anyway? Don't you have your English class tonight? I thought you were coming from school."

He tossed the keys and caught them. His voice came lower, but no less caustic. "I quit."

"Why?"

"Because it was a stupid idea."

"Why was it stupid?"

"Because I *said* so. Who do you think you are, my goddamn mother?"

He came charging around the front of the car and stood less than a foot from her. She felt unbearable terror come up in her chest and yank her stomach. "Calm down, Paul."

He hit her arm, backhanded. Her leg twisted and she groaned. "Man, I have had it with you. Go to college. Don't be late. Little Miss Varsity."

"Okay, forget it."

"Shut up!" He struck her with a vicious backhand swing that clanged against her jaw. She saw double, and wondered why nobody ran to help her.

"Please...," she moaned. "Don't hit me again...."

"Lay off me," he screamed, and she thought he hit her in the ribs, but there was so much pain in her body that she couldn't tell. He kept screaming at her, but the words blurred. He pinned her against the car. She tried to avert her face, but he kept slapping her, and every time he screamed.

"Stop...," she said.

"SHUT UP!" With a motion so swift that it stunned her, he rammed his open palm against her ear and cracked her head against the window of the Oldsmobile. The crack became silvery branches that speared her skull and lanced through her head. She vaguely saw the parking lot, but everything hummed, and fragmented.

She thought she heard him saying something like, "All right, all right, take it easy, Jesus, don't fall down, get in the damn car..." She thought the car door opened and she sat in the front seat. It seemed to be happening, but the humming and the fragmented images persisted. She felt detached from her body. She couldn't remember what had just happened, or where she was, or why she was feeling this way. There was a roar, or many roars, and a sensation of movement and passing light. It was all very far away.

Chapter Nine

LILLIAN WAS THE VICE-PRESIDENT OF THE SENIOR CLASS, and when she needed warm bodies to prepare for Homecoming Weekend, she got Heather and Casey to come down on a Saturday. It was the second weekend in October. A warm south wind blew clouds across the sky.

In the gym lobby, Casey and Heather knelt in front of a banner of brown butcher paper. They were painting "Westfield Warriors Rule!" in big block letters. Casey dipped a long brush into a jar of red tempera paint and laboriously began to fill in an *e*. The light made the paint glisten and she couldn't really see what she was doing.

"Hold it still," Heather told her. Heather was doing the exclamation point.

"The floor's slippery," Casey said.

"Well, I'm getting this all over the place."

The vast lobby echoed with voices. One of the cheerleaders stood on a wooden ladder and stapled a cardboard sign to a doorway. Another girl steadied the ladder, and all the while the two of them yammered. Guys from the football team kept stampeding up the stairs from the locker room, since there was a game at Hillside in two hours. Casey liked the noise and all the people.

She wore an old gray sweat shirt over shorts, and old sneakers.

Lillian and Mrs. DiLauro came down the long, empty corridor into the gym lobby. Mrs. DiLauro was one of the senior class advisers. She taught Math, Casey remembered.

Lillian was complaining about how she wasn't getting cooperation. Casey said to Heather, "Listen to her!"

"Forget it," Heather said sourly. Her tongue moved along the rim of her upper lip in the direction of her paintbrush. "She gives me a pain."

"What's she bitching about now?"

"I think she's bent about the Drama Club and the Newspaper selling candy at the same time."

Casey listened intently. Lillian was saying, "We made a rule, and we printed forms, and everybody's totally ignoring it. We have no credibility."

Mrs. DiLauro listened, though her eyes darted around the gym lobby. She answered Lillian in a modulated voice and Casey couldn't make out the words.

"That was *Lillian's* rule," Casey said, "not everybody's. Lillian decided to gain control of the fund-raising situation."

"I wish she'd gain control of her life," Heather said. She sighed and sat back on folded legs. She had on a ripped pink sweat shirt over a white T-shirt, and she'd chopped her hair.

"I can't sit this way," Casey decided. She dropped the brush into the paint jar and stretched out on her stomach. She felt her bare skin touch the cool floor as her sweat shirt rode up.

Heather dropped her hands into her lap and looked misty-eyed. About twelve football players suddenly charged out of the stairwell and ran with a clatter past the girls. Casey watched them go outside, where a yellow school bus waited. She hadn't seen Glenn yet.

"What's the matter?" Casey asked.

Heather shook her head, but she was crying.

Casey grunted as she sat down. She discovered blobs of

wet tempera paint on her fingertips and wiped them on the butcher paper. "Come on."

"It's Jon," she sobbed.

"He broke up with you?"

Heather sucked in a long, tragic breath and let it out. She looked toward the ceiling and bit her lip. "He's so cold to me when he writes. His letters used to be beautiful. He'd wrap a flower in Saran Wrap and put it in the letter, so I could pin it up."

"Wow," Casey said. "So what happened?"

"I don't know," Heather said. "What am I supposed to think? I mean, does he *have* somebody?"

"Did he say he did?"

"No." That was more of a whimper. "But how could he fall out of love so fast? What do I do, Case?"

Casey wished she could tell Heather that Jon had probably gotten sick of her smother-loving. But she couldn't.

"Why don't you sort of hint around in your next letter?" Casey suggested. "Ask him what's going on?"

Heather picked up her paintbrush again. "If he thinks he doesn't need me now, fine. He's still very immature, no matter how old he looks."

Casey stifled a laugh. Suddenly, Lillian's cylindrical legs, in powder-blue sneakers, appeared on the other side of the butcher paper.

"Didn't you get any further?"

Casey looked up. Lillian was scrutinizing the banner. "We just started."

"Well, you hardly did anything. What are all those smears on it?"

"What smears?"

Lillian pointed. "Over there, and over there. Are you going to paint over those?"

Casey looked at the smears. "I don't know. I didn't get to them yet."

"Well, I hate to say it, but it's a week until Homecoming

and we've got a lot of work to do. I mean, this is just one stupid banner."

Casey dropped the brush into the paint jar. "Yeah, you're right," she said. "It's a stupid banner." She stood up and wiped her hands on her shorts.

"Oh, come on," Lillian said. "Don't get insulted."

"I'm not insulted," Casey said.

"Yes, you are."

"No, I'm not."

"You know, *I've* got all the responsibility," Lillian said. Her eyes suddenly glistened. "I did the whole darn showcase in the center hall by myself, eighth period, every day, and nobody gave me a hand."

"I've got Math eighth period," Casey said.

"Well, there are nine hundred other seniors. I have to handle the fund-raising, and Homecoming, and the banquet, and the trip, and, by the way, I have a six-period schedule and college applications. I'm supposed to be starting a research paper today. I'm not going to get *near* it." She hugged a clipboard to her pillowy chest and looked away with a tightly set mouth.

Casey said, "Well, Lillian, if you want help, then don't come around and harass people."

"I'm sorry if I was harassing you," she said frozenly.

"You were being a snot."

"Thanks."

"You want us to make the banner?"

Lillian looked back at Casey. "I'd like it to look decent, not like a total mess."

"It'll look decent, don't worry. Half the kids in the school can't read it anyway."

"Very funny."

Casey dropped down to the floor again. "Why don't you get lost for a while, Lil? Go bother the kickline girls. Tell them you see a varicose vein on their legs and watch them freak out."

Heather cracked up at that, and her brush, hovering

over the paper, dripped. Lillian said, "Darn it, Heather! Watch what you're doing!"

Heather stared at her. "Oh, suck ice."

Lillian tried to stare her down, but couldn't. "Remind me not to ask you for any favors again."

"Okay," Heather said. "We'll remind you."

Lillian flounced away, viciously making some marks on the pad she carried. Heather watched her. "Twerp."

"She's okay," Casey said, as she tried harder to paint within the lines. "She's just insecure."

"Oh, yeah, make excuses for her." Heather swirled her brush in the paint. "She thinks she's Mother Superior. Between her holy-holy attitude and her phony injuries, I don't know why anyone talks to her."

Casey smiled. "Well, we like her."

"*You* like her," Heather said. "Then again, you like Paul VanHorn, so we can't go by your taste."

Casey stopped painting and stared at her. "Thanks a *lot.*"

Heather's face reddened. "I'm sorry. I didn't mean it."

"Boy. Sorry if I ruined your life."

"Back off," Heather said. More football players came up and stomped outside. Casey could hear the bus chugging and the thin, raucous voices of the guys.

She went back to painting, her head throbbing. She hoped it wasn't another one of the headaches she'd been getting. "I notice that everyone stays away from me lately."

Heather turned. Her paintbrush dripped again. Casey pointed, and Heather put the brush into the paint jar. She wiped her hands on a paper towel. "You want it straight?"

Casey felt herself knot up inside. "Sure."

Heather licked her lips. "Okay. Nobody cared that you started going out with him even though he's a fruitcake. But *you're* different."

"How?"

Heather shrugged. "I don't know. You were always

pretty deep, but you were normal. Now you're just—I don't know, *sad* all the time. Like we say let's go to the mall and you go"—she did a mock sigh—"'Oh, I don't think so.' Or we go to the deli to get lunch and you go, 'Oh, no, I'm not up for that.' It's like you're too old for us." She exhaled. "Well, you wanted to hear it."

"I know." Casey pushed the brush down into the jar until she felt the bristles squish on the bottom. "I didn't think I was doing that."

"Well, you are. I mean, Faye's supposed to be your best friend and she's been going out with Ed Reese for about two weeks and you don't even know about it."

The headache intensified. It burned inside her skull, where Paul had banged her head against the car. "Who's Ed Reese?"

"He's in the Drama Club. Kind of tall, with glasses and blonde hair."

Casey shrugged, defensive now. "I don't know him."

"I know you don't. That's the problem."

The team bus ground its gears and Casey turned to see it move away from the curb. She'd missed Glenn totally. She'd wanted to wish him good luck before he got on the bus. That made her feel lousy, too. "Faye didn't tell me."

"She's mad at you."

"Tough."

"You *asked* me to tell you, Casey."

"I know I asked."

She wanted to smash the damn jar of paint all over the banner and maybe ram the broken glass into her wrists. Or into Heather's eyes. Or somewhere. What a laugh. Did they all know she hadn't seen Paul since he'd beaten on her in the parking lot? Not a phone call, nothing. Not that she was about to call him. Forget it. One time, you overlooked it. Not the second time. If he was sick, let him get help. Obviously, he didn't need *her* assistance.

Heather said softly, "You're sore now, right?"

"A little."

"Well, can't you be with Paul *and* us? Where do you two go, anyway? Nobody ever sees you anywhere."

"We go places."

"Like where?"

"None of your business!"

"Go to hell," Heather muttered.

"I'm sorry," Casey said to Heather. "I'm feeling rotten." She stood up, tingling. She folded her arms across her chest and took quick breaths to try to stave off the growing agony in her head. Great. She could go to the bathroom now, but when Mom came to pick her up, she couldn't fake being okay. Already her stomach rolled with nausea. Heather kept painting. Casey said, almost to herself, "Paul's a moody guy. He's got a lot of problems."

"So do you," Heather said.

"Forget I said anything."

"You got it."

Casey had to walk to the nearest showcase and lean against it. She tried to focus on the color photos of the football team behind the streaked glass. She found Glenn's picture. He seemed too cheerful and mischievous to be a jock. But he looked mint standing there in the sunshine. She wished he could step out of the picture and hold her.

Maybe she should have called Paul. Not that he had any excuse for hitting her again, but the guy *had* walked into Little Tony's dead tired, and she'd dumped all over him for forgetting her stupid birthday. He was breaking his rear end, and she was being a princess. She'd told him she'd stand behind him. Some loyalty.

She wanted to talk to Faye about it, but she didn't know how, and anyway, Faye had Ed Reese, so forget about her as a friend. So what? Casey was used to being alone. It was like Paul said: You did tricks to make people like you and then they kicked you anyway. He knew what he was talking about.

"Casey," Heather said. "Are you okay?"

Casey's eyes fluttered open. She forced herself to straighten up and to rest her back against the showcase. "Yeah. I just have a headache."

"You look terrible," Heather said. She touched Casey's forehead. "Oh, man, you're sweating like a pig."

"Thanks."

"Want me to drive you home?"

Casey shook her head. "My mom's coming at one."

Heather glanced at a clock high up on a wall. "It's only eleven. You'll never make it."

Casey wavered. Her stubbornness made her resist. "No. You've got stuff to do."

"What do I have to do, paint Lillian's banner?"

"She'll have a fit."

"That makes my day. Come on."

Casey couldn't answer because the right side of her head was pounding too hard. Each throb made her wince. She stepped gingerly over the banner as Heather guided her toward the doors.

Casey was daydreaming in Homeroom two days later when Mr. Adelman called her name. She turned her head sharply; she'd been gazing out the window, past the twisted venetian blinds. "Me?"

Mr. Adelman held out an envelope. Casey got up and took it, wondering what it was. Some of the other kids watched.

Casey turned the envelope over as she went back to her seat. The envelope was a plain white one, and on it was Casey's name. But it wasn't a school envelope.

Casey slid back into her seat and tore off the end of the envelope. Behind her, Mike Leonard leaned forward. "What's that?"

"I don't know yet."

She took out a doctor's bill and a folded piece of lined paper, the kind that came from those writing tablets you bought at Cheap John's.

"Who sent it to you?" Mike asked.

She gave him a sharp look. "Do you mind?"

She faced front to block his view and opened the doctor's bill. It was from the State University Department of Psychological Services. It was for ten dollars, for an initial consultation. And it was charged to Paul.

Casey's heart jumped. With fumbling fingers, she opened the lined paper. It was a note from Paul. It said, *A long journey starts with a single step. But I can't walk alone.*

She folded the note over for a moment, her mouth dry. She realized just how much she'd been depressed that he was gone. Not just that he was gone, but that she'd screwed up everything.

She let out a long breath. This wasn't anything to get crazy about. He had a lot to prove. She looked at the note again, and it asked her to meet him at the beach at Smith's Point, tonight at sunset. He wrote out directions to the exact spot.

"So?" Mike asked. "What's up?"

"Nothing," she said crisply. A voice crackled over the P.A. She slid the note and the bill back into the envelope and stuffed the envelope into her pocketbook. "Pledge," Mr. Adelman called out. She stood up, as thirty other chairs scraped, and absentmindedly pressed her palm to her blouse. For some reason, this time, she wasn't afraid to see him again.

When she got home, Mom was in the kitchen, looking at a bunch of The Budget Gourmet TV dinners. "Casey, I need to talk to you," she said.

Casey had one foot on the carpeted stairs, her pocketbook slung over her shoulder and her schoolbooks balanced against her ribs. "One minute."

"Now, please."

Casey whispered a curse and dropped all her junk on the landing. She heard JoAnne out in the backyard with her friends. She went into the kitchen and stood impatiently, one hip thrust out. "Yes?"

Mom was dressed up, and Casey's stomach knotted. Mom looked from one box to another, through her reading glasses. She smelled of freshly sprayed Shalimar. "Which do you like, Casey, chicken with broccoli and cream sauce or sweet and sour chicken?"

"Either one," Casey said. "What's up?"

"Well, you can have either one. JoAnne won't eat a TV dinner, so you can microwave a hamburger for her."

"Are you going somewhere?"

Mom said, "Your father and I are going out to dinner and then we're going to start looking for a new dining-room set."

"Tonight?"

Mom looked at her. "Yes, tonight. Why? Did you have an appointment?"

Casey bit down on her teeth and tried to control her panic. "I had some plans, yeah."

"Sorry. I didn't think you'd have plans on a Monday night. I need you to watch JoAnne."

"Can't you get a sitter?"

Mom stared at her. "No, I can't get a sitter. You can reschedule your appointment. You know, I wish, just once, you'd say, 'Okay, Mom,' without giving me a hard time."

"Yeah. Okay, Mom." She bit off the words.

"Go to your room," Mom said disgustedly. "I really don't want to see you right now."

Casey stormed out of the kitchen, picked up her stuff, and pounded upstairs. She slammed her door hard enough to make it shake. She lay on her bed for half an hour, as the sun slanted across her wrists. She had Paul's phone number. She could call him and change the date. But she didn't want to. Defiance burned under her skin. She was almost seventeen, and she had a license, and she resented having to stay with JoAnne. She resented not having her own car, even though she worked fifteen hours a week. She hated JoAnne's guts for being alive.

What scared her was her flat-out fury. This was the first time she just felt *mad*. Not mad as in cry on her bed with the light off and the stereo playing. Not even mad as in write a poem that made smoke come off the page. Mad as in, screw everything and be free.

So she sat up and dialed Lisa's number. When Lisa got on, Casey said, "I need a big favor, Lise. Really big."

"What?" Music blasted in the background, and the McGuires' beagle howled.

"I'm supposed to watch JoAnne tonight, but I have to go out. It's incredibly urgent. Can you fill in for me? I get paid tomorrow and I can pay you on Saturday."

"I was gonna do my nails tonight."

"You can do them here. *Please*, Lisa. I've got to get out."

There was an agonizing silence, with just the hard rock and the howling in the background. Finally, Lisa said, "Yeah, I guess so. What time?"

"Oh, God, thanks! You're a lifesaver. About six-thirty."

When Casey hung up, she couldn't concentrate on homework, so she forgot about it. She knew she was going to be in deep trouble if she got caught sneaking out, and she'd never done anything like this, but she wanted to meet Paul *tonight*. She tried not to think about how she was lying to her parents, and disobeying them. It was up to them to listen to her a little and not mess up her life.

Lisa came over about ten minutes after Mom and Dad left. Casey had showered and put on a soft lemon-colored blouse, jeans, and lavender sneakers. She wore her dark blue Westfield windbreaker. JoAnne was at her friend Connie's house.

"Give JoAnne a hamburger or something," Casey said, as she fingered her keys. "Let her watch TV or whatever she wants to shut her up. She goes to bed at eight. She's supposed to, anyway."

Lisa wore old sweats, and she methodically set up her

nail stuff on a stack table in the family room. "What if your folks come home?"

"Yeah, what if?" Casey said. She was breathing too fast. "Tell JoAnne, and my folks, that I *had* to go to my friend's house, that my friend's mom got really sick and she was all alone."

Lisa smiled. "What friend?"

"I don't know yet. I have to get whoever it is to back me up tomorrow. Okay?" She hugged Lisa. "Thanks a billion. You're terrific."

Lisa made a face. "What's with you, anyway? You don't do this kind of stuff."

Casey blew out a nervous breath. "Well, it's important. I'll try to be back before my folks."

Lisa seated herself on the couch. "Okay," she said, unscrewing the cap from the polish remover. "Have a good time."

"Thanks," Casey said. She was practically chewing on her heart.

"Taking the Toyota?" Lisa asked.

The Toyota was the family's second car. "Yeah," Casey nodded. "I have the copy of the registration. Daddy keeps it in a cubby in the hall closet."

"You're stealing the car?"

"Don't remind me," Casey said. "I won't get stopped."

She looked around the house as if leaving it forever. Suddenly, she was struck by the enormity of her actions. She had a tremendous urge to send Lisa home, to stay here, to forget the whole thing. At the same time, the need to see Paul, the need to go through with it, pulled her as if she'd been brainwashed.

She shook off her hesitation and went out the front door. The sky was flooded with cherry light, darkening to a deep blue horizon. Casey heard JoAnne's squeal three houses down. As she unlocked the Toyota, she prayed that she would get through this in one piece.

Suddenly, words flooded her racing mind.

> *I am settled, and bend up*
> *Each corporal agent to this terrible feat.*
> *Away, and mock the time with fairest show:*
> *False face must hide what the false heart doth know.*

Her fingers stopped on the car key. *Macbeth.* They were lines from *Macbeth,* from last year! And she'd remembered them, and they fit the moment.

She turned the key and warm air rushed through the vents, but she shivered in her windbreaker. She wished she could tell Mr. Young that she'd actually thought of a literary reference at a critical moment. He'd be so happy. But it wasn't something she wanted him to know about. And she didn't like equating herself with Macbeth, of all people!

With a quick intake of breath, she shifted into drive, then sped around the corner toward the crimson sky.

Chapter Ten

CASEY STOOD NEXT TO THE TOYOTA AS SEA WIND BLEW her hair across her face. The hood of the car was hot under her palm. She stuffed the keys in her windbreaker pocket and got a little chill thinking about being the only car in the whole parking field. The sky was split into bands of turquoise and black and looked like it went on forever.

Casey scanned the empty beach. Wire wastebaskets etched their grids against the dying light. A lifeguard stand tilted. The sand glowed pastel pink, and far down at the shoreline, luminous foam broke with a distant hiss. The wind blew stiffly and spray wet her lips.

I'm an idiot, she thought miserably.

She leaned against an iron post where the concrete walk ended and slipped off her sneakers. Her bare soles felt cold on the hard sand. She tied the laces together and slung the sneakers over her shoulder. She rolled up the cuffs of her jeans, then took a deep breath and started walking.

She'd seen the beach at night before. She smiled a little as she remembered some wild parties they'd had out here. She could visualize bonfires and kids dancing.

She could hear blasting radios and see Glenn and his buddies strip down to their underwear and dive into the water. She remembered salt kisses and sea-cold skin.

Her heart ached at the memories. Why did things have to change so much, anyway? Why did you have to become different?

Her throat tightened, and her head throbbed. *No,* she raged. No headache now. Even if Paul didn't show up, she had to drive home.

She had a sudden thought: What if he beat up on her again and left her lying on the beach? What if she couldn't get home until morning? What if she lay too close to the ocean and she drowned at high tide?

She stopped and made a disgusted face. "Quit it!" she said out loud. She blew out an exasperated breath, shook her head, and went on.

Far down the beach, a bright yellow fire twinkled like a star that had fallen but still burned. And she thought she heard music, but maybe it was somebody else's radio, or just the way the ocean sounded.

As she walked along the shoreline, spent waves unrolled over her bare feet and she enjoyed the startling chill. Seagulls hovered over the water.

Casey reached the fire. It spat and cracked, throwing a mask of light over her face. But the spot was deserted. She stood before the fire, soaking up its warmth, and felt her heart sink. Had he been here and left? Or was this someone else's fire? She blinked as smoke stung her eyes. She felt cold disappointment. She had really thought that he would be here.

She turned to go, but paused. She strained to hear a faint sound, counterpointed against the steady boom of the surf. It sounded like drums, but so low she could hardly tell.

The smell of the fire tickled her nose and its heat warmed her back. The packed sand was damp beneath her feet. The drums grew louder. Their persistent rhythm echoed in her chest. She looked around, frightened. She couldn't see anything. The blue band of sky was darkening. The first stars faintly gleamed like candles lit a million miles away.

Louder...! How were those drums getting so close when she couldn't see...

"K-R-E-E-E-E-E-G-A-A-A-A-A-A!!!!!"

She screamed and her heart played paddleball in her throat. A male figure *leaped* out of the darkness into the firelight. He had war paint on his face—yellow and green streaks. He was naked except for a flowered cloth around his middle. He held a torch. The fire made flickering lights on his glistening skin.

"Jesus, Paul!" she croaked.

He looked so totally ridiculous that she couldn't sort out her reactions. He stared at her wildly, as the drums kept hammering.

Then he started to dance! It was the stupidest thing she'd ever seen. He kept *flinging* himself into the air, and twirling, and waving the torch. As he danced, he did a chant in time to the drums: "YUKKA doobie doobie hunga bunga BOOGA BOO!" or something that sounded like that. She could hear his breath rasping as he knocked himself out.

Laughter came rushing from Casey's terrified insides, in gasps and flurries. She clapped her hands over her mouth and trembled with relief.

When she could produce a coherent sound, she said, "Stop, Paul. You'll kill yourself." He finally quit and stood there, with his chest heaving.

"Turn off the drums," she said, and started laughing again. He nodded and marched off down the beach a few yards. She could barely see him, since he was out of the firelight and it was just about dark. The drums stopped, but her ears still vibrated. She heard the muted crash of the ocean once more.

He came back and tossed the stick into the fire. "Ugh," he grunted. "White woman foolish to seek Mgoomi village at night." He gestured grandiloquently at the wavering black sky. "Full moon mean sacrifice of virgin."

"Too late," she said dryly. "Take me to your leader."

He made an elaborate shrug. "No leader. Me whole village."

"You whole fruitcake," she said, and felt new mirth bubbling up. She fumbled in her windbreaker pocket for a tissue to wipe her eyes.

He scurried past the rim of firelight again and returned with a towel. Roughly, he began to wipe off his makeup. "Glad you came," he said in his normal voice.

"I can't believe you did all this."

"Well, I had to make it good." He toweled himself vigorously for a minute, then rubbed his hair so it got all tousled. He stood looking at her, with streaks of yellow and green still on his face. "It's good to see you."

"It's good to see you, too," she said.

"Wait here." He disappeared for a third time, and she heard him dragging something along the sand. His flowered tush came into view, and then the rest of him, hauling a cooler. He straightened up and breathed hard. "Damn thing has only one handle."

"What is it?" she asked. "More wine and cupcakes?"

"Nope."

She pushed back her hair as it blew across her eyes and mouth. He opened the cooler and she heard ice rattling. He held up a big bottle with foil at its neck. "What is it?" she asked.

"Champagne."

"Get out of here."

"No." He stripped off the foil and used the towel to twist the cork as he held the bottle under his arm. She winced in expectation of the pop, but the cork came out with just a little rush of air. Paul dug into the cooler and came up with a real wineglass. He gravely poured the champagne. He stepped to her and handed her the glass.

She took it by its stem and stared into the dark, diamond-flecked liquid. The fire heated her cheeks. He poured a glass of champagne for himself, put back the bottle, and held up his glass as he stood in front of her.

"So what do we drink to?" he asked.

Emotions spun inside her like a whirlpool. "I don't know."

"To new beginnings?"

She took a steadying breath. "I've heard that before."

"I know," he said.

The fire popped. The smell of sea salt grew strong. "I'm glad you went for help. If you know you've got a problem, that's a start."

"Yeah."

"How was the session?"

"Great. It's like I've been walking around with this pain inside me, making me crazy. And now I'm taking medicine for it."

She felt herself soaring with his words. "That's great, Paul."

He looked deeply at her. "You did it for me."

"Come on..."

"You showed me I was worth something. You had the right to get a gun and shoot me."

She nodded, smiling ruefully. "Yeah."

"Jesus, it's good to see you."

She lifted her head and sniffed and concentrated on holding on to the glass. "Same here."

"So let's toast you. For saving a guy who wasn't worth it."

She met his eyes with full force, and she gulped champagne. It fizzed in her mouth and hurt her raw throat.

Almost instantly, it went to her head. "I didn't save you," she said.

"Yeah, you did. And I'm going to make it."

"I hope so," she said. She finished the champagne in another gulp and gave him back the glass. She knelt down in the sand and watched the blinding dance of the fire.

He put down both glasses and sat near her. The firelight picked out the curve of his muscles and the flatness of his stomach. She could smell his perspiration and the pungent grease of his makeup. "I don't blame you for not believing me," he said.

She dug up cold sand and sprinkled it through her fingers. "It gets harder every time."

"I need a chance."

"Yeah, and I need a doctor for my headaches."

He looked away from her. She could see how hurt he was. "I'm not going to lie about it," she said. "You messed me up. You could have killed me."

He still said nothing. Fireflies danced in her blood. "Why do you get that way, Paul? It's okay to get pissed off, and to yell, but why do you hit me?"

His silence became unbearable. She hugged herself, aware of the vastness of the beach around her. "Nothing to say?" she asked.

He looked back at her and said, "Come on, let's take a walk."

She drew back, stiff with fear. He stood up and extended his hand. She looked down at the flickering sand, paralyzed.

"Come on," he said.

She stood up slowly and brushed the sand from her jeans. The wind got under her jacket and made it billow. Mutely, he began to walk. She followed him at a few paces.

They walked into the planetarium of night. The moon was really full, like he'd said. Its whiteness glimmered coldly on the black ocean. On the opposite rim of the sky she saw the reddish glow of civilization.

She could barely see him next to her, except when they walked through a slat of moonlight. At those times, he looked like a savage warrior, the way he walked so lightly and the way his smooth skin seemed to glide over his bones. Her throat closed and she couldn't stop shaking inside. She'd never felt this much need for anybody, ever in her life. It was drowning her, like an undertow that turned her over and over.

"Stop here," he said.

"What?"

He raised his arms and chanted, "HOY-a, HOY-a, here lies treasure...."

She laughed. "Not again."

He gestured. "Take a look."

Puzzled, but expectant, she followed the line of his arm and saw something big and bulky, propped against a wire wastebasket. "What is that?"

"It's the treasure of my whole village."

"You don't have a whole village."

"Well, it's a small treasure."

She laughed again and knelt to examine the bulk. Her fingers timidly reached out and touched what felt like wrapping paper. She looked up at him. "Give me a hint."

"It's a friend."

"What?"

"Go ahead. Look."

Eagerly, she tore away the paper. The moon sailed between clouds and flooded her with icy brilliance. She was looking at an immense Paddington Bear, about as big as JoAnne. "Oh, my God, Paul!" she squealed. She threw her arms around the bear and hugged its new-smelling plushness against her, as hard as she could. She buried her face in its side, and its fibers tickled her nose.

"Happy birthday, Casey."

She cried idiotically into the bear's synthetic fur, and

she heard him chuckle at her display. She stood up, finally, and looked at him. "Jerk."

"Thanks."

She laughed and sniffled at the same time. "I love it, Paul. It's gorgeous. I can't believe you did this. It's better than anything."

"Even gold?" he asked.

Her cheeks hurt from all her laughing and crying. "I never asked for gold."

He gestured. "Paddington's got something else for you."

She stared at him, then turned back to the bear. She dropped to her knees again and felt in its fur, stopping at its left paw. Her fingertips touched thin, light metal. "What is this, Paul?"

"You can take it. He doesn't wear jewelry."

Her fingers shook as she undid the delicate clasp. She stood again, holding the glittering chain up to the moonlight. She could see a charm dangling from it. She could tell, just from holding it, that it was expensive. She lowered the chain and looked at him. "Why did you do this? You can't afford it."

"I can't afford to lose you."

"Oh, man." She bit her lip hard. Then she took a breath and clasped the chain behind her neck. He looked so happy, and so like a boy, as he stood there.

"I owe you more than a birthday present," he said. "I'm going to lick my problem."

She wiped her eyes and cheeks with her fingers, smearing what was left of her eye makeup. "I believed you before. I've got to think of it like probation. One day at a time."

He nodded. "That's fair."

"Well," she said. "How about some more of your bubbly?"

He laughed. "You're getting to be a real alky."

"Very humorous," she said. "What do I do with the bear?"

"He'll wait for you."

She turned to the bear and said, "Don't get too cold,

Paddy. I've got a nice warm bed for you tonight." And a nice lie to come up with for Mom and Dad.

She stretched out her hand and Paul took it. They walked slowly through the wet sand. Casey enjoyed the wind in her hair and the smell of fish. Paul had lit millions of little stars inside her.

They reached the fire again. It had burned low and begun to redden. Paul took wood from a stack he'd obviously gathered earlier. He threw more chunks on the blaze, and it flared, awhirl with cinders and sparks.

He came to Casey and stood right in front of her, close enough for her to see streaks of sweat on his ribs, and his belly button. He was about a head taller than she was and she had to look up a little to see his eyes. He placed his hands tenderly on her hips, just under the hem of her windbreaker. She reached up and touched his face. It was chilled.

"Let's stay by the fire," he said.

She rested her hands on his arms, and he worked his hands under her jacket. She closed her eyes and began to breathe more rapidly. Without saying anything, she unzipped the windbreaker. He pulled her against him and she kissed him. She wrapped her arms around his fire-hot back.

She became acutely aware of sounds: the steady spit of the fire, the rush of waves, the ragged wind. She'd never felt more free and more beautiful in her life. She was conscious of every cell of her skin. It was like being unchained after a hundred years, and she didn't care what happened when she got home or what Heather thought or even if he killed her tonight and the cold ocean rushed into her lungs. She almost longed for it, because only that beautiful, romantic death would fit this moment.

Casey guided the Toyota onto the double driveway. Paddington Bear rolled around in the backseat. She'd taken off the chain and zipped it into a windbreaker pocket.

She doused the headlights and stopped the car. She sat back against the vinyl seat. Her head pounded and her body ached. All the joy of the night had faded, and now she coiled into a spring at the thought of facing her parents.

Viciously, she pulled the key from the ignition and got out of the car. She shut the door softly, on the wild chance that everyone was asleep. In anybody *else's* house, everyone would be asleep. Her friends snuck in and out all the time. Only Casey's mom and dad had radar.

The night air was warmer and thicker here. She looked up. The moon had long since gone down, but she could still see stars, dim against the streetlights.

Tired, and scared to death, she opened the storm door, let it rest against her back, and tested the front door. It was open. She cursed.

She went inside. The lamp on the family-room table was on. She stood with her hand on the doorknob for a minute, wondering if it was worth trying to sneak upstairs and into bed.

"Casey?"

It was Mom's voice. Casey felt like a plug had been pulled in her feet and everything was draining out of her. "Yeah."

She heard Mom whisper, "Thank God." Dad said, "Get in here, please."

Already, the rage was building. But she knew it was her own fault. She hadn't had to stay with Paul all night. She had just wanted to. Nothing had mattered, then.

She stopped by the entryway to the family room. Mom sat in one of the club chairs. She wore a nightjacket over her nightgown. Her hair was a mess. She wore her glasses, and she had a book on the table. Dad sat on the couch.

"Are you all right?" Mom asked.

"Yes."

"Where were you?"

"I had to go out."

"Casey, you'd better tell the truth," Dad warned.

Casey's intended lie shredded in her mouth. She couldn't think fast enough to come up with a friend. "I had to meet somebody."

Mom took deep breaths, trying not to lose it. "What should we do, Casey? Right now, at three in the morning, what should we do? Do we beat the living daylights out of you? Because that's what I feel like doing."

Casey shrugged.

"Or should we act civilized? I'm trying to go that route. I'm so...outraged, and disgusted, and plain spitting *mad*..." She was overcome.

Dad looked more bewildered than angry. "I'm really disappointed. I really, truly thought we'd raised you better than this."

Casey's own anger came up in her throat. "Oh, for God's sake, I didn't sell my body on the corner."

"Shut up!" Dad screamed. Casey shuddered and felt her face redden. "Don't you *dare* open a mouth like that. We nearly had the police out for you. I'm infuriated."

Mom folded her hands in her lap. "You were told to watch JoAnne. You totally ignored what we said. You had the...*nerve* to walk out of this house, on a school night, and leave your little sister."

Casey wanted to run upstairs and curl up in bed. She couldn't take this. Not after tonight, not after being so free. "I'm sorry," she mumbled.

"No," Mom snapped. "Sorry won't cut it. Thank God you had at least enough intelligence to get Lisa to watch JoAnne. We paid Lisa ten dollars. That comes out of your pay."

"All right."

"We have a lot of thinking to do," Mom went on. "Apparently, we had the wrong idea. We thought that, even if you were a little lazy, you were at least grown up. Well, you're not. You can't be trusted, you can't be depended upon, and you can't be treated as anything but a willful and selfish child."

Too much. Too much. She was going to break.

"You are going to be punished so that you never forget." Mom's voice was like a needle, poking and poking. "You are going to remember—"

"SHUT YOUR MOUTH!" Casey screamed. "Who do you think you are? God?"

Mom went dead white. "You *dare*—!"

"Get off my back," Casey said. Her whole body shook. "I *told* you I had to go out tonight. I *asked* you to get a sitter. But you didn't even care what I had to say."

Dad stood up and jabbed a finger at her. "You may not talk back to your mother that way."

Mom gave him a sarcastic look. "Don't start now to teach her, Ron. Where were you all these years?"

Dad's eyes flared. "How did this become *my* fault?"

"Stop it," Casey pleaded. "I can't stand this."

"Oh, can't you?" Mom said. "You're going to have to stand a great deal more. This is not going to be forgotten."

Casey felt so low she could have crawled. Guilt stifled her. It wasn't any use to blame them. She'd lied, and she'd left JoAnne, and she'd illegally driven their car. Standing here now, with her head swimming, she couldn't believe she'd done it. Not even for Paul.

"Look, I'm sorry," she said. "I know I was wrong. I just needed to get out."

Dad exhaled angrily and rested a hand on the lamp table. "God, if you'd been in an accident..." He looked at her sharply. "Were you drinking?"

"*No!*" Oh, man, another lie. She couldn't stop.

Dad pushed a hand through his wiry hair. "Well, this is a big, big problem. You have to be severely punished, and we have to find out what's lacking in your ethics."

Casey slumped against the doorway. "There's nothing wrong with my ethics."

Mom sat up straight. "This is useless. It's much too late to discuss it. Casey, get to bed. I want signed notes from your teachers tomorrow attesting to the fact that your homework was done properly. Please come straight home from school."

"I have a Literary Magazine meeting."

"No, you don't," Mom said. "You're grounded. That's the beginning. Come straight home and remain inside. We'll get this straightened out."

Casey bit back her anger. It wasn't any use to argue. She had no arguments, anyway. At least they hadn't grilled her about who she was with and what she'd done. She guessed that would come tomorrow. But she could sleep first.

"I'm sorry," she said again.

"Yes, I'm sure you are," Mom said tiredly. "Go to bed."

Casey looked pleadingly at her father, who couldn't meet her eyes. She'd never seen him so ashamed or hurt. It tore her up. Her whole, beautiful night was a wreck. The fantasy was over.

But for those few hours, in the dancing light of that fire, she'd mattered. They couldn't ruin that. And Paul was still hers. The Paul she was saving. Paul with his strong, beautiful body and his troubled heart.

Yeah, he was still there. And soon she'd be with him, always important, always loved. She could take her punishment until then. She could take any damn punishment they wanted to give.

"Good night, Casey," Dad said.

"Night, Dad," she said. "Night, Mom."

"Good night," Mom said, without a shred of feeling.

Casey trudged up the stairs. She ached with tiredness and her head sang with memories. She remembered that she had to wake up in three hours to go to school.

She flicked on the lamp in her room and dug the gold

chain out of her jacket pocket. She draped it over her palm and let it catch glints of light. The square charm had a tiny diamond in it, and her initials and Paul's. She dropped wearily onto her bed and held the chain against her cheek. The quiet ticking of her clock relaxed her.

"Happy birthday, Casey," she whispered to herself. "And many more."

Chapter Eleven

AT ELEVEN-FORTY AT NIGHT, CASEY SAT CROSS-LEGGED ON her bed. Some diehard crickets chirped outside. Electric current hummed in her ceiling. Casey wore her frilly baby-doll pajamas and listened to a sad romantic album.

She got off her bed and went to her door. She stood in the darkened hallway and listened hard. Mom and Dad's bedroom was black, and no sounds came out of it. A nightlight, plugged into the wall socket by JoAnne's room, made a bowl of brightness. It looked as if they were all asleep. Casey could hear the kitchen clock ticking downstairs.

She dropped down on her bed again and called Faye. She tensed as she heard the phone ring three times on the other end.

Faye's voice said, "Hello?"

"Hi."

"Who is it?"

"Me. Casey."

"Oh. Hi."

Casey worked a barrette out of her hair. She looked at Paddington, who sat like a furry Buddha in the corner, with Casey's Raggedy Ann and Pound Puppy and teddy bear tucked all around. "Did I wake up anybody?"

"I don't think so. You waited until *late*."

"Sorry. I had to make sure everyone was asleep."

"You really got grounded."

"Mom gets into punishment. I think she's working up some long-term stuff."

"You were a royal jerk," Faye said.

"I know, I know. Anyway, what went on at the meeting?"

"Nothing much," Faye said. It sounded like it was raining outside. "Mr. Anderson made a big speech about fund-raising, and Josh and Bruce and Cynthia stood behind him and made stupid cracks. There were about a hundred people there. Some of them looked like refugees from the Twilight Zone."

"What about being an editor?"

"You have to take a test for it," Faye said. "Next Wednesday, right after eighth period. Going to try?"

Casey shrugged and lightly stroked her cheek and upper lip with the barrette. "I'm not sure I'll have time."

"I'm going to try it," Faye said. "They had all these science-fiction freaks there. You know, Josh's friends. I'd like to have a chance to get some normal writing published."

Casey smiled. Again, it sounded like rain, but only for a second. "Anything else?"

She could hear Faye go icy at the other end. "Gee. I thought we could kind of pursue that theme for a while."

"What theme?"

"My writing. I wanted to show you something I churned out while I was supposed to be doing a lab report."

"Sure. Give it to me tomorrow."

"I thought I'd read it to you now."

"Oh." Again came the pattering noise. Casey looked toward her window. "It's kind of late."

"I know."

"Don't be sore," Casey said. "It's not my fault I had to call at midnight."

"Well, *you* were the one who stole your parents' car and went out to Smith's Point."

"Thanks a heap," Casey said coldly. "I counted on your support, not a lecture."

"Support for what?" Faye said. "Running like an idiot to Paul VanHorn because he wanted you to meet him on the beach? You could have made it for another time."

"That's none of your business," Casey said, trying to keep her voice low. "Everyone thinks I need two mothers."

"Maybe you do."

"Maybe you ought to butt out."

"Fine with me."

More pattering. Casey's chest tightened. "Hold on a minute," she said into the phone. "Something weird's happening."

"Really," Faye said.

"No, I mean it. Hold on." Casey set down the receiver and went to her window. She pulled aside the ruffled curtain with one hand. She couldn't see much; it was a dark, cloudy night. She could make out the whiteness of the patio table and the shadows of trees. The pool was covered for the winter and looked like a black hole.

Then a sudden spray rattled the screen. Casey jerked her face back. That *wasn't* rain, it was *stones*. Someone was throwing stones at her window.

She turned off the record player and pressed the light switch. The lamp by her bed went out and her room sank into darkness. The red numbers on her clock cast a glow on the brass base of her lamp.

Feeling clammy, Casey went back to the window. Now she could clearly make out the backyard furniture. Tree branches shook in a sporadic wind.

"Casey...!"

The voice came from the backyard! Casey nearly choked on her surprise. She thought of running into Mom and Dad's bedroom and waking them up.

She called out in a stage whisper: "Who is that?"

"Me."

"Who's 'Me'?"

"A pronoun."

"Huh?" She pressed her forehead against the screen, straining to see. Then she realized who it had to be. *"Paul?"*

"Right."

"What are you doing back there?"

"I want to see you."

"You can't see me. I'm grounded."

"No," he said. *"I'm* on the ground, you're up there."

She smiled, but she was scared. "You'd better get out of there." It hurt her throat to keep up the loud whisper.

"Come down," he said.

"I can't come down."

"Then let down your hair."

She laughed. She still couldn't see him. "Come *on*. I'll really get in trouble."

"I want to see you."

"I want to see you, too."

"So come on."

"Paul, I can't..."

"Bull."

She felt as if her room was a runaway roller coaster and she had to keep gripping the windowsill to stop herself from being flung into the sky. "Paul, don't do this. I'm supposed to stay up here."

"Come down, or I walk."

The conflict wracked her. It *was* stupid. Her parents would never wake up. What was the big deal? The punishment was unfair anyway. And Paul was risking a lot by coming here. And she wanted to be with him. "I'm in my pajamas," she said.

"Take them off."

"Will you *stop*?" She stood very straight and still, while her mind rolled dice.

"So what's the deal?" he called up. His voice was getting a little louder each time.

"Wait there," she called back.

She moved away from her window and stood in the darkness while she tried to figure out how to do this. She wondered if she should turn her light back on. Then she saw the phone on her bed. "Oh, crap," she said. She lunged for the phone and slapped the receiver against her ear. "Faye? Are you still there?"

She heard a rushing sound. With a curse, she hung up. She'd explain it to Faye tomorrow. She moved cautiously to her chest of drawers and managed to claw out a pair of shorts and an old cutoff sweat shirt. It was a pretty shabby outfit, but she couldn't be choosy.

Casey felt like a burglar, creeping down the stairs one at a time. Even though the steps were carpeted, they squeaked. At the landing, she paused and listened so hard her ears hurt. Nothing. Don't go to the bathroom, JoAnne, she prayed.

She had to fish for the back door key on top of the washing machine. She clenched her teeth when the key made its loud click. She pulled open the door with a vicious tug; the warm weather had kept it swollen. The door made such a scrape that she stopped again and listened.

When she was sure that nobody was stirring upstairs, she pushed open the screen door and guided it edgily back until it clicked shut. The humid night rushed around her. The whole sky seemed to be moving.

"Paul?"

"Here."

She felt her way across the patio. The concrete stabbed her bare feet, and once she squished something slimy. She shuddered and moved on. She could feel her heart beating. She saw him standing against the house, where the kitchen jutted out.

He stepped toward her and she grabbed him and hugged him hard, digging her fingertips into his cape.

His *cape*?

She took a step back. "What are you wearing?"

"My Superman outfit."

She looked at him and a laugh fluttered in her throat. She couldn't see too clearly, but he wore some kind of cape around his neck.

"You're crazy," she said.

"Crazy for you."

"Oh, man." She threw herself around him again and kissed him wildly. He guided her against the shingling of the house so he could lean hard into her, and they made out with silent desperation.

She couldn't breathe by the time they took a break, and her heartbeat was a booming sound. She tried to hook her fingers into his waistband but couldn't get under the cape. "Will you take this thing off?" she said.

"I can't fly without it."

"You want to fly or feel my passionate fingers?"

"No contest." He untied the cape and it fell with a silken rustle to the patio. She hooked onto him and held him against her. He nuzzled her neck. She shrank at the tickling.

He said, "How long are you punished?"

"Three weeks."

"Nice."

She sighed, and idly stroked his arms. "Well, I guess I can understand why they got bent. I never did anything like that before."

"Like what, taking a ride to meet a guy?"

"Stealing their car and disobeying them."

He played with her hair. "Well, they wouldn't give you the car, so you had to take it."

"It still isn't right."

"They treat you like a kid."

She nestled against his chest. "There's not much I can do about it."

"You can do whatever you want."

"You want to tell them that?"

"You already did."

"And got punished."

He held her face between his hands. His eyes were invisible in the dark. "So what? Does it hurt?"

She felt a strange, swirling excitement grow inside her, a wild rebellion that tasted like forbidden liquor. "It's a pain in the rear."

"But it doesn't hurt."

"No, it doesn't hurt."

He rubbed his thumbs against her cheeks. "They can't hurt you, Casey. They can't do a thing to you. You don't need them anymore."

"Well, that's not entirely true."

"Why not?"

She sighed. "Oh, there's a little matter of twelve grand a year for college."

"You don't need that either."

"Who's going to pay it?"

"I meant college."

That startled her. "Paul, I'm not about to give up college."

"Why not?"

"Come *on*."

"Why are you going? For your mother and father? Does it make you happy to go?"

"You're being weird."

His voice was rhythmic and seductive, like an exotic Latin dance. "You never dreamed of being away from your mommy and daddy."

"That's not true."

He kissed her, which she didn't expect. It was a hard, demanding kiss, and even when she wanted to stop he wouldn't let her. She tried to pull away. He jammed the heel of his palm under her chin and pinned her head against the shingles.

"Don't do that," he said.

"I'm sorry."

He released her head. "I'm trying to wake you up."

"I'm awake."

"Not until you say that you don't need them. They just want to own you. They get off on their authority trip. Do you love your parents?"

"What kind of question is that?"

"Do you?"

"Well, they're my parents."

"Do you love *me*?"

"You know I love you."

"Can you feel it?"

She began to tremble. "Yes."

"Do you want me even when I'm not around?"

"Why are you asking all this?"

"Do you need me?"

"Yes."

"Do you need your mom and dad?"

"What kind of question...?"

"Think about it."

"That's stupid, Paul. You're not supposed to feel like that about your parents."

"Why not?" The clouds let through a thin white trail of moonlight. Sticks and leaves blew with a papery noise across the patio. "You felt like that when you were a kid, right?"

"I guess so."

"But things change."

"Yeah, they do."

His hands became intimate. She felt uncomfortable about it, with her mother and father sleeping upstairs. She tried to wriggle away, but he was immobilizing her.

"Are you all grown up?"

"Just about."

His voice harshened. "You're my lady. Are you ready for that?"

"Sure."

"Your parents don't care how you feel. They just want to control what you do. I'm the one who cares, right?"

146

"Probably."

"Absolutely."

"Okay, absolutely."

"You need me."

She nodded.

"*Only* me." He pinched the flesh of her arm between his thumb and forefinger. He dug into the muscle and she gasped in pain. Then he released her. She shut her eyes and rubbed her arm. He touched her forehead tenderly. "Just believe it. We've got something special. But you have to give everything. You can't love me and worry about Mommy and Daddy. Mommy and Daddy don't count. *Capish?*"

"Yes." Then why did she want to run upstairs and crawl into bed with Mom and Dad? But Mom and Dad would tell her to stop being a child and get out. Which meant that Paul was right.

"Good girl." He embraced her warmly and gave her lots of small, sweet kisses. "Just me, okay?"

"Mm hm."

"Nobody else gives a damn. Not even friends."

"Friends count, too," she protested.

"Friends stab you in the back."

"Not always, Paul."

"Always."

She linked her hands around his waist and tilted back her head as he kissed her. She thought about Heather giving her a hard time about her attitude, and Faye getting on her case just now—and hanging up on her. Come to think of it, at Glenn's party, Faye had tried pretty hard to get Casey to break up with Paul. And Lillian was just an obnoxious creep. Casey couldn't really think of any friends who had stood by her side. The girls on the team were all out for themselves. They cheered you when you won, but treated you like slime if you lost.

Casey kissed Paul back with angry eagerness. Her throat

swelled with the pain of her self-pity. "I love you so much," she said.

"Forever," he whispered.

"Forever."

"Don't forget it. I'm here for you."

"And I'm here for you."

"I know," he said. "I want to make your life great."

"You already do."

"Just remember," he said. "You don't need anyone else but me."

"Okay," she said.

"I want to be your whole world, Casey."

"I want you to be."

"Come on. Let's have a drink on it."

She got a cold shiver down her spine. "Huh?"

He grabbed her hand. "I want to toast to us."

"Paul, I can't go drinking..."

"Hey!" He yanked her against him and sharply twisted her forearm up behind her back, just hard enough to throb. "Remember what I said?"

She blinked hard. "But if they wake up..."

"So what? They won't put you in jail. Come on, Case. You have to make your moves. I'm your man. I'm the one who matters. You don't need anyone else."

She looked up toward her parents' darkened window, and then back at Paul. "Just one drink."

He smiled and squeezed her tightly, releasing her arm. "Ten minutes with you is like a lifetime with a zebra."

"What?"

He laughed and hugged her again. A dog began barking. Wind moaned through the electric wires. The night seemed evil and alien and she wanted to be inside, with Paddington. But instead she held on to Paul.

Casey usually hung out in the library during eighth period, but she was so tired from last night that she went down to the music suite and stretched out on a big table in the band room. She made a pillow of her folded jacket and brought her knees up to her stomach as she listened to cars and radios and voices outside.

The noise of the door opening woke her up. The vast room seemed to spin for a moment before she focused on Faye.

"Oh, hi," she mumbled.

"Hi."

Casey sat up and folded her legs. She wore one of her dad's shirts, over a short skirt. Her bones felt rusty. "I'm out of it," she said.

"I can see that." Faye had her flute case with her, and her books. She sat down in one of the folding chairs that were scattered about the room. Black music stands made a tangled forest. The oversized windows were all open to let in hazy sun.

"Lesson this period?" Casey asked.

"Yeah. I'm just waiting for Mr. Small."

"Okay. I'll clear out."

"How come you never got back on the phone last night?" Faye asked.

"How come you hung up on me?"

Faye gave Casey a look. "I waited ten minutes for you to come back on."

"Okay. I'm sorry."

"So what's the story?"

"There's no story. What do you mean?"

Faye hugged her blue-jeaned knees and bent forward. "Was it Paul again?"

"Get lost."

Casey swiped at her jacket and slithered off the table. Her head spun a little from exhaustion. Faye's eyes followed her. "What did he do, come to visit you?"

"I can't believe you're giving me the third degree."

"One question isn't the third degree."

"It's a nosy question."

"Why? What's the big deal if he visited you?"

"There's no big deal." Casey felt her nerves rubbing against each other. "It's just private, that's all."

"Friends tell each other private things. That's the whole idea."

"Maybe the whole idea is that you feel you have to know everything so you can own me."

Faye gaped at Casey. *"What???"*

"Come on, Faye. You wanted me to break up with Paul right from the beginning. So did Glenn and everybody else. You've been working at it and working at it. Well, it's not going to happen."

Faye gave an incredulous laugh and released her knees. "You are *bizarre*. What's he been doing, brainwashing you?"

"I figured that's what you'd think."

"Well, what am I supposed to think? What are you so paranoid about? What did you do last night that you weren't supposed to do?"

"Get off my back, Faye. You're not my mother."

"So stop being afraid of me."

Casey wished Paul were here, so he could help. She couldn't think of answers the way he could. "Paul just made me see things in a different way. He's out of this whole high-school game. He has some perspective, and man, that's what I needed. Nobody went out of their way for me until Paul."

"And nobody beat the crap out of you until Paul."

"SHUT UP." Casey shook with rage. Her voice caromed off the high ceiling, bouncing among the exposed ducts. She felt her face vibrating.

Faye sat erect. Her eyes glistened and her voice quivered a little. "You can yell at me all you want, Casey, and you can tell yourself all the lies you want. I saw what your face looked like the first time he beat on you. Everybody knows about your headaches. And today you have a gorgeous bruise on your neck. Was it fun last night? Do you really *like* it?"

Casey felt wobbly, as if Faye had been punching her. "I can handle it," she said.

"Not unless you take karate lessons."

"You always have a swift remark, don't you?" Casey said. "What about you and Ed? I heard he cheated on you the week after he went out with you."

Faye reddened. "So what?"

"So did you break up with him? Or did you go back with him?"

"What's that got to do with anything?"

"Because where do you get off lecturing me on my relationships? If you love a guy and he needs you, then you love him all the time. You don't give up on him. If you're his whole world you stick by him and you take the bad times with the good times. Paul and I have a commitment. A commitment is for keeps."

"Not if he hits you."

"Or if he cheats on you?"

Faye smacked a music stand, making it clatter to the floor. "You don't understand a thing. It's not the same. The worst I'm suffering is embarrassment. Paul is a psycho."

Casey felt cornered and hurt. Faye's words lodged like red-hot bullets in Casey's heart. But if Faye were even a little bit right, then Casey had nothing. So she fought for Paul, because she was fighting for herself.

"You're dead wrong, Faye," she said. "And you can't see it. I think it's because you had a hard time getting a boyfriend and the one you got is making a jerk out of you."

"Stick it," Faye said grimly. "I don't want to hear this garbage."

"Fine. But don't hand me *your* garbage. You're jealous of me, and so is Heather. You don't have me around all the time to dump on, and it pisses you off. Well, I'm sorry. I've got a *man* who loves me and he needs me to be there for him. A lot of people are going to have to understand that, like my mother and father, and my friends."

"You won't have to worry about your friends," Faye said spitefully. "There won't be any around."

"There never *were* any around," Casey said, wanting to hurt Faye. "Not when I needed them."

"You have some hell of a nerve saying that."

"It's the truth. You weren't there when I stood in the bathroom with my father's razor in my hand and I came this close to opening my wrists."

"Yeah, right," Faye said. "Like we all knew you were in your bathroom with a razor. When did this supposedly happen?"

"After I broke up with Mark Simon," Casey said defiantly. "When you *allegedly* knew how I was feeling. You didn't know a thing about how I was feeling."

"I guess Paul knows better."

"He knows *exactly* what I'm feeling. I never knew what it was like to matter that much to anyone. But I know now. And I'm not giving it up."

"Hooray for you," Faye said. "Just make sure your parents pay up their medical insurance."

Casey made a sour face. "Paul's taking care of his problem, and I'm going to help him lick it."

"I can see that."

The door opened and Mr. Small poked his head in. "You about ready?"

"Yeah. Be right in." The door closed and Faye stood up, gathering her stuff. "See you around."

Casey felt bruised all over. "You know, we can still be friends, Faye."

"Sure. Tell me when you can fit me in."

"Okay, if that's how you want it. Paul *said* you'd drop me if it meant competing."

Faye shook her head. "Unbelievable. I wish you could hear yourself, Casey. I really like you, but I'm not going to cry at your funeral."

"Don't even bother to show up."

"Don't worry, I won't."

Faye balanced her books and flute case while her hand curled around the doorknob and twisted. The door closed behind Faye, and Casey sat down hard on a chair. Outside, she could see white clouds against a soft blue sky and yellow leaves fluttering like tiny flags. She felt a little like she'd had a leg amputated.

She'd given up everything now for Paul. She'd gone drinking with him last night until one-thirty and she was sure she'd recognized a couple of Westfield kids in the bar. Mom and Dad were still asleep when she snuck back home, but Mom had looked at her really strangely this morning. Casey knew she must have looked totaled. So it would all hit the fan pretty soon. And now Faye wasn't talking to her.

Casey heard the faint melodic whispers of Faye's flute in the rehearsal room next door. Then the bell rang shrilly and made her jump. Almost instantly, kids started filling up the corridor and swarming outside toward the waiting buses.

Chapter Twelve

IT WAS TWO MINUTES UNTIL THE 7:30 BELL, AND FOR Owen Young, the craziness was in full swing. He stood behind his desk at the front of the room with his grade book open, a pile of Xeroxed handouts on top of his briefcase, and a crowd of kids around his desk.

"No," he kept saying as the kids tried to drop their essays on his desk. "Don't hand them in now. Wait until I call for them." Some of the kids dropped the essays anyway. The corner of his eye caught Chuck Longano, one of his students.

"Hey, great meet yesterday," Chuck shouted.

Owen smiled back. "Yeah, the girls were terrific. East Harrow is a tough team."

The bell blasted over the P.A. Owen put up his hands and said, "Come on, come on, that's it. Seats! Seats!"

The wailing wall of kids in front of him kept clamoring, but Owen had learned he had to stop listening if he ever wanted class to begin. "No questions. No answers. If you're seated, you're here. If you're standing, you're late. Let's go."

Reluctantly, the petitioners dropped back and shuffled to their seats. Owen felt the air twang from the noise and energy. He jabbed a pencil in the air as he noted which seats were empty.

He saw right away that Casey wasn't there. She hadn't been at the meet yesterday, either, and she hadn't come to him with an excuse. Owen's chest tightened as he thought about Casey. He was losing her fast.

Distracted, he said, "Okay. While you're writing in your journals, I'm going to—QUIET!—I'm going to call your names. Bring up your essay and lay it down. If you haven't got it, don't bother with excuses. Just bring it tomorrow and I'll take ten points off."

He sat behind his desk and felt depressed about Casey being absent. He shrugged off the emotion and began to call names. He liked collecting essays, but he didn't look forward to reading through all of this mud. At least a cold front had brought chilly fall air and brighter skies. As he thought about these things, Casey walked into the room.

At first, he felt his spirits lift, but quickly he frowned. She looked slovenly, which she never had before. Her hair was ratted and her denim jacket and skirt were askew over a half-buttoned white shirt. She glanced at him and mumbled, "Sorry. My ride was late."

She started for her seat. Owen said, "Casey?"

She stopped, her hip jutting impatiently, and looked at him. "Yeah?"

"Don't you take the bus?"

"I get a ride now."

"Well, you know, if your ride is late, school policy says it's illegal."

"Yeah, I know." Her voice was thick with sleep.

"Okay," he said. "When are we going to talk about yesterday?"

"What was yesterday?"

"The meet against East Harrow."

She hissed an obscenity, then raised her face to the

fluorescent lights and sighed. "I forgot. I'm really sorry, Mr. Young."

"We'll talk about it later. Right now, I've got to get this class going."

She moved listlessly to her seat, muttering to herself. She sat down with a thud and touched her fingertips to her desktop as she squinted up at the board. He watched her rummage in her big gray pocketbook and come out with a pen. She flipped open her notebook and began to write.

Owen knew she was dating Paul VanHorn and he knew a lot about Paul. He had seen other bright, terrific girls get sucked into relationships and surrender their morals, their needs, and their personalities. He had never understood it. He couldn't understand it now.

He kept collecting essays, and got to Casey's name. "Miss Gordon?" he said.

She looked up with a blank face. "I don't have it."

Damn, he thought viciously. "Tomorrow?"

"Yeah." She nodded, and looked down again.

He marked a zero in the grade book and felt himself get angry. He felt something similar when he fell a few yards back in a ten-kilometer race and his hamstring quit. He usually coaxed some extra yardage out of the anger. Now the anger would motivate him to look into Casey Gordon's love life.

Casey stopped writing and looked out the window, in time to see Paul's car leave the parking lot. Unsaid words stuck like chicken bones in her throat. He'd deliberately pulled up late the last few mornings. "Don't sweat over it so much," he'd said. "It's no big deal."

But it *was* a big deal to her. Or at least it always *had* been a big deal. She didn't know why. They wouldn't hold back her diploma. Everyone knew you could be a total dirtbag but if your mother cried to the superintendent, they'd cut a deal for you. Nobody didn't graduate.

She balanced her face on her fist. Every time she got ticked at Paul for something, he turned out to be right. It felt kind of nice to walk in late. Man, she was tired of toeing the line. Paul had untied her and she was running free.

A hand poked her ribs and she sat up. The hand belonged to the girl who sat next to her, and it held a folded note. Casey reached down to take the note and glanced at the front of the room. Mr. Young was scrawling "Christendom" on the board.

Casey leaned over her books as she unfolded the note. It was from Dina DeLillo, a curly-haired little girl who sometimes hung out with Casey and Faye and the gang.

Mr. Young's strong voice rose and fell in sturdy cadences as Casey read the note. The sun flattened out against the windows and spilled over desks. It made Casey feel like a sensuous cat.

The note said, *Heather wants to know if you're coming to the School Spirit Dance because if you are she doesn't have to hang out with Lillian all night. P.S. Glenn wants to know if you're coming, too, but don't let him know that you know.*

Casey refolded the note and fought a smile. She hadn't even *seen* the gang lately, Paul had kept her so busy. And he hadn't been hitting her. Boy, she wanted to tell Faye that. He liked to pinch and poke her a lot, and it got annoying, but not one temper fit.

She crumpled the note viciously and glanced over at Dina, who gave her a big smile. For some reason, she *wanted* to go to the School Spirit Dance. She missed everybody. But Paul didn't like crowds. And he'd give her hell for doing this.

Mr. Young was getting worked up over the influence of the church in medieval Europe and how it got drama started. He was crouching and gesturing and making weird voices. The kids were laughing. Casey looked out the window again and watched colorfully dressed girls walk by. A paper cup dropped from a second floor window. She felt her insides draw together and twist around.

She was scared to go. She was scared of Paul hitting her for it. But that was stupid. He wouldn't mind her having a good time.

Casey tore a sheet of paper from her spiral notebook and quickly wrote a note back to Dina saying she probably would go to the dance. Then she folded the note and let it sit next to her pocketbook while she delicately extracted paper shreds from the spirals. She looked up at the clock and saw that the period had four minutes to go.

With a big sigh, Casey leaned into the aisle and jabbed the girl next to her. The girl glared at her, then nodded and took the note. Casey sat erect and blushed as she saw Mr. Young looking at her.

"Ah," he said, "the lateral underhanded note pass. Smartly done." Everyone laughed. As long as you get your jollies, Casey thought.

She slumped in her seat, realizing that she'd lost the stupid composition assignment. Maybe she wouldn't hand it in at all, and see what it was like to get a zero. Maybe she'd flunk everything, right down the line. How long could Mom ground her?

She daydreamed about kissing Paul and she smiled with her eyes half-shut. The bell rang.

When Heather pulled into a parking space the night of the School Spirit Dance, the moon was full and the creatures were out. Heather's Camaro shuddered and burped as she turned it off. Casey peered through the smeary windshield.

"You sure you want to leave the car here?" she asked.

"Where else am I going to leave it?" Heather said. Her white-blonde hair was moussed and gelled and it made her look like a lion-woman from Alpha Centauri. Her long silk shirt helped the effect.

"Good luck," Casey said. They both got out of the car and stood in the chilly night air. The parking lot lights were on, bathing the scene in a lurid pink glow. Muscle cars prowled the aisles, with deep macho roars. The ground seemed to throb with blasting stereos.

As they walked gingerly on the shattered glass that always lined the student parking lot, Casey and Heather breathed the stale smell of beer and the sweet smell of pot. The raw power of darkness and the shuddering energy of hundreds of kids reached deep inside Casey's ribs and beat there like a second heart. She liked it.

At the school entrance stood two security cops, next to their cars. They wore school jackets and caps and held walkie-talkies. "Narcs," Casey said.

"Yeah," Heather agreed. "Let's hide the crack."

They both giggled. Kids hung around outside the school, smoking cigarettes or making out. The stink of nicotine hit Casey's nostrils as she and Heather neared the glass doors.

"What's Carolyn doing with Vinnie?" Casey asked, as she gestured toward one passionate couple.

"Making babies," Heather said. That sent them both into a paroxysm of laughter.

Inside, they were slammed by the heat. The custodians had gone nuts with the boilers. *Whoa,* Casey said, putting up a hand.

"I'm going to die in this outfit," Heather moaned.

The gym lobby was a mass of bodies, including kids and teacher chaperones. Blue and white crepe paper had been strung up wall to wall. The girls presented their tickets and went into the gym, which was dark except for flashing disco lights. Rock music came at them like a runaway train, and the jumping feet of five hundred kids made the polished wooden floor bounce up and down. Casey felt strangely nervous.

"Hey! Casey!" The words were thin over the earsplitting music. She turned and saw Glenn. He wore a black shirt, mostly unbuttoned, and tough-looking pants.

She made eyes at him. "Sexy."

He did body-builder poses and then glided into a raunchy dance step. He gestured to her. She looked at Heather. "Let's dance," she said.

Casey let the driving beat spin up through her legs into her midsection, and she began to move with Glenn. Heather joined in as well. The band members were kids from the school. Casey knew most of them, and they were pretty bad.

After the number was over, Mr. Germaine, a Social Studies teacher, got on the mike and started making announcements. Casey couldn't understand most of it. He said, "My man," a lot, and "What it is!" and "How're we doin'?" The kids screamed and clapped. Casey, Glenn, and Heather went to the concession table.

"Coke?" Glenn asked.

Casey nodded. Her skin tingled from dancing, and the backs of her thighs hurt. She suddenly felt lousy about missing the track meet. It was the first time ever. Not only was she scratched from the next meet, but her legs were killing her because she hardly trained. Paul had asked her why she didn't quit the track team. Casey couldn't answer.

Glenn handed her the wet, cold can. She popped the top and fizz bubbled up. She tipped back her head and gulped the first burning sips of soda. She shivered and pressed the can against her perspiring forehead.

"Whoa," she said. "That felt good."

Heather was drinking a can of Slice with a straw, and Glenn had a Sunkist orange. "Where's Faye?" Casey asked.

Glenn jutted his chin. "There."

Casey looked, and thought she could see Faye and Eddie on the other side of the bandstand. They were touching foreheads, their hands on each other's waists. Casey turned away, feverish with jealousy. Of what?

"So how's it going?" Glenn asked. "Haven't seen you for a while."

"Fine," Casey answered with a shrug. "I've been grounded mostly."

"For what?"

"Search me. How are *you*?"

Glenn looked meaningfully at her. "A little banged up."

"Oh, yeah?"

He laughed. "You really don't know, huh?"

"About what?"

Heather looked up and said, "He got hurt in the game against Northville. Your knee, right, Glenn?"

"Yup. I'm sidelined for another week or so."

Casey felt stupid. "I didn't know. I'm sorry, Glenn."

"It's okay. Flynn made me assistant field coach so I get to call some of the plays."

"That's great," Casey said. "Jesus, I'm really sorry. I've been so out of it."

"I figured," he said. "When you stop coming to the games, I know something's up."

Heather slurped from the bottom of the can. "Casey is obsessed."

"Get real," Casey said.

"She always gets obsessed," Glenn said with fondness. "Even when she was a little kid. Remember when you got into The X-Men? You had every X-Men comic in the world."

"X-Men?" Heather said.

Casey felt her cheeks heat up. "It was this stupid comic book. I just liked it."

"You went psycho over it," Glenn said. "My mom used to drive us to these comic-book conventions so Casey could look for X-Men comic books. You still have those?"

Casey sipped more Coke. "Probably. Unless I threw them out."

"Aren't they worth money?" Heather asked.

"Who knows?" Casey said, wishing they'd get off the subject.

"Casey wouldn't sell any of them," Glenn said. "She just put them in these plastic bags and took them out and read them. That's the way she is."

Casey made a sardonic face. "Thanks. Do I pay you the nickel now or later?"

Glenn grinned. The band started to play a slow song, way off key. Slowly, couples drifted out to the middle of the gym and slid into swaying embraces.

Glenn touched Casey's elbow. "Come on," he said.

"I don't know, Glenn."

"Give me a break."

She put the can on the table. He led her through the maze of warm, pungent bodies, and then turned her around. She relaxed against him and wrapped her arms lightly around his neck. He linked his hands at the small of her back and they pressed together and rocked to the beat. A flow of relaxation massaged Casey's body. She remembered the comic books, and fat little Glenn taunting her about them. She remembered identifying with the mixed-up teenage mutants in those stories, with nobody to love or understand them. Casey used to fantasize that she was a mutant, and she kept giving herself different powers. Sometimes she could pick up cars by telekinesis, and sometimes she could move so fast that everyone else appeared to be standing still.

She molded herself more intimately to Glenn and rested her cheek in his damp neck. She felt miserable for missing the football games. Damn it. Why did everybody make her feel guilty? None of them would stick by her when she needed them. As long as *she* solved *their* problems. Heather wanted Casey tonight to avoid Lillian.

Glenn wanted to make a play for her. Faye was making goo-goo eyes at Eddie. What a farce.

The dance ended, and Casey held on to Glenn for a moment. Then, as if a spell had broken, they parted and headed back to the concession table. Lillian grabbed the mike on the bandstand. She was all frilly in a blue confection with a scoop neck.

"This is such a wonderful turnout..." Lillian was gushing. Most of her words got lost in howls of feedback and the steady roar of the crowd. "Support our student organization... spirit of this senior year..."

"Give it up," Casey said.

Heather's eyes sparkled as she watched. "She's so *into* it. She's got so much *belief*."

"I think it's all phony," Glenn said. "She told Mrs. Markman she didn't do a report because she was made a deacon of her church and she had to run a rap group."

"I *hate* that," Heather said, changing sides. "That's so hypocritical."

"I think she really does believe in herself," Casey said. "I don't think *she* thinks she's a hypocrite."

"It works," Glenn said. "She gets everybody to wait on her."

"It's her serenity," Casey said. "She's just so peaceful."

"Like a saint," Heather said.

"Now Faye would have a great comment on that if she wasn't so busy sucking face."

The others laughed. Heather said. "This is so great."

"What?" Casey said, "Tearing Lillian apart?"

"*No,*" Heather said. "Just *talking.* We haven't done that for so long."

"I agree," Glenn said. "We ought to ditch this dance and go to Little Tony's for two pies and a pitcher of Coke."

"*Yeah!*" Heather said. "Want to do it, Case?"

Glenn said, "Maybe we could even grab Faye."

"Not without Eddie," Heather said.

"So let Eddie come along. I like a drama fag every once in a while."

They laughed at that. The band crashed into an up-tempo number. Casey said, "How about if we just hang out here for a while?"

"Oh, come on," Heather said, disappointed.

"We'll see," Casey promised. She clapped her hands and thrust her arms in the air, getting into the music. Heather sulked, but Glenn joined in. Casey began to spin and shout and do fancy steps. She needed to release the tension and hold on to the mood.

Out of the corner of her eye, Casey noticed Paul. She stopped dancing and made tight fists of her hands. Glenn noticed, too, and looked at Casey. He huffed a little and streams of sweat ran down his temples.

"Did you invite him?" Glenn asked.

Casey shook her head.

Glenn's hand folded over her shoulder. "Don't worry. He won't bother you."

She looked up at him. "Don't be stupid, Glenn."

She wriggled away. Paul wore his old Army fatigue jacket; it had battle ribbons on it. He wore it over baggy pants, and she thought she saw an earring in his left earlobe.

She began to feel ice-cold inside. If she asked Glenn, he would take her home, or even to Little Tony's. She wouldn't have to face Paul. She wouldn't have to be punished. But she couldn't run away from it. She'd betrayed him and he had a right to be pissed off. She felt as if she was four years old again and she'd just drawn big looping pictures on her door with a Magic Marker, and Mom came home.

Casey moved toward Paul, feeling like she was in slow motion. He saw her, finally. His eyes were like fingers hooking into her flesh. She felt sick to her stomach.

With a sudden clap, he contorted his body into a slinky dance step. A slow grin split his face and he glided back and forth, his legs dazzling. He kept his eyes on her.

Other kids started to stare at him. Casey shook. She made herself stand near him.

Paul flung himself around, now low to the floor, now upright. Now and then he'd freeze, then launch back into his dance. A ring of spectators gathered around him, whooping and clapping as Paul performed for them.

The band stopped after an eternity, and everyone applauded and yelled. Paul's chest heaved. Electronic beeps and howls came from the bandstand. Paul said, "You didn't dance with me."

She tried to say, "I'm sorry," but she could barely make her throat move.

"This is a pretty good dance. You should have asked me to come."

She could only shake her head. Beneath her studded blue shirt, her skin chilled.

"You could have handled two guys," Paul said. His voice was louder.

Casey shook her head again. Her throat was paralyzed.

"Any SLUT can handle two guys, right?" Now he was shouting. "That's what you are, right? A little SLUT."

Casey's eyes filled. She was shaking so hard she couldn't see straight.

Paul pointed at her. "You came here without telling me. What kind of crap is that? Huh?"

He shoved her, hard. She shuddered and crossed her arms over her chest. Some guy said, "Hey, buddy, take it easy."

Paul snapped an obscenity at the kid, then turned back to Casey. "What's the deal, slut? Make me look like a fool? You want your head broken? Huh?"

He shoved her again. Out of the corner of her eye, Casey saw Glenn come steamrolling out of the crowd. Paul kind of crouched and hit Glenn in the stomach. Casey could hear the pop. Glenn doubled over. Paul hit Glenn in the ribs and Glenn whimpered. Casey thought she was going to throw up.

Two male teachers elbowed their way in. Then two security guards appeared. It was hard to see with the disco lights. The teachers grabbed Glenn, who was thrashing around and trying to stand up straight. The security guys were crowding Paul, who kept shrugging them off and strutting around. Paul's face was darkly flushed. He looked crazy.

"Get your damn hands off me," he kept saying. His eyes found Casey again. "What's the story, slut? You staying here?"

Casey kept taking deep breaths to stay upright. She tried desperately not to think of everyone watching her.

Paul looked at her sharply. "I'm walking. If I walk and you stay, then you're history."

"Let's move it," one of the guards said gruffly.

Paul moved closer to Casey. "With me or without me?"

Casey needed to get out of the gym, into the air. She thought she heard somebody—Heather? Faye?—saying, "Don't go with him, Casey, don't." It didn't matter. She'd been such a fool to do this. She could have talked it over with him. He probably would have said okay. She was so wrong to just go and not tell him.

She nodded to Paul.

"I'll be outside," he told her. He began to walk away. Then he spun, and screamed at her. "Don't you EVER pull this on me again. You hear me?"

Casey lowered her head.

"ANSWER me, slut."

She formed the word "Yes."

He spun again and strutted between the security guards. Casey forced her legs to move, aware of all the eyes following her and the whispers that struck her like hurled stones between her shoulder blades. She would never come back. She would never let any of them hurt her again.

Outside, the cold air awakened her. She smelled smoke. She stood shivering under the amber lights that outlined the brick building. She couldn't see Paul. There were other kids, in small groups.

Then she saw the taillights of a security car, driving toward the far side of the lot. She began to walk quickly, wanting to be away from the school before Glenn or somebody came after her.

She crossed into the parking lot and she saw him, past the lights, by the chain link fence just where it bordered the playing fields. Casey kept her head down because the wind blew dust at her eyes. Her teeth chattered and her shirt felt clammy against her skin.

The walk stretched out forever, but finally she was out of the light. She heard the distant swoosh of cars on the road, and music. She ran one hand along the chain link, listening to it rattle.

She saw Paul waiting for her, and stopped. He smoked a cigarette. Its orange tip glowed brightly, then ebbed. He dropped the cigarette and ground it out with his heel. She could just see his outline. She jammed her hands into her dungaree pockets and trembled in the wind.

"Get over here," he said.

She shuffled the last few steps toward him. He cupped the back of her head in one hand and then pinched the nape of her neck. "You're stupid," he said. "You never learn anything."

"Don't call me stupid," she said.

"I'll call you what I damn want."

She said, "You made me look like a fool." A new sensation razored through her throat. Anger. Pure, clean anger. "You could have talked to me on the side. You didn't have to pull that crap."

He looked away and laughed with disbelief. "This is funny. You cheat on me and you have the nerve to tell me I'm pulling crap."

"I wasn't cheating," she said. "I just danced with Glenn."

"You don't dance with *anybody* unless I say so."

She could hear faint surges of music that rose and fell

on the night wind. Her anger slipped, but hung on. "You don't own me, Paul."

"I don't, huh? Okay, you want out? Maybe we should just cool it for a while. You want that?"

She shook her head. "No."

"Damn straight. Don't ever try to walk away from me. I'll break your legs. Wherever you go, I'll find you. I'll be there, and I'll be waiting."

The anger drained, and she felt ice-cold. For a moment, she realized what she'd gotten herself into and how terrified she was. For a searing instant, she wanted to be back in the gym, close to Glenn and Heather and Faye. She wanted to scream for help. But being alone scared her so much more. Her spirit sank, and she regretted everything she'd said. She'd been an idiot. What if he left *her*? Where would she go now? How could she face anybody?

She kept her eyes lowered. "I'm sorry. I didn't mean to start an argument."

"You're a piece of garbage, you know that?"

"You don't have to talk that way," she said.

"I don't."

"No."

His fingers tightened on her neck and he slammed her against the fence. She hit with tremendous force and her ears rang with the jingling. He spun and gripped the fence with both hands, imprisoning her. "I don't have to do that. You make me look bad but I don't have to do that. You spit in my face and I don't have to do that. Is that right, huh?"

He punched her in her ribs and she moaned at the stabbing pain. "What don't I have to do, slut?" he spat. "What is it I don't have to do, huh? Huh? Huh?"

With each "Huh?" he punched her. He used sharp, hard jabs, with closed fists. He exhaled hard with each punch. She saw his face, and it looked horrible, like something out of a monster movie. Oddly, she was aware of the parking lot behind him, of individual cars gleaming in the light, of the school building far away.

He punched her in the face and brilliant red lights exploded in her head. Now the punches came in flurries, everywhere, again and again. Her mouth filled with salty warmth. It made her cough. She couldn't get air. Every time she tried, long, pointed sticks jabbed her windpipe. She wondered if she really, truly were going to die.

Then she wasn't being hit. The absence of the punches startled her, almost as if a loud record had been turned off. She could hear her breath gurgling and scraping inside her. She heard his car start, and she heard the tires crunch. She thought she saw his headlights.

Her soaked back became aware of the fence pressing its grid into her. She couldn't feel her face, but she sensed the wind. She found a small pool of anger, and she pumped it into her legs. She was *not* going to sink onto this filthy asphalt with all the glass and old beer and God knew what else. Anyway, they'd be looking for her. She needed to get home and wash up and put some makeup on the bruises. She'd gotten pretty expert at that.

She pulled away from the fence but held on with clawed fingers. She was able to see the dark fields and the school. It was blurry, but she could see it. She coughed and spat up. Then she lurched around the end of the fence and stood on hard-packed dirt. She began to walk. She crossed the open field, breathing through her mouth. She had an awful stitch in her side, but she'd had those before.

She was across the field now, in the open, and the wind swirled around her. She heard the rustle of millions of dead leaves. The moon slid from between black clouds, and Casey saw the cinder track coldly illuminated. She stumbled onto the track and began to jog. Once or twice around the track and she'd have the strength to find her way home. How? She'd come here with Heather.

It didn't seem to matter. At least she didn't feel worried

about it. It was nice to run, and it was almost as if she were floating above the track, like one of the X-Men. Maybe it was true! Maybe that was her power, to fly, to float, to spin over the moonlit track in the cold rushing wind, to race the spinning leaves. Awesome! Wait until she showed everyone.

Only for a brief instant, as unconsciousness swept over her, did she comprehend that she was falling.

Chapter Thirteen

AS SHE PAINFULLY BUTTONED A CLEAN SHIRT, CASEY looked away from her mother and kept her eyes on the green wall of the Emergency Room cubicle. She hurt in about a hundred places, but her embarrassment was worse than the stings and throbs.

"Put the icepack on your eye," Mom said. "The doctor said to keep it on for twenty minutes."

"I know," Casey said.

The icepack sat like a blue island on the white paper of the examining table. Casey sat next to it, and every time she shifted a little, the paper crinkled. Mom sat on a wooden chair, her fingertips brushing a shopping bag stuffed with Casey's bloody clothes.

"How's the hand?" Mom asked.

"Okay." Casey picked up her left hand and flexed it. She marveled at how swollen it was. They'd just finished X-raying her hand, *and* her chest, because she felt like she was breathing over iron spikes. She couldn't figure out how her hand had gotten messed up. She must have tried to fight him off, but she couldn't remember.

"Did you eat anything at the dance?" Mom asked.

"No. I just had some Coke."

"I'll heat up supper for you."

"I don't want any."

"Do you want me to stop and get you a hamburger?"

Casey looked at her. "Yeah," she said. "That'd be okay."

Mom stretched her lips. She looked like she was suffering. Well, too bad. Casey was suffering, too. Why she had to faint on the track, anyway....She sniffled, and that made her whole head burst into fireworks. She forgot there was packing in her nose.

There was a flurry of efficient footsteps and Dr. Cohen pulled aside the curtain that closed off the cubicle. He was a good-looking guy with iron-gray hair and a rugged face, but he wore dopey ties, like the yellow and purple one he had on now.

"Hi, Casey," he said. "Sorry I couldn't get here sooner. I was in Huntington."

Mom said, "Thank you for coming, doctor. It's not that I don't trust the staff here, but I wanted you to check her out."

"I understand," he said. He took an explorer from his jacket pocket and with his thumb lifted Casey's eyelids and shone the light into her eyes. She blinked. His thumb hurt her face. "What happened?" he said.

"Ask *her*," Mom said. "I can't get a straight story."

He looked at the packing in her nose and scrutinized the stitches they'd taken over her left eye and just below her lip. Casey shivered. It was cold in here. "What happened, Casey?"

She said, "I got into a stupid argument and I ran out and decided to do laps in the dark. I kept falling down, but I kept going. I don't know why. I was a jerk."

"Uh-huh." He felt under her chin and pressed her neck and her shoulders. He looked at her midsection. "They taped your ribs?"

She nodded.

The coldness snuck inside Casey and chilled her. She

wished Dr. Cohen would leave. He knew she was lying. Now he'd have a conference with Mom. You had to faint, she berated herself. Just two minutes. That's all she'd needed, to get out of there. But by the time she'd opened her eyes and realized she was laid out on the track, Faye and Eddie and Heather had found her, and a couple of teachers. Then she had to lie there like a jerk while they put coats under her head and told her to keep calm, and the stupid ambulance had to pull right up on the stupid field, and she had to go to the stupid hospital where Mom was waiting in total panic.

She shuddered as she remembered it. Dr. Cohen was looking at her with knowing eyes. She turned her head and marbles rattled in her skull.

"I spoke with Dr. Rau," he said. "It doesn't look like there's any serious damage. No internal bleeding that they can see. You probably have a cracked rib, and if you do, then count on sitting still for about six or eight weeks."

"Forget it," Casey said. "I have important meets—"

"Not with a cracked rib," he said. "Nothing else looks broken, except maybe your hand. You have lacerations and contusions on your face and body, and a couple of loose teeth. You'll have to see your dentist about those. Casey, you couldn't have sustained these injuries from falling, not on a cinder track."

"So what are you saying?" she asked. "That I'm lying?"

"Yes," Mom said emotionally. "Of course you're lying. You truly believe we're all stupid?"

"Get off my back," Casey said.

"And you get off your high horse!" Mom stood up. "How dare you come back at me? You've been insane lately. You've been doing things that I'd expect from a tramp."

"Shut up," Casey snapped.

Dr. Cohen looked embarrassed. "Casey, you should

know that you were hurt badly. The gash over your eye was very close. If you lose an eye, you can't get it back."

"I'm not going to lose an eye."

"Well, as long as you're sure."

He tried a smile, but she stared him down. A white-coated guy with permed hair came in and gave Dr. Cohen a big envelope. Casey remembered that he had been in the X-ray room. The two men talked for a minute, in that low voice that doctors always used when it was bad news. Then the X-ray technician left.

"Let's see these," Dr. Cohen said. He took the X-rays out of the envelope and clipped one onto a light board that was attached to the wall. He flipped on the light and Casey looked with fascination at the eerie gray and white masses that represented her insides.

Mom came over to look, too. Mom had this medical book at home that listed symptoms for every disease, and she always read the science articles in the *Times*.

"There's the rib fracture," he said, pointing to the X-ray. "Hairline. She's lucky." He stood back from the X-ray, squinting at it. "A lot of bruising, too." He took down the X-ray; it made a whooshing sound. He clipped up the other X-ray, and Casey thought she saw finger bones.

"This is her hand," Dr. Cohen said. "I can't tell from this whether there's a fracture. There's too much swelling. I think we'll immobilize the hand for now, and then see if we need to cast it."

"It doesn't feel that bad," Casey said.

"Be quiet," Mom said severely. To Dr. Cohen, she said, "Your honest opinion, doctor. What do you think caused all this?"

He looked pained. "It could be a lot of things. These injuries could happen in a car accident, or a fight. I really can't say for certain."

"What's your best guess?"

"Why don't you torture him for information?" Casey said.

Mom deliberately kept looking at Dr. Cohen. "Doctor?"

He shook his head. "I can't commit myself to an answer, Mrs. Gordon. I wasn't with her." He put both X-rays back into the envelope. He took out a prescription pad and a pen and began to scribble. "I'm giving Casey Vicodin for her pain, and an antibiotic in case of infection. I'll tell Dr. Rau to splint her hand, and I want to see her Monday afternoon. By then, the swelling should be down and we can decide what to do."

Mom took the slips of paper. "Thank you, doctor. I'm sorry you had to be taken away from your social engagement."

"No problem," he said, but he sounded annoyed. "You have major medical, so just fill out the forms they give you. Casey, get some rest. You've been banged up pretty badly. I'll see you Monday."

"Okay," she said sullenly.

Dr. Cohen took the envelope with the X-rays and left. Casey listened to the clash of gurneys, the crying of children, and the babble of voices. The light in here was garish and made her skin look green. She wanted to go to sleep.

"Come on," Mom said tiredly. "Let's find out where they want to put on the splint."

Casey slid from the examining table and stood shakily on the antistatic black floor. Mom stared at her, and she looked ready to cry. "Casey, I'm going to find out what happened tonight."

"Go ahead."

"I can't believe you won't talk to me. Who are you protecting?"

"The Mafia."

"*Stop it.*" Mom was on the edge and Casey knew it was lousy to keep prodding her. "I have no strength left. Somebody has to penetrate that wall you've built around yourself. If you're getting into fights, I want to know why. And if somebody's hurting you, I want to know who it is. This wouldn't by any chance be Paul VanHorn, would it?"

"Give me a break."

"Was he at the dance?"

Casey was cracking inside. "I don't know."

"You don't know? Were you with him?"

"Call him up and ask him."

"Why won't you give me a straight answer?" Mom swayed a little. Casey wouldn't lock eyes with her. "I'm trying to make sense of what's happened to you. Your father is oblivious, but I can't look the other way. You're fulfilling every prediction I made about you. Somebody's got to get through. I can't."

Casey stood mutely through the speech, stung by the cold, accusing words. She vividly relived the moment Paul crashed the dance. Every twinge and needle of pain reminded her of the beating, and she was so frightened of him now. But scared or not, she wanted to be with him. Nobody else could protect her from the world the way he did.

"Don't you have anything to say?" Mom asked.

"No."

"Fine. Tough it out. You're still a little girl, Casey. You think you're strong, but you're not strong. And if you spit on the people who are willing to help you, then there won't be anybody."

She blinked and her eyes grew blurry. She could still taste blood in her mouth.

"Come on," Mom said. "I'm sick of you. I want to take a bath and relax. JoAnne's got a temperature of a hundred and one. Did you know that?"

"No."

"I didn't think so."

Casey wished JoAnne would go into a coma. She followed Mom out of the cubicle and through the maze of corridors to the nurse's station. She began to plan when she could see Paul again. He'd keep away, like he always did after he got crazy. But she'd find him, and she'd stay with him this time and never cheat on him again. She'd learned her lesson.

Owen leaned on the chain link fence that separated the football field from the stands. A swift, cold wind rippled the sleeves of his windbreaker. The boys on the football team were running a scrimmage, and their deep yells were torn by the wind.

The school building glowed in golden afternoon light. Owen loved this kind of weather. He used to take Robbie to the Bronx Zoo each fall. They'd picnic, and he'd tell Robbie that the apartment buildings in the distance were window mountains. The memories stuck in Owen's throat.

He looked back and saw that the scrimmage had ended. He especially watched Glenn Lindstrom. The tall, husky halfback wasn't going to win any Heisman trophies—kids from Westfield High usually didn't—but he had determination and spirit.

"Hey, Glenn," he called. Glenn looked for the voice and saw Owen. He jogged toward the fence. Another kid slapped Glenn and said, "See you later." Glenn waved the kid off.

Owen idly watched the guys trot toward the bench where they'd stowed their stuff. Jack Fischer, the football coach, wore his usual red jacket and cap as he talked to a kid at the far goalpost.

Glenn reached the fence. Twin streams of sweat darkened his temples and his blonde hair was pasted to his forehead. He breathed heavily and smelled of hard play. "Hi, Mr. Young."

"Hi, Glenn. Glad to see your knee's back in shape. Can I talk to you for a minute?"

"Sure." Glenn unlatched the gate and came through. Owen walked to the stands and sat down in the first row.

The sun lowered just enough to flare from the treetops. Glenn stripped off his team jersey and undid his shoulder pads.

Owen said, "I want to know about the dance."

Glenn dropped the shoulder pads onto the long green bleacher. "So does everybody else."

"Well, I'm not the police," Owen said. "I don't care who started the fight."

"I started it," Glenn said. "I just couldn't finish it."

Owen glanced up at him. "You didn't have much of a chance, from what I heard."

"He took me out," Glenn said. "I didn't think he'd whale on me so fast. He's got pretty good moves."

Owen laughed. "That's sportsmanship."

Glenn shrugged and put his jersey back on. He shivered a little in the wind. "Next time I'll know."

"You're going after him?"

"Well, I can't go after him or I'll get bounced off the team. But I can wait him out. He's going down. Doesn't matter when."

Owen could feel Glenn's restrained fury. He wished he could use physical violence as an answer. He remembered how good that felt, how cleansing. "I'm asking about it because of Casey Gordon."

"What about her?" Glenn asked. He leaned against the fence.

Owen rubbed his dry, cold hands together and chose his words carefully. "I'm not Sherlock Holmes, but I've been considering some pieces of evidence."

"Yeah?"

"Changes in her behavior, things like not doing homework and coming in late—I mean, every kid does that now and then, but it's the *way* she's doing it. I see this stuff happen when a girl gets crazy for a guy."

He could actually *hear* Glenn tighten up. "So? You know she's going out with VanHorn."

"Yeah, I know. And I was all ready to live with her

craziness. I have an all-girl team and I've been through it before. But I think it's more than just lovesickness."

"Like what?"

He moistened his lips and exhaled. He knew it was dangerous to share these thoughts with a student, but only through the students would he get confirmation. "Casey missed practice, and a meet. She has a cracked rib and more bangs and bruises than a tackling dummy. She says it happened after the dance, when she was running laps."

Glenn's fists were clenched against the fence and he was fighting to keep his face impassive. "I know."

"She said she felt so embarrassed about Paul crashing the dance that she had to run it out."

"So?"

The sun blazed at the horizon. "I'm not an M.D., Glenn, but I deal with sports and injuries. She didn't get those bruises falling on the cinder track."

Glenn said nothing. He just stood against the fence, helpless in his strength.

"I think this guy's hitting her. I think he beat her up that night. I think he's beaten her up before last night. I want to know what you know about it."

Again, silence. It was the kind of silence that said, oh, man, are you right. But Owen couldn't do anything with silence, even if it agreed with him.

He stood up and approached Glenn. "I know all about the teen code. You guys are worse than the Black Hand. But if I'm right, you're protecting slime."

Glenn turned his head, and kept it lowered. He mumbled, "I'm not going to protect anybody."

"What do you know?"

Glenn was struggling to remain composed. He was almost crying, or maybe he was crying already. Owen folded a reassuring hand over Glenn's muscled shoulder. He felt the boy shake.

"I want to do something about it, Glenn. Besides beating the crap out of Paul VanHorn. You can take care of that; I can't. Casey's more important than he is."

Glenn bit his lip and then looked up. His eyes glistened defiantly. He fought to keep his voice steady. "Everyone knows he's hitting her. The whole school knows."

"Great," Owen said sardonically. "Any proof?"

Glenn shook his head. "It's like you just know it's happening."

"Anybody talk to Casey?"

Glenn gave a little, bitter laugh. "Yeah. Everyone's talked to her. She doesn't want to hear it. She thinks he's an okay guy."

"Why?"

"How the hell do I know why? He cursed her out at the dance like she was some kind of whore, and she went after him. She wants to die. She's always been like that. She was always so deep inside herself. I don't know. I never understood her mind."

Owen smiled. "Neither do I. You're pretty crazy about her, aren't you?"

He smiled back. "Good guess."

"It doesn't take much talent to see it." He wrestled with the rage and frustration seething in his heart. Everything made sense. He could see how this intense, too-serious girl who didn't like her looks could keep going back to a boy who beat her. Somehow, Paul VanHorn must have offered Casey the feeling of being pretty and important and worthwhile that she needed so desperately.

But that was glib psychology, and it really didn't explain very much. And Casey sure wouldn't listen to it. He couldn't save her by having a heart-to-heart. He'd have to go through other channels and risk losing her respect and affection. That was going to be the toughest thing.

"So what are you going to do?" Glenn asked.

"I'm going to talk to the school psychologist."

"Forget it," Glenn said. "You think Guidance is going to do anything?"

"Ease up," Owen said. "I'm not saying they're going to wave a magic wand and fix the problem, but they have access to other agencies, to the law, to things I don't know about. If VanHorn is abusing Casey, it's a legal matter *and* a psychological problem."

Glenn looked off toward the parking lot. "She's going to freak."

"You might be right," Owen said. "But what's the alternative?"

"I'll cripple him," Glenn said coldly. "He won't touch her again."

"Then another guy will." Glenn whipped around and his eyes glared. "Don't get sore at me, Glenn. You know it's true. VanHorn isn't the problem. We've got to get to Casey. Make her know she's worth it. Show her who *really* cares about her."

Glenn thought about that for a while. Cars roared into life as other team members started for home. The sun sank another notch, and black branches made patterns across its glaring light. "I don't understand her."

"Well, most people worth loving aren't easy to know."

Glenn looked with admiration at Owen, and seemed to let out some breath and some tension. "Anything you want," he said.

"I'll try to keep you out of it," Owen said. "I just needed to know I wasn't up the wrong tree."

"No. You were right."

Owen slapped Glenn's shoulder and jammed both of his hands into his jacket pockets. As the sun dipped, the air turned sharply colder. Definitely a taco night. Tacos and a cold beer. And some compositions to grade. Couldn't beat the single life for adventure.

"Go home," Owen said. "Don't go nuts over the fight. Going after him made you a man. Getting hit just made you stupid."

Glenn laughed out loud. Owen gave him a last friendly tap and started to walk away. Glenn called, "Mr. Young."

He turned. "Yeah?"

"Help her. She's the greatest lady I know."

Smiling at Glenn, he said, "Don't worry." He turned again and breathed in sharply as he walked. Dusk shadows folded over the stands.

Chapter Fourteen

WHEN THE STRANGE GIRL CAME INTO THE BAND ROOM, Casey was all the way up near the window, and the room was mobbed with chattering kids from Concert Choir. But Casey saw the strange girl right away, and a ball of fear formed in her chest. She *knew* the girl was here for her.

Ms. Carlin, the director of the choir, took attendance on her green upholstered stool down by the piano. Everyone was acting like a jerk, as usual. Tom Verdun was shoveling Sweet Tarts into his mouth; Evelyn Greene was dashing up and down the tiers, getting people's music; Heather was doing grotesque movements from her jazz dance class.

Casey sat in front of her music stand and pretended to scan the *Timete Dominum* by Michael Haydn, but the notes were just squiggles. She was looking at the strange girl, who was going into shell shock at the screaming and pigging out. Half the kids were selling candy for clubs, and the rustle of plastic bags sounded like a forest fire.

Ms. Carlin noticed the strange girl, who was thin and neatly dressed. Casey felt her heartbeat quicken. Faye sat two seats down, leaning over to giggle with Eddie. Casey felt a twinge of sadness when she remembered how she and Faye used to be the buddies of Concert Choir, whispering like cats and pulling everyone apart.

Ms. Carlin looked at Casey and gestured. It would have been pretty useless for Ms. Carlin to say anything in this racket.

Casey slipped her pocketbook strap over her shoulder. With a light toss of her hair, she scooped her books into the cradle of her arms and got up. She knew everyone was watching her, even if they pretended not to. More and more, she hated the kids at school.

She clumsily made her way around sprawled feet, candy bags, books, and music stands and got to the bottom of the room. The strange girl looked at Casey with curious eyes. Ms. Carlin said, "You have to go to Guidance, Casey."

That was a surprise. Casey had figured it would be the assistant principal's office, for cutting. Before the School Spirit Dance, she had met Paul a few times during each school day. "Should I take everything?" she asked.

"Maybe you'd better," Ms. Carlin said.

Casey hefted her books to make them lie more comfortably. With her chin on the topmost book, she slid her music off the pile and gave it to Ms. Carlin. "Here."

"Thanks," Ms. Carlin said.

The strange girl waited politely, then turned and led the way out. Casey followed her.

They walked past the art rooms, hooking a left into the gym lobby. Mr. Gross, her physics teacher, was on hall duty near the glass doors. He looked up and smiled through his beard. "Hi, Casey."

"Hi," she said. It used to give her a warm feeling when teachers recognized her. Now she didn't like it. She knew there was pity behind the smiles.

Casey liked the hallway in the middle of a period. She could glance into the rooms on either side and see kids hunched over or grabbing naps or looking out the window, and teachers walking back and forth or writing on the board. All the voices blended into a soothing babble.

They turned left at the main staircase and headed for the office area. Casey's hand throbbed in its Ace bandage. She was glad it wasn't broken. Her mouth really hurt, and Dr. Irving had said she'd need a bridge. Her rib was doing okay. She wanted to tell Paul that he was a wimp with a flabby punch. He'd laugh and get embarrassed.

She began to feel apprehension as they got to the Guidance suite. The secretary at the desk looked up and nodded. Wow. *Nobody* got into Guidance without an official pass, but Casey was being ushered right through. Pretty important.

"Mr. Burton's office," the strange girl said.

Mr. Burton was Casey's counselor. Casey saw that his door was closed. Some kids sat on the couches, waiting for their appointments.

She knocked on the door and Mr. Burton's muffled voice said, "Come in."

Casey got a good one-armed grip on her books, flexed her knees, and turned the knob. When she pushed open the door, she saw her mother sitting in a chair. It made no sense. Casey looked for Mr. Burton and saw him standing against the window, and then she saw her dad, in a chair against Mr. Burton's bookcase.

She stopped dead, with her hand still curled around the doorknob. "What's going on?"

"Come in, Casey," Mr. Burton said.

Casey's heart started to pound. Wild lies began to form in her mind. She said to her mom, "What are you doing here? Why is Daddy here? What happened?"

"Please, Casey," Mr. Burton said.

She stepped into the small, carpeted office and nudged the door shut with her shoulder. As the door swung closed, Casey saw Mr. Young in a third chair. She looked desperately from one face to another.

"I don't get this," Casey said.

"You can drop your books on my desk," Mr. Burton said. Casey looked at him, and set her books down on the cluttered desk. She slipped her pocketbook from her shoulder and let it slide to rest near the books. Her bruised face felt like it was flashing on and off.

Mom stared at Casey. Mr. Burton pulled his own chair out from his desk and turned it. "Sit down, Casey."

Casey said, "I want to know what this is about."

"Sit down first."

Casey *hated* when people did this. Mom and Dad had pulled this crap when Grandma Esther died. She came home from fourth grade and Mom and Dad were sitting on their bed. They made Casey sit in the green velvet chair and get hives while they had their big dramatic moment.

Mr. Burton said, "Casey, Mr. Young came to me with something very disturbing. I thought it warranted a conference with your parents, and I thought it might be best to have it here, on neutral ground, with Mr. Young and myself present."

"What did I do?" Casey asked desperately.

"This is not because you did anything wrong," Mr. Burton said. Now he smiled a little, under his moustache. "Casey, you've been dating a boy named Paul VanHorn."

Rage and terror spiraled through her so fast it left her breathless. "Is *that* what this is about?"

"Calm down, Casey."

Casey shot to her feet. "I can't believe this. What kind of stupid crap...?" She looked at Mr. Young. "Who the hell do you think you are, sticking your nose in my personal life..."

"Sit *down*, Casey," Mr. Young said. His brusque words stopped her cold. She stayed on her feet, her mouth open, staring helplessly.

Mom began to shake. "I can't believe it," she said in a shivery voice. "I can't believe any of this is happening. It's a nightmare."

"Calm down, Ellen," Dad said. His voice sounded exhausted, like he was dying.

Mom turned on Dad like an attack dog. "Don't you *dare* tell me to calm down. Are you a total idiot?"

"Shut up," Dad said.

"Don't tell me to shut up. You're a waste, Ron. You've been a waste since she was born...."

"That's enough," Mr. Burton said. His own voice sounded uncertain, and his face was red. Casey shook convulsively now.

Mr. Young stood up, and he seemed to fill the whole room. He said, "Casey, you can hate my guts, but do it sitting."

Casey couldn't help a tiny, reflexive smile. She sat down, fighting nausea. Mr. Young looked for a moment at Mom and Dad. If you were freaking out, Mr. Young could just look at you and make you really uncomfortable. He said, "I know this is a nightmare. But what's happened to Casey is not rational, so *we've* got to be rational."

Mom subsided, and fished for a tissue from her purse. Dad twiddled his fingers in his lap and looked down. Casey was fascinated; she'd never seen anyone get the best of Mom. It looked so weird to see both of them here in school.

Mr. Burton gave Mr. Young a grateful look. He said, "Casey, Mr. Young came to me because he was very concerned about your health and your well-being. He's pretty certain that you've been abused by Paul VanHorn."

"He's out of his mind," Casey said softly.

"Have you been abused?"

"No."

Mom gave a disgusted sigh. "This is worthless. The girl needs psychiatric help."

Mr. Burton gave Mom a filthy look. Mr. Young, back in his seat, said, "Casey, you know that I'm pretty good at diagnosing injuries, yes?"

Casey didn't answer. She tried to focus on the millions of yellow Guidance passes and other papers on Mr. Burton's desk, and on the hard white sunlight against the window and the big shiny calendar on the wall.

"Casey?"

"Yeah."

"You know I'm a trained EMT."

"So?"

Mr. Young leaned forward just a little. He always did that, too, when he knew he'd broken down your defenses. "So I know that your bruises and cuts came from being hit. I've seen enough kids in fights to know that. You didn't fall after the dance. You were beaten up. And those other times you came to school with black and blue marks, they were beatings, too. You can't lie when your body is telling the truth."

Casey felt ice-cold inside. She pulled the sleeves of her yellow knit sweater over her hands and hunched over. "What do you want me to say?"

Mr. Burton said, "Tell us what happened the night of the Spirit Dance."

She sighed, and a cold, black wind rushed through her heart. She wanted to be with Paul, so badly. "Nothing happened."

"Nobody hit you?" Mr. Burton said.

She turned away, but there was nowhere to turn. "I got into a fight."

"With who?" Mr. Burton said.

Mom shifted and her wool suit rustled. Dad cleared his throat. They were so close to her right now that she felt suffocated. "Some girl."

"Did you know her?" Mr. Burton asked.

"No."

"How did the fight start?"

"I don't know."

"No memory at all?"

Casey exhaled with open disgust. With the fingers of

her right hand, she traced the wrapping of the Ace bandage on her left hand. She pressed down at times to make pain shoot through her wrist. "She made some remarks and I told her to screw off and she said she'd be waiting for me outside."

"That's where you had the fight?" Mr. Burton said.

Casey nodded. "I forgot about the whole thing but she was waiting with a couple of her friends."

"So you fought her?"

"Yeah," Casey said. "It wasn't exactly a fair fight. If I got in a punch, one of her friends kicked me down. They left me lying there."

"Did anybody witness the fight?"

Casey shrugged. "I don't know. Nobody helped me. And it was out where the fence ends, at the end of the parking lot."

Mr. Young said, "Why did you walk all the way out there if you knew someone might be waiting?"

Casey looked up at him. "I don't know."

"You don't know?"

"I wanted to be alone. I wanted to run for a while. I don't know, I just walked out there. Give me a break, huh?"

Mr. Young leaned back. Mr. Burton sighed a little. Mom said, "What is this leading to? Was there a reason for my taking time off from work to come here?"

Mr. Young said, "Casey, why did you neglect to mention that Paul VanHorn crashed the dance?"

Casey lowered her head. "I didn't think of it."

"Or that he publicly insulted you, cursed you out, in front of everybody, and called you a slut."

Mom sucked in a sharp breath. *"What?"*

Casey rocked back and forth in the chair, shutting her eyes. "What's the difference?"

Mr. Young kept on, relentlessly. "Or that he told you to follow him outside?"

Casey couldn't answer anymore. The questions tormented her because they made her sound so stupid.

"And you did follow him, didn't you?" Mr. Young asked.

Casey bit hard on her lower lip.

"We know you followed him because everyone saw you follow him. And then, a half hour later, they found you beaten up, lying on the track. There wasn't any girl, and there wasn't any fight. Paul VanHorn beat you up because you went to a school dance and he didn't want you to go."

Her throat wrenched as she cried. Mr. Burton said, "Take it easy, Casey."

"Let her go," Mr. Young said. Casey could hear Mom crying softly. She began to be terrified. She visualized Paul and kept his face in her head, not ever wanting to forget it. She vowed that she'd tie bedsheets together and escape from the nuthouse if they put her there. She'd run barefoot in the snow and cut her feet and die and then they'd understand that it was her life and not theirs.

Dad spoke. "What do we do about this?"

Mom said, "You aren't ashamed to ask that? What in God's name is wrong with you? Why aren't you hunting that animal down and breaking his neck? He beat up your daughter, and you sit there asking what to do? I want him dead. I want his hide nailed to the wall. And if you don't have the guts to do it, I swear to God I'll hire a hit man."

Her voice had risen higher and higher and the little office sang with it. Mr. Young said, "I know that makes the most sense right now, but it won't work. If you, or Mr. Gordon, or anybody you hired, were to hurt Paul VanHorn his parents would sue you and they would win."

Mom gave a vicious little laugh. "But we can't do anything to *him*?"

Mr. Burton said, "That depends. If you wanted to have Paul VanHorn arrested for assault, Casey would have to testify before a judge that he attacked her." He paused, and the silence framed his embarrassment. "The court might ask a lot of personal questions...if there was any intimacy..."

Casey looked up, her head stuffed from crying. Mom stared at her. "What does that mean?" she asked. "Sex?"

Mr. Young said, "Only she can tell you."

Mom kept her eyes on Casey. "How about it, little girl? Did you?"

Dad said, "Take it easy, Ellen."

"Keep quiet," she said. "I'll handle this, just like I handle everything else. Answer me, Casey."

Casey absorbed the hatred from her mother's eyes, and shook with it. "Yeah," she said nastily. "We did it everywhere. And I did it with sixteen other guys."

"You little piece of garbage."

"Same to you," Casey said.

Mr. Young said, "Mrs. Gordon, Casey has been abused by her boyfriend. If you attack Casey for being attacked, she's going to run back to the guy pretty quickly."

"No, she won't," Mom said coldly. "She won't go anywhere near him. If she does, I'll have her institutionalized, and she knows I'll do it."

"For Christ's sake," Dad said.

"I'm not even listening to you."

Mr. Burton sighed heavily. "Well. I'm sorry it's turning out this way. We want to help Casey. I'd like her to see our school psychologist first, and then she can recommend further counseling."

Mom snapped her purse shut and primped her hair. "Yes. I agree about the school psychologist. In fact, let's make that a condition for Casey to remain in this school."

"That's your prerogative," Mr. Burton said.

Mom said, "Do you understand that, Casey?"

"Yeah," Casey said.

Mom turned to Dad. "Do you have anything to say at all, or do you just intend to hide your head in the sand?"

Dad's face was frozen and he sat very still. Casey could

see so much in his eyes. There were major hurricanes going on in there. "No," he said. "I don't have anything to say. I have to think about this."

Mom shook her head and turned away. She looked at Casey again, but this time with bewilderment. "How could you let him touch you? How could you allow that, Casey? You're intelligent and talented and...I don't understand. It's so horrible...."

Casey huddled in the chair, feeling more bruised and beaten than after Paul had finished. "You wouldn't understand."

"I'm *trying* to understand. I really want to."

Casey pushed hair out of her eyes. She felt hungry, and she wished she'd bought some candy from one of the kids in Concert Choir. "It's not important."

Mom looked at Mr. Young. "This is what I have to deal with, Mr. Young. This girl was tested at the age of four and she's gifted. My aunt was a concert pianist. My cousin is a full professor at Yale. And Casey is willing to trash all that. Every year, we received notes from her teachers saying that she didn't pay attention or work up to her level. And now this. She wants to flush herself down the toilet, and you know what? I'm going to let her. Because I'm too damned tired to fight anymore."

Mom stood up, and Casey heard the vinyl cushion hiss back into shape. Dad got up, too. His face looked white, almost like a china plate. He said to Mr. Burton and to Mr. Young, "Thank you. I'm glad you brought this to our attention."

Mr. Burton looked like he'd run a marathon. "Well, it isn't pleasant, but we have a responsibility toward the welfare of our students."

Mr. Young said, "Try to remember that we *can* help Casey."

"Thank you," Mom said. To Casey, she said, "How are you? Do you want to come home with us now, or stay in school?"

"I'll stay," Casey said.

"Are you sure?"

She nodded.

Mom said to Mr. Burton, "If she collapses or anything, call my neighbor, Mrs. Dolce. She'll come for Casey. I'll be at work."

"All right," Mr. Burton said. "I think she'll be okay."

"Yes, I'm sure she will." Mom looked at Dad. "Ready?"

Dad nodded. He coughed into his hand. Mr. Young opened the office door and Mom and Dad left. Dad walked kind of hunched, and Casey felt a throb of worry about him. She'd begun to like him more. He didn't talk to her any more than he used to, but Mom ranked on him all the time now, and Casey felt sympathetic.

The room seemed to take a deep breath and expand. Mr. Burton said, "I have to see someone for a minute. You want to take her back to class?"

Mr. Young said, "Sure."

Mr. Burton touched Casey's shoulder. A shock of static electricity made her jump. "Casey, I know that you're angry at us now, but we're on your side. We're not going to lock you up and we're not going to make this public. Do you understand?"

She nodded. "I'm not angry."

"Good." He patted her shoulder and left the office. Casey didn't want to look Mr. Young in the eyes.

"Want to go back to class?" he asked her.

"In a minute."

She heard him stand up. She felt numb, as if they'd shot her full of novocaine. But she also felt pretty decent. She'd sat here and taken it all. She didn't have to pretend anymore. She loved Paul as much as before, and she knew she'd be with him soon, and always. And once she could live with him, she could love him more. That was the one thing she'd failed to do.

"How are you doing?" Mr. Young asked. He leaned against the open door.

"Okay."

"Want to take a punch at me?"

She looked up at him and shrugged. "No."

"Don't hate me?"

"I guess you had to turn me in."

"I didn't turn you in, Casey. You're not the criminal. He is."

"Yeah, I know that's what you think."

Mr. Young took a tight breath. "You're going to defend him, aren't you? Your sense of values is so twisted now that you truly, truly believe that he's an okay guy and what he does to you is okay."

"It's nothing you'd understand," she said.

"No, I guess it isn't." He glanced out at the crowded office, and back at Casey. "But I'm going to try to understand. I'm going to stick with you, because I care about you."

She smiled. "Thanks."

"You don't believe that. But it doesn't matter. If I can't do anything else, I can show you what caring is supposed to sound like and feel like. I'm going to show you every day that caring doesn't hurt. That if it hurts, it isn't caring. At least you'll know that."

His words bothered her. She fought them off, the way she shivered away the first cold splash of a shower. "Can I go back to class now?" she asked.

"Yup."

She got up stiffly, her rib burning with pain. Mr. Young gathered up her books. She slipped her pocketbook back on her shoulder and reached for the books.

"I'll carry them," he said. "It's been a lot of years since I carried a pretty girl's books."

She smiled and said, "Thanks."

"Come on." He touched her back with gentle fingers and guided her toward the door. She walked a little awkwardly, trying to minimize the pain in her side. The voices and faces of her mom and dad stayed in her imagination, vivid and threatening. She dreaded going home today. Dinner would be cold and silent, and she'd get all those stupid looks. She'd get grounded and lectured and driven to all kinds of shrinks.

So what? It would be a major hassle, but she'd get through it. All the hurting would be over pretty soon, with Paul at the end of the tunnel. And if they stopped her from reaching him, then she'd make sure they couldn't touch her ever again.

Casey let Mr. Young open the door for her, and she went out into the hallway again. Afternoon sun streamed in through windows and made dusty white slabs on the floor. Tired, Casey walked with Mr. Young back toward the music suite.

Chapter Fifteen

FOR A WEEK, CASEY WAITED FOR PAUL TO PHONE HER.
Every day she came home from school and twisted the
doorknob to get inside fast, in case the phone rang. She
knew Mom would never give her a message. At night, she
moped over her homework, her nerves tensing. Every
time the phone rang, she scooped up the receiver. It was
never Paul.

She knew this was part of his game, and by midweek,
she was pissed off. What if she *didn't* call him back? What
if she started going out with her friends, and showed him
that she wasn't going to be pushed around?

But he'd kill her if she cheated on him. She always
wondered if he was parked across the street when she
talked to Lisa, or if he was somewhere in school, watching
her. Sometimes she wished that he'd die in a car accident
and set her free.

After a week, Casey couldn't take the waiting. She sat
up in her room at eleven o'clock on a Tuesday night and
rummaged through her folder. It was hopeless. She had
to do fifteen notecards for her research paper, rewrite
the essay she'd flunked because she'd scribbled it in the
cafeteria ten minutes before class, and do *another* essay—

and that was just for English! Her first quarter grades would be a disaster.

The mass of paper on her desk made her frustrated, so she thought about Paul. She needed him now. She wanted to hear him say that school was a game and that she didn't need the grades. She dug her wallet from her pocketbook and found his phone number, behind a snapshot of him on the beach.

She got the idea to go see him, but she realized she didn't even know his address! Still wearing her cotton top and warm-up pants from school, she turned out her light and went downstairs. Mom was in the master bedroom, with the door closed. A strip of light under the door showed that the TV was on.

Casey flipped on the kitchen light and got the phone book out of a drawer. She clunked her elbows on the counter as she flipped pages. She found Paul's phone number listed under a James VanHorn. His dad. She couldn't really picture him as some guy's son.

She noted the address and then slid the street map from its pocket in the back cover of the phone book. She stood up straight to unfold the map, and bit the tip of her tongue as she traced lines and squinted at street names.

Footsteps made her look up. Daddy came into the kitchen, from his office in the basement. He looked at her with surprise.

"Hi," he said.

"Hi."

"Whatcha looking at?"

"Nothing."

Dad had on his old, grungy, blue sweat shirt and dungarees with holes at the knees. His face was all pinched and worn.

"Planning to run away?" He indicated the open map.

She felt her face warm. "No."

He seemed to be waiting for her to say something else. When she didn't, he sighed, and sort of nodded to himself, as if he knew he was right about something. "I'm just getting my milk and cookies."

She smiled encouragingly. "Okay."

He really *did* have milk and cookies, every night. She watched him take the milk out of the fridge and pour a glass of it. Then he took the bag of chocolate chip cookies from the pantry and counted out four cookies. Casey stifled a giggle. He was so *serious* about it.

He picked up *Newsday* from the counter and dumped it on the kitchen table. Casey saw him look at her, and she said, "I'll get out of your way."

"You can stay there."

"No. You like to be alone with your milk and cookies."

He looked sheepish but grateful as he sat down by the table. She folded up the street map and put the phone book back in the drawer. Daddy was still looking at her, with a faraway expression.

"What's wrong?" she asked.

"I get depressed when I look at you."

"Thanks a lot."

He smiled. "That's not what I mean. It's just so weird to see you grown up."

She tried to smile back politely, but she really wasn't in the mood for a Daddy's Little Girl scene. "It *feels* weird."

"You look so pretty right now."

She was getting embarrassed. "I look like a wreck. I don't even have any makeup on."

"I like that," he said. "I don't like makeup, anyway. Or those long phony nails, or sprayed hair, or perfume. I like plain, healthy skin and long, shiny hair and straight, unpolished nails."

"You'd probably fall in love with a nun," she said.

He laughed. "Not the nuns I used to know. We lived near a convent, and we'd see the nuns walking down the street. They were always big, with heavy black robes, and they all had rimless eyeglasses and warts on their chins with hair growing out of them." He seemed to enjoy the memory. "We were scared of them. We figured they knew all the bad stuff we were doing."

"Yeah?" she said, not knowing how to answer.

He remained lost in his memory for a minute, then rubbed his nose and shook his head. He looked like he was going to cry.

"You should get some sleep," she said.

"Tell me about it."

"You'll get another heart attack."

He laughed. "Everyone tells me that. Except your mother. She thinks I'm doing this deliberately, to get sympathy."

"That's stupid."

"Well, who knows? Maybe it *is* self-pity. I'm too tired to know what my motives are."

He dunked a cookie into the milk and held it there, watching it. Then he lifted it out and sucked at the wet part. Casey held the folded map in her hand and she could actually feel the invisible wall between them.

"Well, take it slow," she said.

His eyes watched her sadly. Wet cookie clung to his lip. "Casey, I just want you to know I'm on your side."

"Okay."

He paused. Then he said, "Your mother really cares about you. She's not always good at showing it, but she does care."

"Yeah. I know."

"Casey, give her a break. Do you know what it's like to hear that your daughter is being knocked around by some animal? You're our *kid*." He held his second cookie over the milk. "I still look at pictures of you in your little green velvet dress, when you were five years old. You used to give me octopus hugs. You wrapped your arms and legs around me and held on and I'd let go and you'd just cling. It's hard to see you now, and think about you...doing those things, and getting beaten up...." His eyes glistened suddenly and the cookie slipped from his fingers and plopped into the glass.

"Daddy, don't freak," she pleaded. He kept his hands on the table and he bit his lip.

She went behind him and touched shaking hands to his shoulders. His shirt was warm and damp and he smelled stale. Her feelings flooded her, and impulsively she hugged his neck and pressed her cheek to his stubbled face. Her skin felt his tears. He grabbed on to her hands and held them. Stop crying, she begged him silently.

Casey straightened up and tenderly massaged his shoulders. "Don't take it so hard," she said. "They made such a big thing out of it at school. It wasn't any of their business."

"I don't know what to do," he said. "I don't know how to handle this."

"There's nothing to handle," she said.

He took a deep breath; she could feel it. "How's it going with the school psychologist?"

"All right."

"What do you talk about?"

Casey shrugged. "Not much. Mostly about Paul, and what I like about him, and where we go on dates, and what my plans are, and how my college applications are going. It's not too interesting."

"We're going to have to do something," he said. "We can't let you get killed by this jerk."

She made fists of her hands and moved away from him. "I wish you'd all just leave me alone."

"Don't stay with him, Casey," he begged. "Get away from him. Please."

He spoke intensely. For a minute, hugging him, she'd had what she'd dreamed about since she was a kid. But it didn't mean anything. He was still sore at her for taking up his time.

"I'll be okay," she told him. "Don't sweat it."

"Well, I *am* sweating it," he said. "I can't make believe it isn't happening."

"Take it light, Dad," she said. Already, she was inching

out of the kitchen. She was polite enough to wait in case he had anything else to say, but he just looked at her, totally miserable. She said, "You dropped a cookie into your milk. Don't drink it."

He looked at the glass, then said, "Oh. Thanks."

She smiled a little, at how much of a little boy he was. Casey couldn't hate him. She wanted to tell him to pack up and leave, because that was what he wanted to do more than anything.

"Night, Daddy," she said.

"Good night, Casey."

She blew him a kiss and went back up the carpeted steps. Mom's door was still closed. Casey turned on her room light and lay down on her bed, still holding the street map. She rested the map on her stomach and stared up at the ceiling.

The next afternoon was cold and nasty. Pewter clouds plated the sky and a bitter wind scoured the trees. Casey got off the bus and looked around. This was an old part of Westfield. Once, these little Cape Cods and ranches had been bright and new. Now they were falling apart.

Casey kept her coat zipped up, but she still shivered. She passed a house with half of its maroon siding ripped off, and a house with a rusting blue car on the grass, and a house with a chain link fence all around it. Dirty-looking kids rode bikes in the road. The mailboxes were all bent at different angles, or hanging off their poles. There were ceramic Madonnas or donkeys and carts on some lawns. Some houses were nearly covered by huge, ancient trees, and some were flanked by soaring evergreens.

Casey shuddered. She saw flapping sheets on clothes-lines, broken fence slats, and twisted swing sets. She got to number 28, Paul's house. She stood and looked at it for a long time. It was a pale yellow house, not too ugly, with a little yard all around it. The grass was dead and had bald patches. A pickup truck was parked under a carport. A torn paper shade hung in a downstairs window.

She felt her heart pounding, and her legs wavered. This was stupid. He'd get furious about her coming here. He was probably ashamed of where he lived.

But she wanted to visit him. When you had a boyfriend you came over to his house and he came over to yours. She wanted Paul to watch a football game with her dad, and she wanted to have Thanksgiving turkey with his mom. Her friends always talked about how they went shopping with their boyfriends' moms, and how their boyfriends practically lived at their houses, and she wanted that. She knew none of it would ever happen, but at least she'd meet Paul's folks.

Casey walked to the door, which was at the side of the house. The air smelled of smoke. She knocked on the storm door. When nobody answered, she stood on tiptoe and pressed her nose against the greasy glass to see inside.

She knocked again. This was totally dumb.

Then the door was yanked open. Casey looked down at a little boy, maybe seven or eight years old. He had black, shiny hair and deep black eyes. He wore a sweat suit with food stains all over it.

"Hi," Casey said. "Is Paul home?"

"*Ma!*" the kid yelled. "Somebody wants Paul!"

Casey tried to smile at the little boy. Paul had never talked about any brothers or sisters. She looked into the house. The door opened into a tiny living room, and Casey's throat clutched at the ugliness of it. Dirty clothes covered the carpet, which had once been mustard yellow but was now nearly black with dirt. A torn, stained couch was the only furniture to sit on. There was a big television set opposite the couch, and it was blasting "He-Man." The walls were bare Sheetrock, defaced with dirt streaks and burn marks.

A woman came to the door. She looked about forty-five, with uncombed iron-gray hair and a bony shape. She wore a Mets sweat shirt and pink stretch pants. Her eyes looked burned out and her face was all angles and lines.

"What's the matter?" the woman asked. Her voice was harsh, the way a smoker's voice sounds.

Casey thought she was going to faint, she was shaking so hard. She said, "Hi. Are you Mrs. VanHorn?"

"What is this?" the woman asked.

"I'm Casey Gordon," Casey said. "Paul and I are…going out together."

It sounded completely idiotic as she said it. Mrs. VanHorn stared at Casey. The little boy remained in front of the woman, leaning against the storm door.

"So?" Mrs. VanHorn said. "What do you want?"

"I was hoping Paul would be home."

"Was he expecting you?"

"No," Casey said, feeling more and more ridiculous. "I wanted to surprise him."

"He ain't home," Mrs. VanHorn said. "He's working, I think. I'll tell him you were here."

Casey's hair whipped around her windburned cheeks. "Okay."

Mrs. VanHorn seemed amused. "Where did you come from?"

"I live off Broad Avenue, near Route 25."

"That's pretty far. You drive?"

"No, I took the bus."

Mrs. VanHorn seemed to soften a little. "You want a cold drink or something before you go back? I feel bad Paul's not here. You should've called."

"I know," Casey said. "I was dumb."

"Come on in," Mrs. VanHorn said. "I'll give you a drink."

Casey half wanted to come in and half didn't, but she let Mrs. VanHorn hold the door open and she went inside. The house smelled sour and burnt. The TV slammed at her ears. Casey saw that there was another little kid, a girl of about nine or ten, sitting on the couch and watching. The girl didn't move. Only her eyes darted, as the colored glow shifted on her face. She wore pajamas.

"What do you want?" Mrs. VanHorn asked. "Pepsi? Orange juice?"

Casey really didn't want to drink anything here, but she knew she had to be polite. "Pepsi is okay."

"Want some cake or something?"

Casey shook her head. "No, thanks."

Mrs. VanHorn ambled into the kitchen and got a plastic bottle of Pepsi from an old refrigerator. Casey hugged herself as she looked around. There was nothing here, no decorations, no pictures, nothing. The room was cold, too. Casey remembered seeing liquid gas tanks up against the side of the house.

"Here," Mrs. VanHorn said, as she came back with a blue plastic cup. Casey took the cup and held her breath as she sipped. The soda was warm and fizzy.

Mrs. VanHorn pushed back her stringy hair as the little boy grabbed her around the legs. "Cut it, Joey," she said. "Go watch TV."

"Hi, Joey," Casey said to the boy.

"You're in love with Paul?" Joey asked.

Mrs. VanHorn lifted her hand threateningly. "Shut up!" Joey smirked and took a flying jump onto the couch. "I'm sorry," Mrs. VanHorn said. "He's got a motor mouth."

"It's okay," Casey said.

"So how long are you and Paul going together? He never mentioned you."

Casey's heart took an elevator to her knees. "It's been a few months."

"Yeah? Where'd you meet?"

"He delivered some fence sections to my house, and I remembered him from school."

Mrs. VanHorn laughed a throaty laugh. "Yeah, everybody remembers him from school. So how old are you?"

"Seventeen."

"You look nice. Don't feel bad that Paul didn't say anything. He never says anything. He could be going to jail and he wouldn't tell us." She laughed again. "He did that once. Got sent to the work farm out in Yaphank and called us two weeks later that he was there. Maybe you can make him act human."

She said all this in a perfectly flat tone, with no emotion. She didn't seem bothered at all by the earthquake volume of the TV. Casey's palm perspired around the plastic cup. The walls seemed to move in toward her. It was so bizarre not sitting down. But she didn't want to sit down here.

"Paul's a good talker with me," Casey said. "He's pretty funny."

"Yeah, like polio," Mrs. VanHorn said.

Perspiration broke out on Casey's forehead and the back of her neck. Her head began to throb. "What's your little girl's name?"

"Diane, say hello. This is Paul's lady friend."

Diane looked at Casey with a deep, unfathomable gaze. "Hi," she whispered.

"Hi, Diane. Like to hang out in your pj's?"

Diane just stared, uncomprehending. Then she returned her attention to the TV. Casey said, "She's pretty."

"She's always sick," Mrs. VanHorn said cheerfully. "She had rheumatic fever and now she has to take penicillin every day. Except I can't afford it so she's probably going to die."

"Oh, no," Casey said. "There must be some way you can get it...."

Casey didn't expect anyone to come to the front door, so she gasped when it swung open and slammed shut. She looked, and tightened her grip on the cup. A man stood looking at her. He was dark and muscular. He had a rough, raw neck and cropped peppery hair. A cigarette jiggled in his mouth. "Who are you?" he demanded.

Mrs. VanHorn said, "This is Paul's girlfriend."

Mr. VanHorn took the cigarette from his mouth. He smelled of gasoline and liquor. Glistening stains across his nose and forearms showed that he'd been working on a motor. "Girlfriend?"

"That's what she says."

Mr. VanHorn scrutinized Casey with cold eyes. "Paul ain't here."

"I know," Casey said. "Mrs. VanHorn offered me some Pepsi."

"Oh." It was a grunt, not a word. He turned his attention to his wife. "I need a rotor and wires. I'm going to the AID store."

"Okay," Mrs. VanHorn said.

Mr. VanHorn stood there, holding the cigarette at his side. He had a tattoo on his left forearm. "Come here," he said to his wife.

"What?" she said.

"Come here."

She made an annoyed sound through her lips and went to him. He grabbed her elbow and spoke in low, knifelike tones, but Casey could hear everything he said.

"What are you, stupid?" he scolded her. "The place looks like a zoo. What are you bringing in people for?"

"I just gave her a Pepsi."

"You don't bring anyone in when it looks like this, huh? I told you to clean the place, didn't I? Didn't I tell you to clean it?"

"Yeah, I'll clean it. I got nothing else to do."

"Don't talk back to me," he hissed.

"Don't tell me what to do. I'm working two jobs off the books so you can stay on welfare and fix your car. You want to clean it up, clean it up."

"I'll smack you silly," he said.

"Yeah, right in front of the kid. Show her what a brain you are."

Mr. VanHorn slapped his wife, a quick, angry, back-handed slap that cracked loudly even over the TV. She twisted away from the slap, but didn't put her hand to the red blotch on her face. Her eyes glistened, but her voice stayed firm. "Do it again, jerk. Maybe she didn't catch it the first time."

Mr. VanHorn looked at Casey, and Casey turned to ice shavings inside. Joey and Diane stayed on the couch, watching "He-Man." They didn't even look at their parents. Casey heard a car pull up outside, and she heard a door slam.

"You gotta go," he said to Casey. "Finish the soda."

"She'll finish it when she wants to," Mrs. VanHorn said defiantly.

"Shut your mouth," he said, and he rapped her face again, not as hard this time.

Casey gripped the plastic cup in both hands and gulped the horrible warm soda. Her stomach lurched at it. She looked around desperately for someplace to put the cup. She wanted to breathe fresh air, as fast as she could.

Then Paul opened the door and came inside. He wore his work clothes from the mall. He looked from his parents to Casey, bewildered.

"What are you doing here?" he asked.

"I came to visit you," she said.

"Are you nuts? You didn't even know if I'd be here."

"I wanted to meet your mom."

Paul looked almost delicate next to his father, but Casey could see the resemblance in the eyes and in the way both men stood. Paul looked again at his parents. "What are you doing, having a ten-rounder?"

"Don't be wise," Mr. VanHorn said.

Mrs. VanHorn said, "How come you didn't mention you had a girlfriend? She's pretty nice."

"It wasn't any of your business," Paul said.

"You're cruising for a bloody nose," Mr. VanHorn said. "Why don't you take her and get out?"

"Why, so you can finish on Mom?" Paul said. "Why don't you let her go first?"

Mrs. VanHorn said, "Let it alone, Paulie. Do what your father says."

"When he lets you go."

"Paulie..."

"No way."

Casey felt long, sickening waves of fear roll from her throat to her knees. Paul looked like a little boy facing down a street bully.

"You want me to let go?" Mr. VanHorn said. "Pull me off."

"Cut it out," Mrs. VanHorn pleaded.

Paul tensed and then lunged, hooking both hands onto his father's wrist. With a swift, brutal movement, Mr. VanHorn flung his wrist outward and threw Paul back against the front door. The door made a loud cracking sound and Paul seemed to hang there, stunned. Mr. VanHorn threw a vicious backhand slap at Paul's cheek and Casey screamed at the impact. Paul rolled sideways and moaned. Mr. VanHorn shook his hand vigorously and yanked the door open. He let it shut behind him.

Paul leaned against the wall, working his mouth and breathing hard. Mrs. VanHorn looked weary. "Honey," she said, "do me a favor and don't come around anymore."

Casey nodded, not in agreement, but just to do something. Snapped bowstrings were twanging inside her stomach. She looked at the two kids, still watching TV. She put the plastic cup down on top of the set, no longer worried about looking stupid.

She went to Paul and stood by him. He glared at her, and his hands were over his mouth. She could see bright blood at his lips and between his fingers. She'd never seen him as a victim, and it scared her.

She touched her fingertips to his shoulder, shaking with the expectation of being hit. "You want me to stay?" she asked.

He just kept glaring. She realized how hurt and humiliated he was. Nothing worse could happen for a guy than to be hit by his father in front of his girlfriend. She had to be careful not to say anything wrong.

"I love you," she whispered to him. "I'll be here for you, always."

He turned away. He was crying, she knew he was. She hugged him as much as she could with him leaning against the wall. She kissed his neck and she stroked his damp, thick hair. As scared and stunned as she was, she felt a warm happiness flood her. Finally, he was helpless and she was strong.

"Stay here," he said, in a low voice.

She hung on to him with all her strength, shutting her eyes and crying and smiling all at once. You and me, Paul, she thought fiercely. We'll beat 'em all.

Chapter Sixteen

CASEY SAID, "STAND OVER THERE, RIGHT BY THAT WILLOW tree. I want to get you against the sky."

Paul glanced over his shoulder to make sure he didn't back up into the pond and shuffled in reverse. "Here?"

Casey squinted through the eyepiece of her camera as hair blew across her cheeks. She saw a tiny Paul and a tiny tree. "A little to your right. No, *left*."

"Make up your mind."

"Left."

She saw the tiny Paul take two dainty steps to his left, which brought him right into the willow branches. She laughed and at the same time shivered from the icy wind that plowed across the duck pond. "Sorry. Three steps to the right."

He dutifully stepped to the right.

"Two more," she said.

He took two more steps. She laughed again. He was deliberately taking faggy steps and making faces. "Okay. That's pretty good." Now she could see the luminous sky behind him, rich blue lit with golden fall sun. The whole scene looked like one of those oil paintings where everything was drenched in sunlight.

"Smile," she said. He made a goofy face, with his tongue curled to the side and his eyes crossed. "Come on." He replaced the grotesque expression with a natural smile. She pressed the shutter.

"Now you take *me*," she said. Her Westfield jacket billowed in the wind, and her ears burned from the cold air. Her eyes drank in the ice-blue pond, surrounded by trees that were pale amber, rose flush, and brown. The ducks still glided on the water, but the fall wind riffled their brown feathers and they looked cold. The grass beneath her sneakers was pale yellow and brittle.

Paul trudged back up the bank to where she stood. She smiled brightly at him. He wore a long, flowing tweed coat with big leather buttons, and he'd cut his hair in a semi-punk style. He took the camera. "How many pictures do you have left?"

"I think three," she said.

"Good."

"Oh, come on," she said, grabbing onto one coat lapel. "I want to have some memories of this place."

"Why? Is it going to burn down?"

"Just do it."

She stood on tiptoe and kissed his cold lips. He returned the kiss and she shut her eyes and drifted for a moment. Then she released his lapel and said, "Take me by the pond, too, but get the ducks in the picture."

She ran down the bank and looked for the ducks. She knelt on one dungareed knee; the ground felt wet. The wind was at her back and she could hear it ripple her jacket. She kept pushing hair out of her eyes and smiling up at Paul, who peered into the viewfinder. His coattails furled behind him like condor's wings.

"A little to your left," he called to her.

She kind of waddled to her left, not wanting to ruin her pose. She could hear the ducks honking behind her, and the rush of the water. In the distance, she could hear cars.

"Okay," Paul said. "Raise your head a little." She lifted her chin. "Now take off all your clothes and look excited."

"*Paul!*" she cried.

"All right, all right, I got carried away. Just stay there. Don't move. I have to wait for the ducks. Come on, ducks. No, no, the *other* way."

She tried not to giggle, but it wasn't easy. Finally, he said, "Say pizza."

"Pizza."

"Got it." He looked up from the camera. "I got the ducks, but I cut you out."

"Very funny," she said. She stood up and looked around. The tip of her nose felt as cold as a puppy's snout. "I want to get a picture of the two of us."

"Who's going to take it, the ducks?" He ambled down to meet her.

"No, I can set the camera for time release. How about down by that rock?"

"This is stupid," he said.

"Come on. This is our special place."

"Okay, don't go hysterical. We can have a whole album of it."

She smiled at him. "I like that idea." She went to him and hugged him, slipping her hands beneath his coat and over his ribs. She pulled him tightly against her and felt the fabric of his coat scrape her windburned face.

He forced his own hands under the elastic waistband of her school jacket and rubbed her lower back. She felt a nameless sadness possess her body. She couldn't identify it, but she didn't like it.

"I'm freezing," he said. "We'd better go."

"Just a few more minutes," she said. "It's so hard to be alone with you."

"I know." He kissed her a few times and she nuzzled his neck. "Your mom and dad really clamped down."

"Well, my stupid coach had to try to save me," she said. "I'm so pissed off at him. I know he means well, but now

I'm punished for three months. No Senior Banquet, no driving privileges, no going out on weekends. I have to see the stupid psychologist twice a week, and get this, I have to go to the doctor once a month to get examined."

"For what?" he asked.

"For *bruises*," she said. "I can't stand it. It's like I'm a master criminal. I feel so degraded."

He was quiet for a moment. He slid his hands from under her jacket and held her head, tenderly. His eyes looked sad. "It's my fault."

She sighed. "It isn't anybody's fault. Why am I getting punished for getting beaten up? It's my problem, anyway, and if I want to keep seeing you, that's my choice."

He smiled bitterly. "Forget it. You don't get choices like that."

"Tell me about it." She backed out of the embrace and took the camera from him, swinging it by its strap. "Let's go by the rock."

"Okay."

She walked down the embankment to a huge, smooth boulder that tipped precariously toward the pond. The sun gleamed from its brown surface. "If we sit on the rock, where would I put the camera?"

"In the tree?"

"Be serious." She looked around, piqued by the challenge. "We could put the camera on the rock and stand there by that tree, the one with the red leaves."

"It's a nice tree."

She looked at him. "You're humoring me, right?"

He nodded.

"You used to be romantic, Paul. What happened?"

"I'm romantic," he said. "By a warm fire."

"Two minutes." She scouted the tree, considering the angles. "Anyway, you're the one who suggested we come here."

"And I'm the one suggesting we go back."

She laughed. Then she felt the sadness again. "There's

nowhere to go back to. I'm forbidden to see you. Mom swears she'll lock me up somewhere if I do."

"She can't."

"Don't bet on it."

He sat down on the boulder, and the way his coat spread made it look like he was a stork hatching an egg. "You're doing it again, Case. Giving them all the power."

He made her feel guilty. "I know, I know. But I'm scared to fight them. It would tear Daddy apart."

"Since when is Daddy worth your tears?"

"Don't be mean, Paul. He's as miserable as I am. I can see it more and more. He just works all the time and does whatever Mom tells him to do. He doesn't love her, but he's afraid to walk out."

"It all sucks, Casey. I told you that."

She stood in front of the tree, hearing its leaves swish. "Well, now I know *why* you feel that way. Boy, I see you so differently."

He seemed to stiffen, and his face, drained white by the cold, reddened at the cheeks. "I don't want to talk about my family."

"I know," she said hastily. "But just knowing about it—Paul, it explains everything, don't you see that?"

"I don't see anything."

She went to him and knelt in front of the rock, setting the camera on the grass in front of her knees. "I've been reading about it, Paul. Please, don't get uptight. I love you."

"Sometimes you make it tough to believe."

She felt her eyes burn. "I know. But it's just that I'm confused, too. Or I was. I couldn't figure out why you went crazy sometimes. But now I know."

"Oh, yeah?"

"Sure. It's because of the way you grew up, and what you saw, and what you went through."

"Bull."

"It is *not* bull. It's true. Your dad is sick, Paul. An

alcoholic is sick, and so is a person who hits people. You have to read this stuff. It's a physical sickness, and it might even be some chemical imbalance in the brain, something they can fix some day. But it gets passed on. That's why you hit me."

He looked down at her with a puzzling, half-angry expression. "So what's the point?"

She breathed back her frustration. "Okay, I won't push it. But I'm really glad I went to see your folks. I know *you're* not glad. I know you're embarrassed and mad at me, but I don't care. I *know* you now. I really, really know you, and it makes me feel so close to you."

He looked to the side and narrowed his eyes. "I still don't know what that means."

"In what way?"

He looked back at her, a little fiercely this time. "Does it mean you pity me?"

"*No,*" she said emphatically. "Please don't think that."

"Does it mean I'm a project for you?"

She felt her chest tighten. She seized both of his rough, icy hands in hers. "Stop it, Paul. You're not a dummy. You like to act like one, but you're smarter than I am. You know what I mean."

"I want to hear it," he said.

"Hear what?"

"That you're my lady."

His words, and his tone of voice, recalled savage memories that sent shivers through her. "You know I am."

"What about the dance?"

"I was pissed at you, Paul. You made me look like a fool."

"You made *me* look like a fool."

"Okay, so we're even. I don't want to fight about it again."

"You told your mommy and daddy I was beating on you."

215

"I didn't tell them. They figured it out." Why was this going downhill? She was scared, and baffled.

"Well, word's gotten around, Casey. I got laid off at the mall."

"Oh, no."

"Yeah. No explanation. My foreman said the management was cutting back."

"Paul, I can't believe Mr. Young or Mr. Burton would spread that around. Not even my mom and dad."

"No, it was probably your zit-faced little girlfriends, the ones who were screaming for you not to go with me. Made me feel like real dirt."

Casey stood up and let go of his hands. She turned around and folded her arms tightly across her chest. The sun burnished the trees so that each individual leaf stood out like hammered gold. "I don't know what my friends did. They're not my friends anymore, anyway. You ought to be willing to take some responsibility if you got into a mess."

Her back shuddered, waiting for his attack. After a long time, he said, "Casey, I'm falling through space, you know? I've got nothing to hang on to."

She turned and looked hard at him. He seemed to be shaking. "All you have to do is reach out, Paul."

"But I have to know I can count on you."

"You *can*. I keep telling you that."

He was lit up by the sun. "I mean all the time. I have to know you're there for me, only me, not Mom, not Dad, not anybody, just me."

"I will be," she said, and some small piece of her said that these promises were stupid. But she sensed that she could stop him from hitting her, that she could keep him the way she wanted him, just by saying what he wanted to hear, and she was willing to say it again and again and again.

"I have to know you won't cheat on me. You have to

listen to me, Casey. You have to run to me. I have nothing else to hang on to."

"I'll be yours, Paul," she said. "Just trust me a little."

He stood up. "I'll trust you when you prove that I can trust you. I need total commitment."

She nodded. "I promise."

He observed her carefully, as if deciding. He shoved a purplish hand into his coat pocket and came out with a small, wrapped package. "Come here."

She stepped to him, feeling breathless and very cold. She felt as if she was out in an alien field, being enslaved, and nobody knew it. She felt as if she was going to be taken away in a ship and Mom and Dad and Faye and Mr. Young and everybody else would never know where she went.

He grasped her wrist and pressed the package into her palm. He curled her fingers up over it. "Open it up, Casey."

He was so serious now, like a solemn altar boy. Casey's hands shook as she tore the striped wrapping from the box. She knew it was a piece of jewelry. She still had his gold necklace and charm hidden in her room. Paddington had been put out front with the garbage after the Guidance Office conference. She'd cried like crazy over that, and didn't know how to tell Paul.

The wrapping was off. Casey could barely move her stiff fingers as she opened the blue velvet box. She felt her heart stop as she saw the small ring with its tiny diamond chip.

"What is this, Paul?"

"I want to marry you," he said. "Right after you graduate. Even if we have to drive down to Maryland and do it ourselves."

Her blood thundered in her temples. "I won't be eighteen yet...."

"So we'll do it when you're eighteen. But meanwhile we'll live together. We'll get an apartment."

His words were like garbled shouts in her ears. "I don't know...I have to think...."

"That's what I figured," he said bitterly.

"No." She looked hard at him. "I don't mean I have to think about marrying you. But about the rest. It's a lot to digest right away."

"Tell me when you're ready," he said.

She clenched her jaws and clutched the ring box in her hand. She envisioned her parents screaming. She imagined her Grandma Lena under sedation and her aunts and uncles scolding her. She saw the college applications on her desk, the neat, ordered life that she and her friends were planning, being thrown in the garbage can at the side of the house. She imagined driving with Paul down dark, new roads, afraid and alone and cold.

"Can't I have a day to think?" she asked.

"About what? You're my lady or you're not. What do you want? You want to go back to your buddies and go to the Prom? You want to be a kid, Casey? I can't commit myself to a kid. Get lost if you can't decide. I'll go home and remember all your promises."

"Don't lay a guilt trip on me," she said angrily. "That isn't fair. I've given everything to you."

"What have you given *only* to me, Casey? And to nobody else? Man, you saw my life. I'm not going to stand in line for any girl's attention."

She shuddered. The sky was darkening to a copper shade, and she had to be home soon. He was right. Why was she backing out? She'd promised him that she'd be there, that she'd help him. And he was putting it all on the line. He was offering his life, too. This was her chance, probably her only chance to change direction. Always, she'd been too scared to take risks. Always, she'd given in, surrendered, been a punching bag. Now Paul had offered her a new future. All she had to do was take it. She'd never be alone again. Oh, man, that sounded good.

She nodded jerkily and used her numbed fingers to tweeze the ring out of the box. "Put it on," she said.

He smiled thinly at her, took the ring, and supported her outstretched hand. "Be there for me, Casey," he said, and worked the icy ring over her finger.

The metal of the ring seemed to burn its circle into her skin. She held up her hand and looked at her engaged finger against the brilliant sky. Rays of sun touched the tiny chip. Warmth filled her, and a sudden rush of optimism.

"Paul, I'm so happy," she said, and held him with savage tightness. He hugged her just as hard and she kissed him with long, desperate kisses. She whispered in his ear, "I want to be with you tonight."

"What about Mom and Dad?" he asked huskily.

"I don't care. I'll make up something. I love you."

He made a gratified sound deep in his throat. She clung to him as long as she could, until her arms burned with the effort. Her head ached throbbingly.

He said, "Still want to take the picture?"

She nodded, brushing at her eyes with the back of her hand. "I want a million pictures. We'll have our first album, and we can look at it years from now, sitting in front of the fire, with our kids asleep upstairs."

"That'll be nice," he said.

"It's going to be beautiful. I love you, Paul."

"I believe you."

She scooped up the camera, annoyed that the strange sadness had not left. Her heart ached as if he'd told her good-bye forever, and at the same time her blood sang with promise. Well, of course it wasn't going to be easy, but love was worth it.

"Come over by the tree," she ordered.

He strutted to the fire-red tree and stood in front of it. Casey set the camera's timed release with fumbling fingers and carefully positioned the camera on the boulder. She squinted through the viewfinder to frame Paul's midsection. "Kneel down," she said. He knelt and his head came into view. "Okay. Stay right there." She pressed down the lever and sprinted over to Paul. She knelt down next to him and threw her arms around him.

"Smile," she said.

"I feel stupid."

"Just smile." The camera whirred and then clicked. She whooped and punched a victorious fist in the air. "Geronimo! We did it."

"Screw the camera," he growled. "I want my woman." He twisted and threw her down on her back. She linked her hands around his neck and pulled his head to hers, shutting her eyes tightly. *I love you,* she said to him silently. It was as much a prayer as a declaration.

Chapter Seventeen

CASEY SHOWERED AND DRESSED WITH A POUNDING HEART on Monday morning. As she brushed her hair, she avoided her eyes in the mirror. She was *still* worried about what her friends would think, after everything Paul had said about them.

Casey tried hard to gag down a buttered bagel, but she finally had to dump it in the garbage. She looked out the kitchen window as she slurped cold coffee, and her eyes enjoyed the show of red and gold in the woods. It was a blue fall morning, with a breath of white frost on the lawn. It made Casey feel almost serene.

But she kept remembering that she was *engaged;* engaged at seventeen like all those dumb Doras in school with teased hair and heavy perfume and tight pants. Casey recalled, as she jammed her arms into her jacket sleeves and slung her pocketbook over her shoulder, that she'd decided against marriage at least until the age of thirty. That was last year, after Mark Simon.

JoAnne was flushing the toilet upstairs as Casey wrenched open the front door and slammed it behind her. The fragrant chill of the morning woke up her cheeks and ruffled her hair as she hurried toward the bus stop on the corner.

For just an instant, her life flashed in front of her. She'd grown up in this house, ridden her Strawberry Shortcake bike up and down the cracked sidewalk, thrown snowballs at the Carters' house across the street, played with her toy stove on the oil-stained driveway. Even then, she remembered, her friends used to flat leave her. She spent a lot of time sitting at the redwood table in the backyard, making up stories.

Foolishly, the memories filled her with pain. She ran the last few yards, her heels clacking in the gutter.

Casey's bus rolled in along with two or three others, and she had to jostle and elbow her way into the building. She said perfunctory hellos to people she passed, and when she turned the corner to go to her locker, she saw Faye and Heather already there. Kids lined the corridor, twisting dials and kicking stuck doors. The scene reminded Casey of gamblers lined up at slot machines.

Faye looked at Casey as she bounced and caromed off bodies. Gangs of kids were already knotting up in the middle of the corridor. Girls shrieked as they saw each other. Guys bellowed. In all the movement, Faye remained still, her eyes curious.

"Hi," she said as Casey reached the locker. Casey, Faye, Heather, and Lillian had managed to get lockers near each other for three years running.

"Hi," Casey said. She leaned in toward the locker and twisted the dial. She kept her eyes on the putty-colored steel.

Heather was stuffing her blue coat into her locker, but turned now. *"Casey,"* she said.

"Hi, Heather."

Faye said, "What happened to Paul?"

"Nothing," Casey said, as she yanked open the locker door. She still had the picture of Thomas Hardy Scotch-taped to the inside of the door. That was a big joke last year when they all had to read *Jude the Obscure*. They decided to make Tom Hardy their pinup boy.

"So how come you're early?"

"What's the big deal?" Casey said airily. She shrugged off her jacket and jammed it in. Library books were piled on the floor of the locker. She was supposed to be taking notes for her research paper, but she hadn't taken the books home yet.

"No big deal," Faye said. "We're just surprised."

"Oh, yeah?"

Faye's eyes narrowed. "What's going on?"

"Nothing," Casey said, and slammed the locker door. She pulled open the door of the top cubicle and slid out her copy of *A Midsummer-Night's Dream,* along with her battered English notebook and folder.

Heather had just shut her own locker. Hundreds of kids were streaming into the building, making the hallway roar. Casey kept her left hand more or less concealed behind her folder. Her stomach cramped in anticipation.

She realized that she didn't want to show the ring. As long as it was just her and Paul, alone, the dream shimmered. But she didn't know if the dream could survive being laughed at.

The warning bell hooted through the din. The floor rumbled as teachers pushed AV carts with TV sets and tape recorders. Fluorescent lights flickered on in classrooms. "Gotta hurry," Casey mumbled, as she shut the top door of her locker.

Faye said, "Whatever you say," and tried to read something in Casey's averted face. But Heather's eyes caught the furtive movements of Casey's hand. She followed the hand as Casey shut the top locker, and the dim corridor light glinted for an instant on the diamond chip of the ring.

"What's *that*?" Heather asked.

Casey's skin froze. "What?"

"Is that a *diamond*?"

Faye's eyes darted to the hand. "Diamond?"

Casey felt her whole body throb, like a heartbeat. She held her books now, so her ring was underneath.

"Did Paul give you that?" Faye asked.

Casey nodded. "Yesterday."

Faye gave Casey a level, frightened look. "Are you *engaged* to him?"

Casey nodded again.

Heather's eyes widened, and her mouth dropped. "Oh, my G-O-D-D-D!" she gasped. Her fingers fluttered to her mouth.

Kids turned around. Casey could feel warm blood rushing into her ears. Heather shoved Faye aside and threw her arms around Casey. Casey was still holding her books and she had to hang on tight.

Heather finally released Casey and just stood there, gaping. She clutched Casey's hand, forcing Casey to balance the books against her ribs. "It's *gorgeous*," Heather gushed. "I can't believe it. This is so awesome. I can't believe it."

"You said that," Faye pointed out.

Heather looked at Faye, to see if Faye also couldn't believe it. Tears glistened in Heather's round eyes. She looked back at Casey. "When did he ask you?"

"Yesterday," Casey said.

"And you said yes?"

Casey nodded.

"Oh, my God," Heather said again. "When are you getting married?"

"I don't know," Casey said. She tried to lower her voice because everybody was looking at them. Kids were now moving toward classrooms, and Casey felt herself causing a traffic jam.

Heather said, "This is so fantastic."

Faye caught Casey's eyes. "Do your folks know yet?"

Casey shook her head. "I'm scared to death to tell them. They're going to freak."

"Really." Faye shifted her own books against her chest, hugging them with both slender arms. "Are you sure, Case?"

"Yes, I'm sure."

"Is he going to control himself?"

Casey smiled. "Yes. I know he's done crazy things, but you don't really know him."

"I hope *you* do."

"Don't worry about me." Casey took a deep breath, feeling suddenly flushed. "Will you come to my wedding?"

Faye looked sad and tired, as if she'd lost a race. "Sure."

"Don't hate me?"

This made Faye smile one of her secret smiles. "No. I couldn't compete."

"Huh?"

Faye shook her head. "Never mind. I was being stupid."

"So you'll come?"

"Yeah."

"You can bring Eddie."

Faye laughed. "I don't know if he'll be around. Long-range plans give me hives."

Casey felt like hugging Faye but since they were both lugging books, she couldn't. She turned to Heather. "You're coming, too, right?"

Heather looked as if she were about to cry. "Sure I'll come. Oh, man, I'll miss you, Casey."

"I'm not getting married next week," Casey said.

Heather impulsively hugged Casey again, giving Casey a noseful of sexy perfume. Then Heather's eyes went wide as they looked beyond Casey. *"Lillian!"* she cried out.

"Oh, no," Casey said.

Casey spun and saw Lillian, with her head down, hurrying toward them. Lillian was chronically late for everything. "I can't believe it," Lillian said as she arrived at the lockers. "The car wouldn't start. I had to have my next-door neighbor jump-start me. Now I don't know if it'll start after school, and I have to be at the church by three."

"And that's the news for this morning," Faye intoned. "Now for the sports."

Lillian glared at Faye. "I'm not even supposed to be running around like this. I'm having nerve surgery in a week."

With a toss of her head, she started on her combination. Heather said, "Lillian, Casey is engaged to Paul."

Lillian looked up, angry that nobody had responded to her announcement. "Who?" she asked.

"*Casey,*" Heather said. "She just got a ring. Isn't that outrageous?"

Lillian stared at Casey. "You're engaged to *Paul?*"

"Yeah," Casey said.

"Isn't he the one who hits you?"

Casey felt irrationally angry. "No."

Lillian shrugged, barely noticing the ring. "You're out of your mind. Boy, I have enough pain in my life to know that I don't want any more."

"You *are* a pain," Casey said.

"Well, excuse *me,*" Lillian said. She reddened and forced her eyes to stay on her locker dial.

"Oh, Jesus," Faye said. "I've got one minute to get across the whole building. O'Connor is going to have my head."

"I'm sorry," Casey said.

Faye managed to free a hand to put on Casey's shoulder. "Good luck, Case. I hope you're happy."

Casey felt her throat tighten. "Thanks." She leaned in toward Faye and they shared a clumsy kiss.

Heather waited her turn and grabbed Casey again. "I think it's great," she said. "Everything's gonna work out."

"Thanks," Casey said hoarsely. She gritted her teeth to endure another Heather-hug.

Teachers were in doorways now, idly yelling out for the

kids to move on. Couples remained against lockers, in desperate embraces. Casey watched a guy and his girlfriend. Their eyes were shut and their jaws worked like crazy. A teacher made a remark and they broke the kiss. The girl was chewing gum, and she didn't miss a beat. Casey shuddered. That was simple love. Swap spit against the lockers but never lose your gum.

Faye and Heather were gone; the hall was emptying. Lillian closed her locker and looked pityingly at Casey. "I'm sorry if I hurt you."

"It's okay," Casey said.

"I'll pray for both of you."

"Thanks."

Lillian gave Casey a tight "hang in there" smile, and then turned and shuffled back down the hall. The late bell rang, and there were curses and scufflings. Casey stood by her locker, with her arm full of books, and felt bereft. Everybody had been so decent and still it hurt. She knew that they all thought she was insane. There'd been no joy in showing her ring.

Paul was right. They didn't matter and they didn't care. Casey let her anger come to a good, rolling boil as she swung off down the hallway and framed an excuse to give to Mr. Young.

That night, Mom made supper for the family. "It's been a long time since we had dinner together," she announced. Casey knew this would be her best shot at telling them.

She sat in her chair at the butcher block table and poked her fork into lettuce leaves wet with dressing. She shivered, even in her sweat shirt, as cold night wind snuck into the house. JoAnne stretched to grab a piece of garlic bread from a wicker basket.

"Don't do that," Dad said. "Ask for it."

"I already got it," JoAnne said, and gnawed off an end. Dad gave her a reproachful look. He sat at the head of the table, with his back to the bay window. He had on his good shirt and slacks and looked pretty neat, but Casey could see how tired he was.

Mom brought a bowl of spaghetti to the table and set it down on a trivet. "It's hot," she said.

Dad slopped spaghetti onto JoAnne's plate and then poured sauce for her. Casey kept looking down at her salad, and she felt her stomach cramp. She hated family dinners. Mom made this big deal about eating together and everybody wound up fighting.

Dad said, "Up for the big meet?"

"Huh?" Casey said.

"Northville."

Casey remembered. It was so strange; a couple of months ago, she had lived to run against Northville. She had kept imagining how the hurdles would feel, with her legs throbbing and pumping. She had envisioned herself sprinting to the finish line. But now, it seemed stupid.

"Yeah," she said. "That's this Thursday."

"Doing the four hundred?"

Casey didn't really know. She'd missed a few more practices, and she'd run way off her time in the meets. She didn't know if Mr. Young would use her. Suddenly, she felt guilty about that.

"Casey?" Dad said.

"Huh? Oh, sorry. Yeah, I guess so."

Dad sipped at his water. "Is something wrong?"

Mom had sat down now and was filling her own plate. "She's been in her own world lately."

Dad kept looking at Casey and ignored Mom. He did that when he didn't like what Mom had said. "Is there anything wrong at school?"

Casey shrugged. "No."

"Work piling up?"

"Kind of. The research paper is killing me."

JoAnne said, "Can I have more garlic bread?"

"That's three pieces," Mom said. "Eat some veal."

"It's too tough."

"It is not tough, it's tender."

"I want *bread*," JoAnne insisted.

Dad sighed and gave JoAnne more bread. Mom put down her fork. "Does my word mean anything around here?"

"Let her eat the bread," Dad said. "It'll shut her up."

Mom gave one of her sarcastic smiles and shook her head.

Casey's cheeks burned. "Could you two stop it? Just for a minute?"

Mom said, "What's *your* problem?"

"Nothing."

Dad said, "If it's the research paper, what you have to do is organize your time. Break it up into small tasks. I have a whole system I can show you."

A vise was squeezing Casey's ribs tighter and tighter. "It's not the research paper. It isn't anything."

"Don't bother asking her," Mom said. "I make one family dinner a week, and I don't want it spoiled by her sulking."

"Oh, right," Casey said. "My sulking. Little Queenie over there stuffing her face and whining doesn't bug you."

JoAnne made a taunting face. "Stuff it up your nose."

Casey banged a fist on the table. "Shut *up!*"

Dad raised his voice. "Casey, cut it out. She's eight and you're seventeen. You should know better."

Mom said, "The day she acts her age will be the day we can expect her to know better."

Casey felt like she was trapped in an airless cave where she couldn't move or breathe. "This place is a zoo."

"Casey, at the moment you're grounded for three months. It can be six months."

Casey said, "What about my whole life? Want to chain me in the basement?"

"Leave the table," Mom said.

Dad said, "Can we calm down here?"

"I want her away from this table. I am not eating until she leaves." Mom put down her fork with a bang and sat back, her arms crossed.

Dad was getting agitated. "Ellen, this is overreacting."

"Too bad. Get her out."

Casey felt the salad lurch in her stomach. She said, "I'll be happy to leave the table. But I thought before I went, you might want to know that Paul and I are engaged."

Damn. She'd said it spitefully, and at the worst time. Mom gave a little laugh. "Did he give you a ring?"

"Yes." With shaking fingers, she dug it out of her jeans pocket and put it on. She held out her hand.

Mom stared at the ring, then at Dad. "Is this serious?"

"Yes," Casey said.

"Excuse me," Mom said, in a cold voice. "This isn't possible. You've been forbidden even to see Paul VanHorn."

"Well, I've been seeing him anyway."

"When?"

"Different times." Inside, Casey churned. She suddenly felt reckless and immortal.

Mom looked at Dad. "Do you have something to say?"

JoAnne watched in fascination, chewing the crust of her garlic bread into a wet pulp. Dad stared at Casey, and Casey had to keep her eyes averted. She could look at Mom, but not at Dad.

"When did you become engaged?"

"Yesterday," Casey said. "We're going to get married after I graduate."

"After you graduate what?" Mom said. "College?"

"High school."

Mom took slow, deep breaths to calm herself. Then she said, "I see. You've come to the conclusion that you have been mistreated in this house and that you are going to do what you damned well please."

"Easy," Dad said.

"Shut up." Mom kept looking at Casey. "I went the

route of the school psychologist. I tried grounding you. But you're going to be a real hellion, huh? Okay, missy, you opened fire on the wrong enemy. Number one, knock that stupid engagement idea out of your head. I will have any marriage annulled before you can blink. I will also have Paul VanHorn arrested for rape. And I will have you put away. You're going to learn one tough lesson."

Casey rocked back and forth in her seat, her fists clenched. "Stop it," she whispered.

"Where you even get the *nerve...*" Mom stopped herself. "It's unbelievable. Absolutely unbelievable. If anybody had told me that a child of mine would turn out this way..."

"That'll do it," Dad said.

Mom stopped talking and looked at him. "Ron, you'd better open your eyes and see what's happening."

He looked awful. There were blotches on his face and his eyes were glassy. "I see what's happening," he said. "Casey's gotten engaged."

Mom's eyes looked baffled. "What's your point?"

"No point," Dad said. "Except that there's not much we can do about it."

"I'll talk to you later," Mom said.

"You don't have to." Casey's heart paused, and she stared at Dad. He said, "You can annul a marriage until her next birthday, when she can marry anyone she wants. And if Casey doesn't think Paul hurt her, you can't arrest him. And sure as hell, I won't let my daughter be sent *anywhere*. So we're kind of stuck, aren't we?"

The kitchen seemed to tingle, and Casey could hear the buzz of the fluorescent light. Mom was shaking her head slowly. "Are you out of your mind?'

"No. I'm just tired. I've been getting angina pains again. I want the nonsense stopped."

"Then tell your daughter—"

"No." He shook his head to cut off her words. "I'm not

telling her anything. I'm sick to my heart that she's done this. I'd like to find that piece of scum and run him over. I'm going to pray to God, every night of my life, that she gets away from him. But I'm through punishing her. As far as I'm concerned, she's not grounded, and she's not restricted, and she's not under guard. Whatever happens to Casey is her responsibility."

Casey shredded a napkin in her lap. She felt like a little girl having a bad dream.

Mom seemed to shrink in her chair. Unexpectedly, her eyes glistened and two wet streaks ran down her face. "She's throwing her life away," Mom said brokenly. "She's wasting it..."

"I agree," Dad said. "But I'm tired of fighting her. We did our part. She's not ours anymore." He looked at Casey now, and she bowed her head. "Look at me, Casey."

She forced her head up, but his eyes uprooted her. He said, "Casey, I think this is the most boneheaded thing you've ever done. I think you're going to be so badly hurt that you'll be scarred for the rest of your life. But I can't figure out what makes you hate yourself. I hope you'll be happy with Paul. Maybe he'll straighten out."

Casey had to choke out her words. "Daddy, I want you to come to our wedding."

He looked so far away. "I don't know if I'll be able to do that. But it doesn't matter."

"Yes, it does," she said, crying. "It does matter."

"No. *You* matter, to me. But if you're going to cut off your parents and your friends and your own good brain, then you're going to be all alone. I hope Paul gives you everything you want and need. He's made you believe you don't need anybody else. He's made you believe it's okay for you to be abused. If you believe that, there's nothing I can say that will make any sense. That's fine. But don't ask me to come and watch you commit suicide."

Casey sobbed. JoAnne was sitting very tiny and quiet, clutching her crust of garlic bread.

Mom said, "So what are we doing, Ron?"

"Nothing," he said quietly. "Casey is engaged. She's begun her own life."

Casey felt the room spin. She pushed back her chair and stood up. Through hot, blurred eyes, she looked at her parents. "Paul and I will last forever," she said defiantly. "And we'll do it by ourselves."

"I hope you do," Dad said. He cut and ate a piece of his veal, chewing with effort.

Casey tasted her tears and rubbed angrily at her cheeks. She turned and stormed out of the kitchen. Daddy's words burned deep, smoldering brands into her heart. But it was weird; he'd torn her to pieces and she felt so strong. Suddenly, other words lit up in her mind. Faye's words. Mr. Young's words. Glenn's words. She was confused and shaken, so she put on the loudest rock album she could find and threw herself onto her bed as the music hammered her skull.

Chapter Eighteen

FOR THE MOMENT, NORTHVILLE HIGH SCHOOL WAS AGLOW with fall sunlight, but thick clouds glowered on the horizon. In the student parking lot waited the BMWs, Mercedeses and Corvettes that belonged to the Northville kids. Today, they were parked next to the Chevys and Fords from Westfield.

Casey sat on the bench, in her sweats, and clapped her hands together. Other girls from the team screamed support as the four-hundred-meter race pounded past them. Casey listened to the thud of sneakers on the track and the huff of breath on the air. Mr. Young stood near the track, screaming his throat out.

The kids and parents in the stands yelled and Casey could feel the noise in her stomach. Janie Barker, from Westfield, was pulling up on a Northville girl. Those Northville girls ran gracefully, with long, pistoning legs. It was like they all took hormones or something. But Janie was catching up, and Casey felt excitement in her throat.

"Yeah!" she screamed. "Go! Go!" She leaped up and punched her fist in the air.

The whole field shook with screaming now, as six girls

closed in on the tape. A Northville girl threw back her head and her sneakers seemed to leave the ground. Janie pumped her arms. Mr. Young was practically on the track, urging Janie to win.

But it was obvious that Janie wouldn't make it. There was one moment in a race when you could make your move and a miracle could happen. The moment was gone. Northville put empty space between her and Janie, and the Northville crowd bellowed with joy as their girl windmilled through the tape and thrust her arms high in a two-fisted salute.

Janie stumbled to a walk, and Mr. Young grabbed her around her shoulders and walked with her, talking low. The other girls straggled over the finish line. "This sucks," the girl next to Casey said.

"I know." Casey looked with anger at the Northville bench, where the girls were hugging and high-fiving each other.

Casey caught herself getting emotional over the meet. It surprised her. She'd avoided thinking about it all day in school. But the girls sang songs on the bus, and gossiped, and the sun was hot through the bus windows. It all brought back the feeling.

The girls were stretching out now for the next heat of the four hundred meters. Then came the hurdles. Casey had asked Mr. Young on the bus if she was running the event, and he said, "There ain't nobody else."

She blew out a calming breath and leaned over on the bench. Her thighs ached and her knee creaked where the cut had healed. Her rib had knitted pretty well, and she'd done her morning run the last three days. She tried to probe her joints and muscles mentally. The air was becoming wetter, and that made her aches worse.

Just as the girls took their places at the blocks, Casey saw Paul's Oldsmobile pull into the parking area. She was surprised to see him. He'd *never* come to watch her run.

But she was also scared. And to her surprise, she was angry. She didn't want to give up her time with the girls on the team.

He got out of the car and looked for her. He wore his sunglasses and a leather bomber jacket and jeans. The gun went off, making Casey jump. All the girls on the bench were on their feet, edging toward the track and screaming. Casey sat alone, surrounded by nylon gym bags and folded coats.

For a moment, she huddled on the bench, hoping that he wouldn't see her. It was so weird how she cherished this stupid track meet. It was like a remnant of her old life, when her mom and dad still talked to her and she hung out with Faye and Heather and Glenn. If she just sat here on this bench and cheered her heart out, then she would be back in time, before Paul.

She remembered seeing him for the first time, carrying the fence section into her backyard. The whole fence was together now, and the pool was covered, and it was as if it had always been there. Paul, too. When would it stop hurting to be in love with him?

Angrily, she stood up and waved to attract his attention. Her ears still heard the thudding feet and the screaming, but she didn't look at the race. She walked briskly away from the bench, past spectators who hung around in little groups. Paul saw her and waved back.

A shadow swept across the earth and chilled the colors. She hurried to Paul and hugged him. She liked the smell of his jacket. He held her at arm's length, and she felt the pressure of his fingers in her arms.

"Hi," she said. "What brings *you* here?"

"I went to school to pick you up," he said. "I figured we'd drive down to the beach, walk on the dunes."

"That would've been great," she said.

"I waited fifteen minutes," he said. "Everybody came out of the building except you. Then I walked around the place for ten minutes."

A chill rippled through her, partly from the damp wind that had sprung up. "Well, I was here. I told you about the meet."

"Never."

"Yeah, I think I did, Paul."

"I don't remember it."

He dropped his hands and jammed them into the pockets of his jacket. She said, "Well, you never were very interested in my track meets."

He didn't answer. He took a crushed pack of Marlboros from his jacket and stuck one between his lips. His hidden eyes swept the field as he cupped his hands to light the cigarette. It took him a couple of matches. Casey turned to watch the small figures as they sprinted around the far turn. Clouds advanced across the sky, and only patches of blue showed.

Paul blew out smoke. "So let's go."

"Huh?"

He smiled. "To the beach."

She looked up at the sky. "Well, it might be kind of wet by the time we get out of here."

He bent his head and scuffed his boot toe on the concrete. "Casey, wake up. I meant *now*."

"I can't go now," she said. "I'm running next."

He sighed. "Boy, you get me tired."

Casey heard loud cheers, and spun. People were blocking her view and she couldn't tell what was happening. Mr. Young would be looking around for her. Mr. Young might also freak if he saw Paul, and Casey got scared at the idea of the two of them fighting.

"Paul, don't pull a scene now," she said. "You *know* I can't leave the meet."

"Why not?"

"Because I'm on the *team*. And I've got to get back for my race. Why don't you watch me?"

Paul dropped the cigarette and ground it out with his heel. "I didn't drive here to watch you run races."

"Paul, don't do this."

"I need you," he said.

"I can't walk out on them."

"Then you walk out on *me*."

"No." Her anger pumped her full of energy. "It's not that simple. You always make it a choice."

Mr. Young's voice sailed through the air like a grappling hook and caught Casey's back. *"CASEY!! Let's GO!"*

Casey felt like a car was dragging her along a road. "I have to run, Paul."

He looked at her with a frozen expression. "If I walked away now, you'd stay here?"

"I have to, Paul."

He scratched the side of his mouth. "What about after the meet? You going out with the girls?"

Her heart leaped. "No! I mean, not if you want me to go with *you*."

He nodded. "I'll hang out. We'll go for dinner later."

She felt breathless. She grabbed him and pressed her mouth against his in a grateful kiss. She felt him stiffen and not give it back.

She folded her hands over his shoulders. "I love you."

Mr. Young yelled again. *"CASEY!"*

She stood on tiptoe and kissed him again, then turned and ran with long strides back to the team bench. The girls milled around and stared at her with open disgust. Mr. Young held his clipboard and his mouth was a thin line.

"Sorry," she panted. "How'd our girls do?"

"Dolores won," another girl said coldly.

Casey noticed Dolores on the bench, head between her legs. "Way to go, Dot!"

Dolores didn't look up. Casey could feel the deep freeze. She stripped off her sweat pants and folded them over her gym bag, then took off her top. Mr. Young said,

"We're ten points behind. We need the hurdles. How do you feel?"

"Good," Casey said.

"Stretch out," he said. "I'll stall them."

Casey nodded. She looked around at the other girls, red-faced. "My idiot fiancé," she said. She stretched out one leg and bent gracefully over it, sliding her fingertips to the ankle. "I tell him I've got to run and he keeps yakking."

Nobody said anything. Blow away, she thought viciously. She stretched the other leg, then jogged in place. She walked through the raw air to the starting line. The official looked at her like she was a toad. She drew a Popsicle stick from his clenched hand and saw that she had the outside position. Her heart sank.

Mr. Young was waiting as she walked to the blocks. He grabbed her around the shoulders. "Don't think about anything but running," he said in a low voice. "You've got the talent to take her."

He squeezed her and let her go. Shivering, Casey knelt by the blocks and glanced sidelong at Northville. She was a slim blonde, not taller than Casey, but richer. You could see by her expensive haircut and her all-over tan. She locked stares with Casey for a moment. Northville's eyes were green and gem-cold. She looked away, with a smirk.

Casey stared ahead, down the black ribbon of track, at the first hurdles. The sky moved overhead, masses of clouds thickening and seething. The wind smelled of rain. Casey ducked her head and flexed. She wondered if Paul was going to watch her or just get a beer and come back. She shuddered from their encounter. She had been sure he was going to hit her right there.

The gun cracked. Casey got a good jump. She glimpsed Northville ahead of her; the satiny red of her top and shorts seemed even brighter under the gray sky. Casey pulled together her concentration and felt her legs moving smoothly. Her sneakers hit hard, sending shocks up her calves. Her lungs burned too soon and she felt perspiration break out on her back.

She ran past the stands, glimpsing open mouths, waving arms, coats, and banners. Then she was out in the open, hearing only the wind rushing past her ears. The first hurdles seemed to race toward her like an oncoming train. Out of the side of her eye, she saw Northville leap. She kept her eyes on the hurdle, bunched her muscles, and pushed off.

Good timing! She landed on her toes, dug, and kept moving. Her form felt terrific, better than ever. But her body was hurting. Suddenly, her cracked rib sizzled with fire, and her groin stabbed her. Breath rasped in her throat. She knew she was out of condition. So did Mr. Young. And he let her run anyway, in a race that meant everything for Westfield. He should have scratched her. What was so important to prove that he had to risk the whole season?

Casey leaned into the first turn, glancing at a leafy wall of brown and yellow woods. It looked dreary and sad under the clouds. But there was a break in the clouds farther down the track. Casey drank in the colors and the smell of her own sweat and the rhythmic thunder of her sneakers. The next hurdles looked a million miles away.

She pumped her arms and thought about Daddy and how he'd whaled on Mom at the kitchen table. She thought of Faye and Heather, who'd wished her luck after she'd turned her back on them. She thought about the changes happening in her own head, that made her feel like she was shedding her skin.

Damn. Northville was way ahead, shrinking into the distance. Casey felt herself get mad. With her head banging, she ripsawed her legs, digging deeper. Every step shot a white-hot javelin into her hip. She moaned as she gasped for breath. She nearly tripped just ahead of the next hurdle, and cleared it by an inch.

She stumbled, and screamed as fire circled her knee. She was around the second turn, all by herself. She ran in her own wind, on her own track. She ran under the break in the clouds and, suddenly, warm pink light flooded her and the sky sang. She couldn't hear her sneakers anymore. She'd run right through her endurance level, into a trance state that numbed her muscles. She felt her arms pump, and she threw her head back, and tears of exhaustion blurred her vision.

She saw Glenn and Faye as if they stood by the track watching her. She saw Glenn charging Paul at the dance, getting hit, and doubling over. She remembered walking with Glenn by her house and Glenn telling her that he loved her. She felt his hands on her shoulders and looked into his clear eyes.

Casey ran through the tunnel of numbness and out again, as her reveries were sheared off by the wind. Agony enveloped her body; fires burned everywhere. The last hurdle was just ahead, but Northville was gone. Casey was running the race alone. Her solo. Her swan song. But she pounded down the track and she scissored her legs and she leaped. She felt her foot knock over the hurdle, but she came down cleanly and grunted at the shock.

She heard the crowd now. She saw Northville, already punching the sky with her fists. Northville tossed back her golden blonde head and her red tank top rippled like a flag. Her flawless bronze legs slowed to a balletic trot as she broke the tape. She seemed to be prancing in slow motion.

Casey could almost see herself gasping and staggering. She could see the purplish blotches on her legs that always came out when she ran in cold weather. She felt ugly and humiliated as she saw the Westfield bench waiting. There were no girls clustered at the finish line to catch her and hug her. The girls sat glumly. Dolores slammed a towel viciously on the bench. Janie turned away.

Casey couldn't feel her legs moving as she ran the last few feet. Mr. Young stopped to her and she collapsed into his arms. He enfolded her, and she shivered in his embrace.

"You're bleeding again," he said. "Come on and sit down."

She sucked in deep breaths, fighting nausea. She looked at the ground, vaguely hearing the applause and the voices. A car sped by somewhere. She felt cold splashes of rain on her cheeks. Mr. Young practically carried her to the bench and guided her to lie down. She braced herself with her hands and stretched out her legs. She saw the trickle of bright blood down her left calf.

The bench was empty. Some girls were getting ready for the next event. Others shoved stuff into their bags. Mr. Young sat next to Casey. "Get your sweats on," he said. "You'll catch a chill."

"I'm sorry," Casey said.

"I'm sure you are."

"I tried my best."

"It wasn't very impressive."

She looked at him, feeling her eyes mist. Exhaustion stripped away her control. She could feel her chest heaving and her shoulders quaking. "What do you want? I couldn't run any faster."

"You could run faster two months ago. You let yourself fall apart."

"So why did you let me run? Why didn't you scratch me?"

"Because you're a member of the team and this is your best event." His voice softened. "And I couldn't be sure what you had inside. I had to gamble on that."

She lifted her sweat top from her bag and draped it

across her lap. "Okay. I had nothing inside. So bounce me."

"No, I won't bounce you. Not for one time. But I'll cut you the next time you do this."

Casey ached with losing, and she stung with the rejection of her teammates. "Look, Mr. Young. I know you want to help me and all, but forget it, okay? I just want to be left alone."

The rain quickened. It was a slicing, chilly rain that pattered on the bench. Mr. Young pushed back his sparse hair and looked quietly at her. Casey had to turn away. The silence seemed to last for a year. Then Mr. Young put his arm around her damp shoulder and pinched her neck affectionately.

"You *don't* want to be left alone," he said. "That's what got you into this mess."

She didn't answer, but she knew he was right.

He took his arm away and sat very still, his hands in his lap. He looked funny in the rain. He was in such great shape, but he looked old. "I was going to be on the Olympic track team," he said. "Back in—" He drew his fingertips over his lips to garble the year and Casey smiled. "Then I got bursitis of the hip." He laughed ruefully. "So I ran in the middle-aged male division of the Empire Games. A profile in courage."

She touched his sleeve, suddenly filled with affection for him. "It *is* courageous."

He shrugged. "No. Just stupid. The pain was so bad I used to faint after a race. But I needed to be a hero."

"There's nothing wrong with that," Casey said.

"It was childish. And I stopped doing it. I run in easier races now, for fun." He stood up, grimacing, and looked balefully at the soggy field. "My wife divorced me a year ago, mostly because I was so involved with my students. She couldn't understand why I preferred to be with a bunch of teenagers rather than be with my family."

"It sounds crazy to me, too," Casey said.

He smiled. "I couldn't explain it. She wanted me to get more jobs, not waste my time coaching girls. Now she's gone. And so is my son, Robbie." He was remembering for himself now, not for her. "You know, I love that kid. He's got some missing teeth, and big blue eyes, and he hugs you with so much love that you just get warm all over...."

He stopped talking. Casey stood up, hissing at the sharp fires in her legs. "Mr. Young, you don't have to talk about this—"

"Yes, I do." He turned to her. "I don't deserve to lose my son, or my legs. You don't deserve to be misunderstood by your parents. We sometimes get what we don't deserve. But it's not our fault. We don't suffer for our sins. Does that make sense?"

"Yeah," she said.

"And hurting yourself is no way to get back at people. Not your parents or your friends or anybody. They won't change for you."

"I know."

"I didn't mean to get into this," he said. "But I'm out of things to say. Somewhere, you figured out that if you hurt enough, you'd earn the right to be happy. And somewhere you figured that you were out there all alone, and nobody knew you, except Paul. You're wrong, Casey. People love you. They don't tell you everything you want to hear, like Paul does, but they love you. Just *see* it. I swore I wouldn't lecture, but I'm losing you and I don't want to lose anybody else in my life."

She felt like she'd swallowed a baseball. "Thanks."

His voice shook with emotion. "You *matter*, Casey. I don't care if nobody on Long Island feels like talking to you. I don't care if you screw up a hundred races. You don't deserve to hurt."

He stopped because it was raining harder. Casey felt the rain slide over her bare shoulders and down her aching legs. "Okay."

He scratched his ear and blinked away raindrops. "Well, good luck to you and Paul."

She impulsively hugged him. His strong arms wrapped around her and held her tightly. She could feel his warmth and his love, and she knew they were real. And Daddy's. And Faye's. And Glenn's. All this time.

"You're terrific," he whispered.

"You, too."

He broke the embrace and his fingers touched her neck. "Get the sweats on, and get on the bus to warm up."

"I can't go home on that bus. They'll throw things at me."

"So duck."

She smiled and he ruffled her wet hair. "Thanks again," she said. Then she remembered. "Oh."

"What?"

"I *really* can't go home on the bus. Paul's waiting for me."

Realizing that she might be wrong, she scanned the area and saw his car, glittering with rain beads. Mr. Young followed her gaze and then looked back at Casey. "He's not your legal guardian. I can't let you go with him."

"He's my fiancé."

"Sorry. Tell him it's my fault. Or I'll tell him."

She shook her head, frightened. "I'll tell him."

Mr. Young lifted her chin with his forefinger. "It's okay to tell him that. It's something he has to accept. You shouldn't be afraid."

She flushed. "I'm not afraid."

"Okay. I have to get back to the action."

She nodded, feeling very much like a small girl. She remembered falling in the playground in third grade and Mrs. Grant picking her up and brushing the gravel from the bleeding scrape on her knee. She remembered crying and feeling stupid and just wanting to be hugged, but Mrs. Grant had kept yelling at her for being a klutz.

Mr. Young walked away, and Casey shivered in the rain. She took a deep breath, heavy-hearted over the lost meet, and started to limp toward the parking area. Yeah, she was scared to death of telling Paul he couldn't take her now. And so glad she was riding the bus.

Chapter Nineteen

AS SHE LOOKED AT THE DIZZYING VISTA THROUGH THE windshield of Paul's Oldsmobile, Casey had the weird feeling that she was waiting for a movie to begin. She blinked as the wavering, winking lights made her eyes tear.

Paul sat behind the steering wheel and tipped a bottle of beer to his lips. Casey's nose flinched at the sour smell. Her veal parmigiana hero lay in her stomach, and her tongue still tingled from the burning red sauce.

She was still scared and didn't know why. Paul had said, "No sweat," when she had to ride the bus. He'd bought her dinner at Little Tony's and now they were up here on the promontory, because this was where you went with your boyfriend. So why did the car feel like a coffin?

"It's so beautiful here," she said. "It's like being in a starship."

Paul said, "I'm givin' it everything I *can*, Captain."

Casey laughed and hugged herself to chase the raw coldness of the night. From up here on the promontory, she could see the whole north shore of the island, like a reflected black sky filled with its own stars. She could hear the wind rattle the car doors and see the frosty haze that rimmed the windows.

"Thanks for supper," she said.

"Took me all day to cook it."

She smiled and looped her hand around his leather sleeve. The fear was still hanging on, like when he came to the meet. And that sadness she'd felt at the duck pond. "Remember our first dinner out?"

"Sure."

His profile looked like a crescent moon. "Yeah? Where did we eat?"

"Clams Unlimited."

"I don't believe it. You remembered."

"Gotcha."

She shifted toward him, leaning against his shoulder. She had seen other cars, and a couple of vans, parked against the low railing. Casey thought about the couples in those cars. Some of them were probably just making out, without any feeling. And maybe some of them were looking at the lights and making promises of forever.

She'd never feel that way. Even if Paul gave her a million giant Paddingtons and a million gold charms and did funny, crazy things every day. She realized this with sudden, shocking clarity.

"Boy," she said, "you embarrassed me that day."

"What day?"

"When you took me to Clams Unlimited. The way you came into the backyard and tried to bull my dad."

"Worked."

"Only because Mom decided to be Mrs. Understanding Parent, and she only did it because it got Dad to freak. Otherwise you would have been history."

He finished the beer, then cracked the bottle down on the dashboard. "Well, we all wind up history anyway."

"Very philosophical." Her body hurt. Running the hurdles had taken all the gas out of her. She thought about losing the meet and her chest tightened. The girls on the bus had given her the silent treatment. Back at Westfield, in the cold rain, she'd listened to them all making plans to go out to Chi Chi's. Then they were all gone, as parents drove them off. Casey had waited by herself because Mr. Young had to go to a meeting. She'd stood just inside the doors, watching the cars come down the road, until Paul finally pulled up.

Now he tapped a nervous rhythm on the steering wheel. "If I started the car now," he said, "we'd go right over."

"Cheery thought."

"Would you go with me, Casey? Double suicide."

"Could we stop talking about it?"

He shrugged and kept tapping.

"You're nervous tonight," she said.

"Got a lot on my mind."

"Like what?"

He scratched the tip of his nose. "Like no job. I have to bring in some bucks or Joey and Diane are going to freeze this winter."

Casey remembered the VanHorn house with a shudder. Suddenly, she was embarrassed to think about them coming to her wedding. She felt guilty for her snobbery. "I feel bad for you," she said. "You've really had it rough."

"No sweat." He flicked on the radio. The music slammed into Casey's head like a truck. Paul sang along with the raucous words, shutting his eyes and imitating a hard-rock guitarist.

Casey tightened her lips and turned down the volume.

He stopped and looked at her. "What was that for?"

"It's too loud," she said. "I want to talk."

"Why?"

"Come on, Paul. Every time we get into a serious discussion about anything you pull an act."

"Oh, *wow*. This is going to be heavy guilt."

"No," she said. "But why can't we ever finish a conversation? I know you don't like to talk about your family, but you can't just act crazy all the time."

He gave her a leering smile. "*You* make me crazy, baby."

"Terrific." She shook her head and stared through the fogged windshield.

He slid his arm around her shoulders and yanked her against him. She yielded and snuggled. He used his index finger to turn her chin and she parted her lips for his kiss. She tasted the beer he'd drunk.

"We have a lot of stuff to talk about," she said into his chest.

"Like what?"

"Like a wedding date, and where we're getting married, and where we're going to live." And why did saying it make her feel strangled? "Man, I haven't even finished my college applications yet."

His fingers toyed with her hair. "Screw college."

"Yeah, I know, you keep telling me that. So then I have no degree and I can't get a decent job."

"I'll work."

"You won't go to college either."

He blew out a breath and leaned back in his seat. "Get off my back, Casey."

"Sorry." She sat up, too. The lights of a car glided across the side windows, making her squint. The Olds kept getting colder and colder.

He reached out and started turning the dial. Casey listened to snatches of songs and static. He turned off the radio with a snap and began to bang on the steering wheel with both hands. "Let's do something."

"What?"

"I don't know. I'm going nuts sitting here."

"So? What do you want to do?"

"Let's just drive somewhere."

"Where?"

"*Anywhere.*" He brought his fist down on the horn. The blare of it made Casey shudder.

"Cut it out," she said.

He kept doing it. Casey's insides bunched. Then he stopped and covered his eyes with his hands. Finally, he looked at her again. "How about if we drive down to Atlantic City?"

"Now?"

"Yeah. Check into a hotel. You've got a credit card, right?"

She didn't know if he was serious. "My mom's Visa card. I used it to buy some pants."

"Great. Let's do it. Hit the slots, play some blackjack, watch a show. What the hell?"

The wind banged the doors, as if trying to get in. "I don't think so, Paul."

"Why not? You said your parents don't care what you do anymore. Let's just drive and have fun and flip out."

"Paul, I can't go to Atlantic City tonight. And anyway, they'd never let us into a hotel."

"Sure they would. You think they care?"

"It's crazy."

"*This* is crazy. Sitting here is crazy. What do you want to do, Casey? Just keep going to school and having pizza? I've had it, man."

She could feel his agitation. "I don't know what to say to you, Paul."

"You never know. You just whine."

"I don't whine."

"Yeah, you whine."

He slumped in his seat, his knees pressing the steering wheel. Casey felt an uncontrollable anger grow in her throat. "Well, maybe if you'd have a normal conversation sometimes, I wouldn't whine."

"Get lost."

"Oh, sure. I won't play games with you, so now you turn me off."

Paul hummed to himself. He casually dug a cigarette from his jacket pocket and lit it. Soon the frosty car filled with rank smoke.

"Are you planning to ignore me for the rest of the night?" she asked.

"Leave me alone."

Casey faced the windshield, so tightly wound she felt as if she would fly away into the night. "I really bother you, right? You don't care about my running, you don't care about our plans, you don't care about anything. Paul, when we started, you made me feel special. You made me feel like I was the most important person in your life. Now I feel like dirt."

He inhaled tightly and released the smoke in a flat cloud. "Jesus, you're a nag."

"Go to hell," she said. She sat shaking, wishing she could get out of the car. Just like the first time he hit her.

He sat up straight again and turned on the radio. He twisted the dial until it came to a soft music station. The sweet strings and muted horns soothed Casey's hot skin. Paul caressed her knee with his left hand. "You like that?"

She kept facing the windshield, fixating on the distant lights. "Yes."

He leaned close to her and kissed her cheek, then flicked the tip of his tongue into the rim of her ear. "How about that?"

"Cut it out, huh?"

"That's romantic."

"Yeah. Wonderful."

He snuggled to her and nuzzled her neck. His stubble rasped her skin. "I'm trying to make you happy, Case."

"Forget it."

"Come on," he purred. He slid his arm around her, still holding the cigarette in his hand, so that the smoke curled past her face. "Tell me what you need."

"You don't want to hear it."

"Sure I do."

She took a deep breath and inhaled some of the smoke. Her chest felt like rocks. "You said you needed me. You said I was the only one who'd ever helped you. I bought that. Every time you hit me, you say you're sorry and ask me to stay. And it's always great for a while, and then you go nuts again."

"How am I going nuts?"

"Come on."

"No, tell me."

His smell was strong in her nose. She was shivering. "You're playing mind games again. You love to do that."

"I'm asking a question. What's the big deal?"

"The big deal is what's happening with us." Her eyes began to water as she gave in to her misery. She longed to be with Glenn, or Faye.

He kissed her chin and pulled her close. "You want to break up?"

"No," she said.

"That's what it sounded like."

"I didn't mean it that way."

"Tired of me?"

"*No.*"

"Still crazy about me?"

She began to cry silently. "Yes."

"So let's drive to Atlantic City."

"Give it up, huh?"

He crowded her now, trapping her against him. Her face was against his jawbone. The saccharine music began to irritate her. He said, "Come on, Case. Cut loose."

"I can't."

"You mean you don't want to, right?"

"No," she said.

"Still want to be a high-school girl. Still want your gang. You want to get rid of me, don't you?"

"I said I didn't."

"What you *said* is a load of crap. You want out."

She felt her veal heave and turn. Yes. Yes, she wanted out. He was wearing off. Like in *The Temple of Doom* when Indy Jones snapped out of his trance. "No I don't."

"No?"

"No."

"Still want to marry me?"

"You know I do."

"Let's drive to Atlantic City."

She tried to push him away, but his right arm still snaked around her shoulder, and he still held her hard. "No."

"Then you want out."

"Don't be stupid."

"You want out?"

"*No*, for Christ's sake!"

"Let's drive to Atlantic City."

She tried to look straight at the windshield. "You jerk."

"Are we going?"

"I can't go."

He seized her jaw between the fingers of his left hand. "Are we *going*?"

She looked at his eyes now and saw something red and dark and crazy. She tried to shake her head. Not again. Please God, not again.

"Say yes, baby."

She couldn't make anything move. She felt cold all over. The radio was playing a dippy version of "Yesterday."

He forced her face to move up and down once. "That's better," he said. "What hotel would you like? Trump Castle? Playboy? You call it. It's your night."

He released her chin. She said, "Could you drive me home, Paul?"

He looked at her almost lovingly. "You don't want to go, huh?"

She kept her hands on her thighs, very still. "No."

"I waited for you to run your asshole race. Then you said you couldn't go home with me. But I picked you up anyway. You're ungrateful, you know?"

"I'm sorry."

"And you're a whining creep, right?"

She nodded.

"And you're still a slut, right?"

"If you say so."

"Not if I say so. For real. Right?"

She felt sick to her stomach. "Yeah. Right."

"But I stick because I'm true to my lady. Only you're not true."

"Paul, please take me home."

He pushed back her hair. "You don't tell me where we go. I say where we go."

"Paul, come on."

He sang. "On the boardwalk at Atlantic City..."

"Shut up!"

There was a stunning silence, filled by the wind and the velvety voice of the announcer doing a commercial. Casey's heart banged. Paul's left hand struck like a rattler, pinning her against the seat. "Don't tell me to shut up," he hissed. "Never."

"Okay," she said.

Casey only barely saw, out of the corner of her eye, the movement of Paul's right hand. Then she felt a small circle of heat on her cheek. For an instant, she couldn't make sense of it. Then the heat made a black hole in her face, and she knew it was his cigarette.

She writhed. "You asshole! Get away from me!"

His left hand covered her rigid mouth. "You got the idea?" he said.

She couldn't even nod.

"We're driving to Atlantic City, right?"

She felt her eyes dart back and forth like trapped sparrows. Her ears rang. How could she get in touch with her mom and dad? She envisioned escaping at a rest stop, running into a gift shop, and begging someone to call the police.

"Ready to go?" he asked.

Her eyes tried to calm him.

"Nope," he said. "Not yet."

She shut her eyes in terrible anticipation and the heat

came again, near her eye. She screamed into his gagging hand.

He stopped again. Sweat dampened her body beneath her clothes. She looked at his face and hated him with all of her soul.

"Ready now?" he said.

Her bones seemed to crack under the pressure of his suffocating body. Her cheek trembled.

He shook his head. "You learn hard, Casey. Man, you are so stupid."

Awareness flooded her. The radio played "Rocky Mountain High." There was a small rip in the vinyl upholstery just over his left shoulder. The willowy profile of the beer bottle gleamed on the dashboard. And she was running again, leaping the hurdles, and this time she had to win. It meant everything, because she knew Faye and Glenn and Daddy and Mr. Young were bunched at the finish line, reaching for her.

Casey sensed his right hand as it moved. The wind rushed into her head, down her throat, into her hands. She swatted upward and felt the heel of her palm strike his wrist.

"Damn!" he said. He jerked back the hand. The cigarette was gone. Casey tried to look down to find it, but Paul twisted her head back. "You're crazy. You're really crazy."

He lifted his left hand from her mouth. For less than a second, relief flooded her. The absence of the burning cigarette and the rush of air into her lungs made her want to laugh. Then he smashed her face with his open hand.

"I'll kill you," he said, or at least she thought he said. Then he began to curse her, in a rhythmic string of filth. He cracked her jaw again. She heard his breath wheeze. She smelled the leather of his jacket.

"*No!*" she said. She tried to intercept his hands. They eluded her. He slapped her ear. She saw his face, hanging like a dark balloon. She made a tight fist and, with all of her strength, she hit the balloon.

Fire raced through her hand. He jerked back, astonished. She said, "Stop hitting me, damn it!"

He threw her against the seat. She punched him in the chest. He began to curse her again, but this time he screamed the words. He grabbed her jacket with both hands and shook her. She tried to grab his neck. He threw her against the door of the car. She hit his face again, this time connecting with the side of his nose.

Then he began to hit her all over, not even aiming. Casey threw her hands around, unable to find him. But she wanted to hit him more. She wanted to keep hitting him, over and over and over. Her eyes rolled back and she saw the ceiling of the car with its stained fabric. Her head banged against the side window. She couldn't feel him hitting her anymore. The last sound she heard was the syrupy announcer talking about the weather.

Owen Young was in his apartment, watching *Return of the Jedi* on the VCR and eating Milk Duds, when his phone rang. It was Jack Logan, the building principal of Westfield High, saying that Casey Gordon had been taken to the hospital in critical condition.

Owen turned off his VCR, rinsed his mouth of chocolate and caramel, put on his shoes and Westfield jacket, and drove to the hospital. In the hospital waiting room, he scanned the tired-looking people on the green and yellow couches.

He went to the admitting window. In the office beyond, women were typing, filing, and drinking coffee. The silver-haired woman behind the window said, "Yes?"

"Casey Gordon," Owen said tautly. "Seventeen-year-old girl, admitted after a beating?"

"Are you her father?"

Odd question, he thought. "No. I'm her track coach."

The woman seemed puzzled. "Oh. Apparently they can't find her father and they told me to watch for him."

"Can I see her?"

"I don't think so," the woman said. She had a fussy voice and demeanor. She checked some records, but Owen couldn't see over the high Formica counter. "I can tell you that she's in serious but stable condition."

"Not critical?"

The woman looked again. "No. It *was* critical but now it's serious but stable."

Owen felt a small rush of joy. "Atta girl, Casey," he said.

"What?"

"Nothing. Any way I can see her?"

"No, you can't. Only family."

"Can I see her doctor?"

The woman sighed. "I don't think so."

"Who *is* her doctor?"

Another sigh, angrier this time. "Doctor Cohen. But he's not on regular duty now. He came in just to see Miss Gordon, but he's probably gone home."

"I'm an EMT. I know Doctor Rau in the ER. I just want some information."

The fussy woman seemed unimpressed by his name-dropping. "I'll call and find out for you."

"Thanks."

Owen turned from the window and jammed his hands into his jacket pockets. He felt empty and frustrated. What a savior he was. Rescuing Casey Gordon because he was so pure and selfless. Bull. He was lonely and bitter and he wanted Casey to need him, just as Paul VanHorn wanted Casey to need *him*. Owen and Paul, both users, both abusers.

No. He stopped himself. He *had* been selfish, but not anymore. He'd honestly loved her, for the first time, after she lost the race. And Casey would never know he was here tonight. He'd come because he was crazy about her, not for stroking, and maybe that meant he'd rescued himself.

Again, he scanned the waiting room. He dreaded sitting among the old magazines with the black night like paint against the windows. The door swung open and a teenaged girl came in. She was thin and had curly hair. She looked really distraught, and her eyes swept the waiting room. Owen thought he recognized her.

He moved through the waiting room and the girl caught his eye. "You're Mr. Young, aren't you?"

"Right. Who are you?"

She worked to calm herself. She wore a red coat over sweats. Obviously, she'd been relaxing at home, too. "Faye Pollack. I'm Casey's friend."

He nodded. "She's mentioned you. How did you find out Casey was here?"

"Glenn Lindstrom called me up. His dad is a volunteer fireman, and he heard it on the emergency band."

"Oh, great," Owen said sourly. "That's the last kid we needed to find out."

"I know," Faye said. "He sounded bad."

Owen exhaled wearily. "I hope he doesn't go nuts."

Faye adjusted her pocketbook strap, which bit into her shoulder. "He said the police were looking for Paul VanHorn."

"Good," Owen said. "Let's hope they get him first."

Faye smiled fleetingly, then looked with anxious eyes at him. "How is she?"

Owen shrugged. "Serious but stable, upgraded from critical."

"Oh, no." Faye said the words as a whisper. Her eyes filled, and she began to tremble. She'd been holding back her emotion.

Owen grabbed her shoulders. "Serious but stable is okay. Casey's going to be fine."

Faye nodded, then shook her head. "What an idiot."

"I agree." He thought a moment, then said, "Your folks know you're here?"

"Yeah. I have my own car. I was supposed to come with Heather but she couldn't get out." Faye looked at him sheepishly. "I guess I'm illegal, then."

"Not if you're not alone. How about a cup of bad hospital coffee, and then we'll figure out what's best to do?"

Gratefully, Faye said, "Thanks."

Owen threw his arm around her shoulder. "Casey's got good friends."

"Stupid friends," Faye said.

"Well, good friends have to be stupid sometimes. Come on. I'll buy you some cake, too."

"This could be the start of a beautiful friendship," Faye said.

Owen laughed softly and gestured toward the small cafeteria. He followed Faye as the distant wail of an ambulance siren gave a mournful air to the waiting room.

Chapter Twenty

CASEY HELD COURT IN THE SOLARIUM ON THE THIRD floor of the hospital. She wore a hot-pink robe over a soft pink nightgown, and she sat in a vinyl chair facing the big windows. Faye balanced on the arm of the chair, and Heather and Lillian flanked her.

"So anyway," Casey said through puffy lips, "they didn't have to take out my spleen."

"*Great*," Heather said. She perched on the radiator, and kept stretching out her leg and touching her toe with her arm.

"Yeah," Casey agreed. "So it's just my broken foot, and I have to get plastic surgery on my face. It must be pretty gross for you guys to look at me."

"It *is* pretty gross," Faye agreed.

Lillian said, "Nice."

Faye gave Lillian a look. "You *do* know I'm kidding."

Lillian said, "Maybe Casey is sensitive about it. What if the plastic surgery doesn't work and she's got to look like that forever?"

Faye bounced up and down as she laughed and Heather giggled through her fingers. Casey smiled but it hurt so much that she had to stop. Lillian blushed furiously.

Casey reached over and patted Lillian's knee. "I know what you're saying, Lil. Thanks."

Heather said, "How did you break your *foot*, anyway?"

Casey shrugged, and that hurt, too. "I think I was trying to kick him."

"Way to go," Heather said.

Casey smiled bravely. Sadness swept over her and she looked through the window. She saw black gravel on the second-floor roof just below, and the parking lot and Route 347 beyond. Somehow, the glistening lanes of cars and the bleached sunlight made her nostalgic. Dr. Cohen had warned her that she might suffer depression.

"So what did they do to you here?" Faye asked.

Casey took a breath. "Well, I don't remember being brought in. Paul threw me out of the car when I went unconscious. He was probably scared that I was dead."

"I wish you were," Heather said emotionally, "so he could fry."

Faye rewarded Heather with a long, withering look. Heather reddened. "Oh, God, I didn't mean that—"

"No problem," Casey said.

Heather covered her face with her hands. Lillian hissed in sudden pain. "What's wrong?" Faye asked.

Lillian shook her head and tightened her lips. She rubbed her knee with both hands. "It goes out on me when I sit too long."

Casey felt a wonderful warmth wash over her. For some reason, it was great to hear Lillian be a hypochondriac and to hear Heather act stupid. It was like waking up from a bad dream and realizing it wasn't true.

Faye stood up and walked to the window. "You were saying, Casey . . . ?"

Casey's mind drifted like a lullaby, and tiredness wound through her aching limbs. "The cops said that a guy in a van called the police on his CB. You realize I don't remember any of this. I mean, I was out."

Heather said, "Well, he almost killed you."

Casey nodded. "Yeah, that's what they say. They had to wash me out with ice water a few times because I was bleeding inside, and they had to do surgery where I was gashed open. Then there was the broken foot and the sprained wrist"—she held up her Ace-bandaged arm—"and my face, which was a mess."

The girls fell silent as they listened. Faye came back to her perch on Casey's chair and rubbed Casey's bathrobed leg.

"So what's the news?" Casey asked.

Faye gave a short laugh. "*You're* the news. Nobody's doing any work at all in school. They keep waiting for Logan to issue bulletins over the P.A."

"All *right*," Casey said. "What about Paul? Did they find him?"

Faye nodded. "The cops picked him up. Your folks filed charges against him so it's going to go to court."

"Good," Heather said.

Lillian looked doubtful as she massaged her knee. "I'd be worried."

Casey considered her feelings. "I am. I'm scared to see him again."

Faye asked, "Will you testify against him?"

The words dug deep and found a wellspring of terror and confusion in Casey's heart. She listened to the muffled clash of carts and the ringing of phones. "Yeah," she said finally. "I will."

Heather regarded Casey with awe. "You still love him?"

Casey said, "I don't know. I thought I did. I *wanted* to. But most of the time I was just afraid, or depressed. And the last month or so, I felt like I was kidnapped or something. Does that make sense?" Faye nodded. Casey added, "But it's crazy. I can feel myself wanting to go back with him."

"*No*," Heather cried.

Lillian said, "If you do that, you deserve what you get."

Faye's narrow face paled with anger. "Yeah, it's so easy

for all of you to tell her what to do. Maybe it's not that easy when you're going through it."

Her words stirred Casey. "Don't worry too much. Remember, I hit him back. I mean, I wanted to tear his face off. I never got that pissed at him before."

"Took you long enough," Faye said.

Casey looked at her. "I'm not proud of it. He needs help. I just screwed him up some more."

Faye said, "It's time to stop the crap, Casey. What he needs is a shrink, for about fifty years."

"Yeah, but look at his family—"

"Oh, give me a break." Faye played an imaginary violin. "Eddie's folks are divorced and he doesn't go around beating on girls. Stop making excuses for Paul. And stop making it your fault."

Casey tingled with the scolding. "But I really thought I'd reached him. I thought I could save him or something." She laughed. "Like the X-Men. Some X-Man I was."

"And that makes you a failure, right?" Faye said. "How come *he* isn't the failure? How come it wasn't up to him to reach *you*? Why is *he* the important one?"

Casey smiled. "Calm down, Faye."

"I can't calm down." Faye stood up and paced. "Where do we all learn this crap, huh? Got to please our boyfriends. I watch it in school. Some jerk walks down the hall and his girlfriend crawls after him, begging him to talk to her. Or some guy curses out his girlfriend in front of everybody because she dares to walk away from him. I'm sick of it. Most of those guys are morons. Let me tell you, Casey, you're smarter than Paul VanHorn, better looking than Paul VanHorn, and worth a lot more than Paul VanHorn. So quit worrying about what *you* did wrong. The only thing you did wrong was going back to him the first time he hit you."

She stood huffing by a window, and the room vibrated

with her fury. Heather said, "Boy, *I'm* through being a doormat for men, that's for sure."

Faye laughed. "Thanks, Heather," she said. "You're an inspiring example."

Lillian had a philosophical look in her eyes as she rubbed her knee. "Well, there are times when a girl has to be kept in line...."

Faye glared fiercely at Lillian. "Don't even start. I don't want to hear it."

Lillian rolled her eyes. "Okay, okay. Forget I even opened my mouth."

Casey enjoyed the byplay but Faye's words burned like coals inside her. Yes, she thought, you're right. But she'd been snowed by *Paul's* words, too. So what did that mean? That she was so insecure that *anybody* could make her a believer? She'd better watch out for cults.

"What about Glenn?" Casey asked. "Is he coming up?"

The girls looked at each other. Faye said, "Well, Glenn's in the hospital, too."

"What?"

Faye leaned against the window. "Not this one. He's at Seaside General. He went ape when he heard about you and he took off to find Paul."

Casey's throat clutched. "Paul hurt him?"

Faye shook her head. "Glenn never made it. He wrapped up his Trans Am and he's got a fractured tibia and a broken leg."

"Oh, no." Casey slumped, feeling all of her aches at once. "That idiot."

"Yup," Faye agreed. "We all came to the same conclusion."

Suddenly, the thought of Glenn lying in a hospital bed, bandaged from head to toe, was wildly funny. "What a klutz. He can't even get to the guy to fight him."

Casey got a chill thinking about Glenn. She ached to hug him. "Are my mom and dad here, too? I remember Mom sitting by my bed."

Again, the girls exchanged glances. Lillian grabbed Casey's wrist. "Casey, listen..."

Casey looked with terror at Lillian. "What's going on?"

Faye abruptly straightened up, her eyes looking behind Casey. "Whoops."

Casey tried to turn around but her neck hurt. She heard Mom say, "Girls, can I just have a minute or two?"

Faye nodded. "Sure, Mrs. G."

Heather jumped off the radiator and Lillian got up. The girls gathered around Casey and babbled their good-byes: "Okay, kid, take care..." "Get better..." "We love you, Case..." The overlapping words played like cool waterfalls in Casey's head. Faye held Casey's hand and met her eyes for a long time.

"Back in a while," Faye said. "You better expect a party when you get out of here."

"I expect an orgy," Casey said.

"No *way*," Heather said, shocked. "I don't believe you said that."

Faye grabbed Heather's hand. "Come on," she said. "Time to go."

The girls filed out of the solarium, Lillian half-limping behind them. Mom came around and sat down in the chair that Lillian had vacated. Mom wore almost no makeup and Casey could see the oldness of her skin. She had on a sweater and jeans, and her hair was hastily pulled back and clipped.

"Hi," Mom said. Her voice sounded husky.

"Hi."

The room grew suddenly silent, missing the chatter of all the girls. The closeness of the solarium began to stifle Casey, and gave her a headache.

"How do you feel?" Mom asked.

"Kind of stiff."

"If you need a painkiller, ask for it. They're supposed to give it to you."

Casey nodded. *This* was painful. Mom had never had a good bedside manner. "I'm okay."

"Well, you're not okay, but you're alive and that's a start." She hesitantly pushed back a loose strand of Casey's hair.

Casey said, "Where's Daddy?"

Mom sighed. "Now listen to what I tell you, and don't get scared—"

"Mom, what's going on? Where's Daddy?"

Mom twined her hands in her lap. "Your father went looking for Paul, after we got the call from the police. I tried to stop him, but I've never seen him like that before. Thank God we don't have any guns in the house."

"Where is he?"

"He's here, in the hospital, in the CCU."

"What?"

Mom nodded. "He had a mild heart attack while he was driving. Luckily, he was stopped for a light. The driver behind him banged into him, and when he got out he saw your father slumped over the wheel. Doctor Halperin says Daddy will probably need a bypass, but the prognosis is good."

Casey became intensely aware of the velvet of her robe and the satin lining against her wrists. She felt her eyes fill. "When can I see him?"

Mom looked a little ticked that Casey was so concerned. "Well, you're in no condition right now, but maybe tomorrow."

"No way. I'm not waiting until tomorrow."

Mom sighed. "Well, we'll see."

A heavy tiredness draped Casey like a blanket. The solarium seemed to hum with it. "Poor Daddy," she said. Then, despite her best efforts, a mischievous picture appeared in her mind, of Glenn and Daddy in adjoining beds. She began to giggle.

"What's wrong with you?" Mom asked.

Casey shook her head. She said, "We'll have to have a

meeting of my White Knights. They're not looking too good out there."

"Excuse me?"

"Nothing," Casey said, tucking the image away for her own enjoyment.

Mom looked down at her hands, rubbing a spot on her knuckle. "Casey, we're going to prosecute Paul."

"I know."

"I'd like your cooperation."

"Okay," she said.

Mom looked at her with some surprise. "Are you sure?"

"Yeah. He's got to get help."

"I was thinking more in terms of jail."

Casey smiled. "I don't hate him that much."

Mom took Casey's hands in hers. "Do you understand now, Casey, how wrong you were?"

The anger rose in Casey's throat. "I wasn't wrong. Maybe I was stupid, but I wasn't wrong."

"How can you be so stubborn after he almost killed you?"

"Because that's the way I am," she said. "I'm stubborn. And I'm not a genius. If you want to spend the rest of your life going nuts because I'm not what you want me to be, go ahead. There are some people around who think I'm okay the way I am."

She couldn't believe she was saying this. Mom's cheeks colored and she released Casey's hands. "Well. Is that your big declaration of adulthood?"

"It's not a big declaration of anything."

Mom stood up. "Casey, I know I don't do all the right things. I'm willing to go for counseling and try to get us to be a family again. I'd like you to meet me halfway."

"I'll try," she said, which was pretty honest.

"Do you want me to take you back to your room?"

Casey shook her head. "No. I want to just sit here for a while."

Mom looped her pocketbook strap around her shoulder. "I'm going to take JoAnne to her Brownie meeting and get her supper, and then I'll be back to see you and Daddy. Do you need anything from home?"

Casey thought a moment. "Could you bring my notebook? I want to write some stuff."

"How about homework? I've called your teachers for your assignments."

Casey smiled to herself. Good old Mom. "Not yet."

"Letting it pile up won't help."

"Mom, I said not yet, okay?"

Mom exhaled. "Whatever you say." She seemed to pause and reflect, then bent down and kissed Casey on the cheek. She held Casey's hand tightly for a moment. "I was worried about you, whether you believe that or not."

"Thanks," Casey said.

Mom squeezed her hand again, then briskly walked out of the solarium. Casey's fingers tingled. Her heart beat a little rapidly at the thought of Daddy almost dying. Poor Daddy, who'd cried over his milk and cookies. Daddy. Glenn. Faye. Mr. Young. Oh, man, she'd missed them while she was out in the cold.

Casey scrunched up in the chair. She felt relief at being free of Paul, and at the same time, she felt the terrible pull of his domination. He was waiting to hurt her again, and she didn't know if she could stay away. Shivering at her nightmare, she closed her swollen eyes and slept.

Casey caught Mr. Young at the edge of the track as he was stowing gear in his gym bag. The December sky stretched in smoky bands over the yellowed grass of the field. A raw wind rippled Casey's jacket and blew her hair.

Mr. Young looked up with a smile as she half ran, half limped up to him. "Take it easy," he said.

She stood, breathing hard, and he laughed at her attempt to talk and get air at once. She liked the mask of coldness on her nose and forehead. "Listen," she said. "You're going to kill me for this—"

"Never," he said.

She smiled. "Yeah, you will. But I have this one last application and you have to fill out a teacher sheet. I didn't even know it was in there until this morning. You're going to kill me, right?"

He nodded with a solemn look. "I think we'll nail you to the scoreboard." He reached out a cold-looking hand. "Let's have it."

"It's in my locker," she said. "I'll put it in your mailbox, okay?"

"Okay."

She grinned. "Thanks a million. You're terrific."

"I know," he said. "Sainthood is next."

She playfully swatted him. He grabbed her and pulled her close and she wrapped her arms around him and hugged him as tightly as she could. He released her and said, "How's the foot?"

"Great," she said. "No more cane."

"I see. Let's look at the face." He lifted her chin with a gentle forefinger and studied her. "Nice job."

"Yeah, the plastic surgeon says you won't even be able to see the scars after a while."

"Not the ones on your face, anyway."

She nodded. "I know. Thanks for letting me cry on your shoulder when I needed to."

"Any time," he said.

She shoved her hands in her jacket pockets. "You're the first person who ever made me feel like I was worth something."

He zipped his gym bag. "Be careful. You once said that about Paul."

"I know," she said ruefully.

"It's only going to work when *you* think you're worth something. You've got to love yourself first. And man, that is not easy." He smiled. "Meanwhile, I'd like you to stay alive so *I* can keep loving you."

She felt the stupid tears come. "Thanks," she said.

He wiped her cheek with his thumbtip and patted her shoulder. "My pleasure."

"I apologize for losing the Northville meet," she said impulsively.

"You *should* apologize. You let us down."

"Now I *really* feel guilty."

He looked tenderly at her. "Good. It's all right to feel guilty when you've done something careless or thoughtless. But remember that *you're* still okay."

She nodded. "Okay."

"Good." He picked up his gym bag, as the wind pushed pewter clouds across the sky. "How's your dad?"

"Fine. Came through the operation great. We're all going to go to Florida for Winter Recess."

"I'm jealous," Mr. Young said. He rubbed her arm. "See you later, Case."

"Okay. Thanks again, Mr. Young, for everything."

"No problem. You're what I'm here for." He hefted the gym bag and walked down the slope toward the parking lot. She yelled, "Mr. Young?"

He stopped and looked up the hill. "Hm?"

"Are *you* going to be okay? Maybe I can get my mom to have you over for the holidays."

He smiled, clearly moved. "I'll be fine. But thanks. You're a good friend."

"You, too," she said.

As Casey watched Mr. Young disappear into the building, a spidery chill raced down her back. She sensed the presence of someone else. She turned slowly and first saw only the deserted green stands and the scoreboard, stark against the sky like some modern Stonehenge.

Then she saw Paul, standing at the far end of the stands. She shivered violently. She knew he'd come back to see her, sooner or later. She was almost glad he was here now. Talking with Mr. Young made her feel ready.

Casey limped along the stands. Her leg ached fiercely. She felt the wind creep under her hair and redden her ears. Her heart pounded.

She stopped in front of him. He wore a denim jacket over a T-shirt. His hair was cut short. His face looked red and pinched.

"How are you doing?" he asked. He was shivering, the idiot.

"Okay."

"You look pretty good."

"Yeah. The doctors did a good job."

He was silent. His eyes looked defeated. All of her need and insecurity came rushing back. She wanted to hold him and listen to him tell her that the world sucked and that he cared.

"Sorry I didn't talk to you at court."

She shrugged. "It's okay."

The hearing had been private. Paul had a lawyer who wore a raincoat the whole time and smelled of cologne. The lawyer pointed out Paul's home life and had Paul plead no contest to hitting Casey. The judge told Paul he had to go for regular psychological counseling and that he had to stay away from Casey. The judge asked Casey if she wanted to keep pressing assault charges and go for damages. Casey's lawyer told Casey's mom it wouldn't be worth it, and her mom agreed. The whole time, Casey avoided Paul's eyes. He'd worn a suit that day and looked like a boy at his first dance.

"I got another job," he said.

"Great. Where?"

"Gas station on Route 25, near the mall. I'm training as a mechanic."

"Terrific."

More silence. Casey heard scraps of band music on the wind.

Paul sighed. "Well, I don't know what to say. I guess I used up all my turns at bat."

"I guess you did."

"I've really got a sickness. Man, doing that stuff to you and leaving you there"—he turned away, his mouth quivering. "I can't figure it out myself."

"Well, that's why you're getting help," she said.

She couldn't find any part of her insides that wasn't twisted. Her skin remembered everything. He kind of leaned toward her as if the wind were blowing him. "Look, Casey..."

"Yeah?"

He searched for words. "Just tell me it wasn't all bad. I mean, we had some good times, right?"

She nodded.

"Remember the picnic with the cupcakes?" He smiled. "One of my better ideas."

"I remember."

"And what about my great performance on the beach?" He did a pale version of his crazy dance. "YUK-a-booga-booga—" He stopped, then shook his head. "You're still the best thing that ever happened to me, Casey."

She felt her insides melting and refreezing. He knew what he was doing. Bringing up all the fun and romantic moments, putting little barbed hooks into her and dragging her back in.

He studied her. "Nothing to say?"

"What do you want me to say, Paul?"

"That it was okay sometimes."

"Yeah, it was okay sometimes."

He laughed. "Thanks."

Cold raindrops were torn from the sky. The earth seemed bathed in a greenish light. Casey shivered at the chill she'd felt every moment she was with him. "I have to go, Paul. I'm glad you're working."

"Hey."

"Yeah?"

"That's it?" He stepped closer to her. "Man, I hoped I could talk to you for a while. I need that. It wasn't fun standing in front of a judge."

"No, it wasn't."

"So let's talk it out. Don't stop helping me now."

Her stomach was flip-flopping. "Paul, there's nothing to talk about."

"You mean you're letting me go under."

She turned away, as the wind scoured her face. "Give me a break, huh? Do you think you can make me feel guilty?"

"I wasn't trying to make you feel guilty."

"Yeah, you were." She turned back to him. "It's one of your games. You knew every weak spot I had and you just went for every one. You never said anything straight from the heart, Paul. It was all to get something."

He pursed his lips. "Tough talk."

"Yeah, I can talk tough. I can hit back, too."

That made him smile. "I know. You clipped me pretty good."

"I'm glad you're impressed."

"I'm happy you did it," he said earnestly. "It kind of woke me up."

She laughed out loud. "Man. You are funnier than Lillian."

"Who's Lillian?"

"My friend. You know, those people you convinced me I didn't need? You got me to drop them all. I guess it was the only way you felt important."

"Look, Casey," he said. "I already have one shrink."

"Okay, sorry." She looked hard at him, through the slanting rain. "I hit you because I don't want to be hurt anymore. You want to know if it was ever fun? I was too scared to have fun. And all these people you said I didn't need—I always had fun with *them*. Pretty bizarre, huh?" She was on a roll now. "When you started on me with that cigarette, I knew that you'd always hurt me, and I can't get into that anymore."

She took a deep breath, wrung out. Paul said, "Well, I'm glad *you* decided it's over. *I* didn't decide it's over."

Her fear shook her, but so did her anger. She kept her hands in her pockets and her eyes on him. "What are you going to do, Paul, beat the crap out of me again? I have the right to say good-bye. I'm a higher life form, you know?"

"Shut up," he said. "You're making me sick."

"Yeah, all right." She blinked rain from her eyes. "I don't want to argue, anyway. I really hope you make it."

He seemed at a loss. "I'm not staying away, Casey. I'm not letting you walk."

"Yeah," she said, with ice in her voice. "You are."

Her shoulders waited for his blows. He looked at her, trying to figure it all out. Casey felt like she was going to upchuck. Finally, he said, "I want all my stuff back."

She laughed. "Okay. I have the ring and the chain at home. Paddington got thrown out, but I'll give you the money for it."

"Yeah. I want the money."

"I have to go, Paul."

"Go ahead," he said. "I'm not ready."

"Whatever you want. Good-bye."

On an impulse, she stood on tiptoe and kissed his cold, wet cheek. He seemed surprised. She turned quickly and began to walk away. Her back felt like a target. She could almost hear his breath. If her heart banged any harder it was going to come flying out and land somewhere on the tennis courts.

She couldn't stand it anymore. She turned around. He wasn't there.

She grinned uncontrollably. And then she suffered a spasm of emptiness. Yeah, she'd broken up with him. She'd broken up with Mark Simon, too. But already she was scared again, and filled with doubts. What would she say when Paul came back? How many days would it take before she convinced herself again that the pain was worth it?

No, this *wasn't* going to be easy. She'd need that shrink her mom had promised. She had to go deep, and learn a lot of stuff. And every new day was going to be scary. She could go under again; she felt it in her broken bones.

The rain came down harder. Casey walked onto the mushy cinder track and began to walk faster, as best she could with her limp. Her foot hurt like crazy. She looked down the curve of the track, seeing the cream-colored school building beyond.

But instead of continuing to the school building, Casey began to jog. It was a pretty clunky jog, since she was limping at the same time. She pumped her arms and watched the white puffs of her breath on the misty air. With each thud of her sneakers, pain shot up through her calf, into her hip.

Yeah, she thought defiantly. *This* was the sweet pain Mr. Young had talked about. And as she jogged in the December rain, Casey thought how good the pain would feel when it stopped.